What was it about Nicole ░░░
that bit him so hard?

He wished he knew; then maybe he could find a way to become immune to it. He didn't want to get involved . . . not with Nicole.

She had so many strikes against her, yet every time he laid eyes on her, he wanted her. And each time, he wanted more. How was he supposed to put his hands on her in public and keep them off in private? It was too much to expect of him.

He cursed Nicole for stirring up urges too powerful to ignore, and he cursed himself for not having the strength to resist the magnetism that vibrated between them.

He knew she was aware of what was going on and that she was fighting it just as hard as he was. He hoped she didn't stop fighting, because he wasn't sure just how long his willpower could hold out.

Dear Reader,

When two people fall in love, the world is suddenly new and exciting, and it's that same excitement we bring to you in Silhouette Intimate Moments. These are stories with scope and grandeur. The characters lead lives we all dream of, and everything they do reflects the wonder of being in love.

Longer and more sensuous than most romances, Silhouette Intimate Moments novels take you away from everyday life and let you share the magic of love. Adventure, glamour, drama, even suspense—these are the passwords that let you into a world where love has a power beyond the ordinary, where the best authors in the field today create stories of love and commitment that will stay with you always.

In coming months, look for novels by your favorite authors: Linda Howard, Heather Graham Pozzessere, Emilie Richards and Kathleen Korbel, to name just a few. And whenever you buy books, look for all the Silhouette Intimate Moments, love stories for today's woman by today's woman.

Leslie J. Wainger
Senior Editor and Editorial Coordinator

DOREEN ROBERTS

In the Line of Duty

SILHOUETTE·INTIMATE·MOMENTS

Published by Silhouette Books New York

America's Publisher of Contemporary Romance

SILHOUETTE BOOKS
300 East 42nd St., New York, N.Y. 10017

IN THE LINE OF DUTY

ISBN: 0-373-07379-8

First Silhouette Books printing April 1991

Books by Doreen Roberts

Silhouette Intimate Moments

Gambler's Gold #215
Willing Accomplice #239
Forbidden Jade #266
Threat of Exposure #295
Desert Heat #319
In the Line of Duty #379

Silhouette Romance

Home for the Holidays #765

DOREEN ROBERTS

was hooked from the moment she opened the first page of a Mary Stewart novel. It took her twenty years to write her own romantic suspense novel, which was subsequently published, much to her surprise. She and her husband left their native England more than twenty years ago and have since lived in Oregon, where their son was born. Doreen hopes to go on mixing romance and danger in her novels for at least another two decades.

To my friends (they know who they are),
for their constant encouragement
and approval.

And to Erin.
Thanks again.
This was a tough one.

And to my husband,
for his unswerving loyalty and support.
Thanks, I needed that.

Chapter 1

Stretching his legs out in front of him, Luke Jordan leaned back in his chair and wished he was anywhere else but in that bleak office. Nothing had changed since he'd left. The stark bareness of the walls, the nondescript beige drapes at the window, the leather-bound blotter covering the cigarette burns on the desk, even the smell of damp clothes and stale tobacco, all brought back vivid reminders of the life he'd walked away from a little under two years ago.

He glared from under furrowed brows at the dark-haired man behind the desk. Captain Grant Sutton was a name that aroused apprehension in the toughest of hearts. Sutton was powerful, in physique, in temperament and in experience, and he was Luke's former boss.

Sutton looked up, sending a piercing blue stare across the untidy desk. "So, how you been Jordan?"

"Fine." Luke uncrossed his arms and rested his hands on his thighs. Sutton was the only man he knew who could smile like that and manage to look deadly. It wasn't that the man intimidated him. There wasn't a man alive who could intimidate Lucas Jordan. It was more the power that Sutton's title carried, and how he could use it.

There was no doubt in Luke's mind that Sutton wanted to use him. They had never been friends. Though they were close in age, both in their mid-thirties, they were too much alike to be friends. Too stubborn and too independent. It was only to Sutton's rank that Luke had conceded. That and the indisputable respect the man commanded.

Luke shifted his weight, sliding his narrow hips farther down in the black vinyl armchair. He was determined to put on a show of relaxed boredom. No way was he going to let the eagle eyes of that shrewd Goliath see his uneasiness. Sutton thrived on weakness and used it to his advantage. Luke knew that only too well. He also knew that Sutton was playing his favorite game.

"Keep 'em waiting, build the tension and watch 'em squirm," he'd told Luke more than once. What really got to him, Luke thought, making a conscious effort to relax his shoulders, was that it worked. All the time. It was working with him now. He could feel the muscles in the back of his neck tightening like drying leather.

Grant Sutton was probably the only person on earth whom Luke Jordan respected. And that, he admitted silently, was why he was sitting here, waiting until the captain decided to tell him what he wanted.

Sutton obliged him by leaning forward to slide a large manila envelope across the desk. "Take a look at that."

Luke reached for the envelope and opened it. He had no idea why he'd been summoned without an explanation, or even why he'd complied. Habit, he thought wryly. All habits, good or bad, died hard. Especially the bad.

He pinched the corner of a glossy photograph and withdrew a black-and-white head shot of a woman. Not badlooking, he decided. He liked the eyes. They stared out at him, wide spaced, friendly eyes, framed in dark lashes. He had the distinct impression that they belonged to an honest, straightforward, no-games type of woman.

A little surprised by his instant analysis, he studied the rest of her. Small straight nose, stubborn chin and a mouth that gave him the impression she smiled a lot. Her hair, dark and thick, was drawn back and fastened at the back of her neck. The style gave her an austere look that didn't suit her.

This woman, Luke thought, would be more at home riding the surf, or on the back of a horse, with her hair flowing wildly behind her. The image gave him a spasm of excitement that was unmistakably sexual.

He looked up to find Sutton watching him, his silver-blue eyes alert and assessing.

"Well?" Sutton rested his elbows on the desk and balanced his chin on his knuckles. "Recognize her?"

Baffled, Luke looked back at the picture. There was something familiar about the face. Maybe the mouth...no...the eyes... Impatient with himself, he shook his head and slipped the photo back into the envelope. He was trying to see what Sutton wanted him to see. He didn't know this woman. He would have remembered her if he'd met her.

Shaken by his conviction of that, he threw the envelope on the desk. "Never seen her before," he said, his voice clearly reflecting his irritation.

Unruffled, Sutton pushed the envelope back. "Look at it again."

Annoyed now, Luke opened his mouth to protest. The look on Sutton's face stopped him. He wore an air of expectancy that Luke knew well. He felt the hairs prickling on the back of his neck as he picked up the envelope again.

"Now," Sutton said, "imagine the hair red and bushy. Heavy makeup, especially the eyes."

Luke stared at the picture. He could see it now, so vividly that he wondered how he could have missed it. It had to be his subconscious refusing to accept it. He must have done a good job of burying that episode in his life, he thought grimly. He looked at Sutton's smug expression. "Opal," he muttered. "She looks like Opal Turner."

"Yes," Grant Sutton said with more than a hint of satisfaction. "I think so, too." He held out his hand for the picture. "Enough to fool Merrill, would you say?"

Luke felt his jaw slacken. He looked down at the picture before handing it to Sutton. "No way," he said as Sutton studied it. "There's a resemblance, but it's slight. This woman is nothing like that cheap tramp. Not even close."

"Ah," Sutton said, laying the photo on the desk. "But she could look a lot closer. Put a wig on her, heavy makeup, trashy clothes . . ." He paused, his brows lifted in question.

"Come on," Luke said in exasperation. "You know it's a lot more than that. There's got to be a hundred differences—the walk, the laugh, the whole voice. This woman has class." He waved a hand at the picture. "She could never pass as Opal in a million years."

"What if," Sutton said casually, "someone were to coach her in those things? Someone who knew Opal . . . intimately? What if that someone taught her how to walk and talk and even think like Opal Turner? What if she never got closer than a few yards to Merrill? You think it could work?"

Now he knew why the back of his neck prickled. Very slowly Luke got to his feet and leaned his hands on the desk. "No," he said clearly. "I do not. I think you're insane to even consider it. I think you're totally deranged if you think, even for one second, that I would have anything to do with this."

Sutton's pale eyes gleamed, but his voice remained impassive as he said, "Merrill owes us one. Wouldn't you like to collect?"

Luke froze. Seconds ticked by while he struggled with his conscience. "Damn you, Sutton," he muttered at last. "You can't guarantee that."

Sutton shrugged his massive shoulders. "You know better than most that there are no guarantees in this business. All I'm saying is that it's a shot. A damn good shot. And almost certainly the only one we're ever going to get."

Luke stared into the hard blue eyes for several seconds, then straightened. "We don't even know for sure if Merrill is alive."

"This is one way to find out."

"What if he doesn't bite?"

"Then," Sutton said evenly, "I'll try something else. When I told you some time ago that we had a possible lead, you knew I wasn't going to give up until I had him."

Yes, Luke thought, he'd known. Sutton had good reasons to want Merrill. Personal reasons. "I didn't know you planned on using a woman as bait."

"The woman is an experienced police officer, and I need you, Luke. It can't work without you."

He hadn't added *and you owe me.* Luke knew he wasn't that kind of man. But it was there between them like a treacherous swamp.

"You can't make me do this," Luke said abruptly. "I'm not on the force anymore. I'm not one of your lackeys you can move around at will."

Sutton nodded, his face devoid of expression. "You're right—I can't make you do this. But you are the most qualified person to do it. You knew Opal well, almost as well as Merrill did. The officer who will double for her will need all the help she can get. Her life may well depend on how good a job she does."

Luke swore. "Does she know that?"

"Yes, she does."

"And she's willing to do it?"

"She's anxious to do it."

"Then she's a lot crazier than she looks."

Sutton nodded cheerfully. "That may be true. You should make a good team."

Luke curled his fists in frustration and moved away from the desk. At the window, he looked down on the wet street outside. Three lanes of traffic crawled up to the stoplight, though it was still early in the afternoon.

Almost June, Luke thought, and it still looked like winter outside. Liquid sunshine, the Oregonians called the incessant rain. It was no wonder they made jokes about rust and webbed feet.

It had been raining that night. The night, almost two years ago, when Mark had died. Mark Wilson, twenty-one-year-old rookie detective, excited as hell to be out on his first assignment.

He hadn't stopped talking from the moment he'd climbed into the squad car with Luke. In less than six minutes, Luke knew more about Mark Wilson than he knew about himself. Less than six seconds later, he watched the kid die from a bullet hole in his side put there by Adrian Merrill's gun.

Yes, Luke thought grimly, Merrill owed him. Luke had been responsible for Mark Wilson's life. Not only had he failed the kid, but he'd also failed to bring his murderer to justice. Yes, he wanted Merrill.

"Would you like to meet her before you make up your mind?" Sutton said behind him.

He thought about it, his stomach churning. What they were asking him to do was impossible. How could he hold himself responsible for someone else's life? How could he take the chance on failing again?

He kept his eyes on the street outside as he said quietly, "Who is she?"

"Her name is Nicole Parker. She's been with this precinct for six months. She's thirty-one years old and has been on the force eight years."

"Married?" He didn't know why he'd asked that. It wouldn't make any difference. Not to an eight-year veteran, even if she was a woman. On the force the job came first; marriage was a poor second.

"No," Sutton said. "She's not married. Relax, Luke. She wants to do this. She was given an option."

"Yeah," Luke said bitterly. "I can imagine."

"Why don't I bring her in?" Sutton suggested again. "You can make up your mind after you've talked to her."

He'd already made up his mind. He couldn't do it; it was as simple as that. As much as he wanted Merrill, as much as he owed Sutton, he could not take on that kind of liability again. He could not be responsible for losing another life.

He knew Sutton wouldn't give up that easily. He'd have to meet the woman face-to-face, go through the motions, pretend to consider it, before delivering his decision. Grant Sutton never accepted snap judgments, unless it was a matter of life and death.

"Go ahead," he said wearily. "I'll talk to her."

The intercom buzzed in the quiet of the room when Sutton jabbed it with his thumb. Outside, once the door to the captain's office was opened, Luke could hear the usual hubbub of ringing telephones, raised voices, rattling coffee cups and clattering typewriters that would make normal conversation difficult. With the door closed, he could almost forget he was in Portland's busiest precinct.

In the outer office an intercom buzzed, and the woman seated in front of it flicked a slender finger at the intercom. "Parker here."

Grant Sutton's voice said succinctly, "He's ready to meet you."

"I'll be right there, Captain." Nicole Parker pulled the report sheet from the typewriter and laid it in the tray. It would have to wait until later. She'd been waiting for this call for some time.

She felt the flutter of excitement and smiled. She was about to launch her first assignment as a detective. And she was dying to meet the legendary Lucas Jordan. The captain hadn't said much about him, but a few discreet inquiries around the station had brought some interesting details to light.

According to her sources, Luke Jordan had been a tough, daring, dedicated cop. Until a young detective, on his first assignment with Luke, had been killed in a shoot-out.

Some said Luke had lost his nerve after his young partner's death; others said he blamed himself for what happened and couldn't face the guilt. All Sutton had told her was that when Luke Jordan resigned, he'd lost the best man on the squad.

Jordan was now head of security at a big fancy hotel, Nicole had learned. She wondered how the captain had talked him into doing this favor for him.

She reached the office and tapped on the door before opening it. Grant Sutton gave her a tight smile, and she returned it. After stepping inside the office, she closed the door behind her, her gaze traveling to the man who stood at the window with his back to her.

"Nicole," Sutton said, "I'd like you to meet Luke Jordan."

The man turned, and she felt the shock of his gaze as steel gray eyes assessed her thoroughly from head to toe. She tried to tell herself that it was natural. He would want to assure himself that she could impersonate Opal Turner, but there was something so intimate about the inspection that her insides still quivered when he looked back at her face.

He was more attractive than she'd expected. Life had not been kind to him, judging by the deep grooves between his brows and at the edges of his mouth, and the black leather jacket he wore accented the tough image he presented.

His face was too unevenly arranged to be called handsome, but that street-smart look, those incredible eyes and a mouth that managed to look both sensuous and hard at the same time added up to the kind of man who could make a woman's heart beat faster just by looking at him.

As hers was doing now, she discovered. Her composure shaken, she managed to give him a cool smile. "I'm happy to meet you," she murmured. "I've heard some nice things about you."

"Don't believe everything you hear."

He made no move toward her, and his expression remained impassive, but she had the distinct impression that something tangible seemed to be drifting between them, vague and elusive and infinitely disturbing.

"I've told Nicole the basics of the problem," Sutton said behind her. "But now that you're both here, we can go into more details."

She was jolted back to earth, having forgotten for a moment that the captain was still there. Sutton waved his hand at the two vacant chairs opposite him and she sat down, aware of Luke Jordan easing into the one next to her.

Out of the corner of her eye, she saw his long legs stretched out in front of him, clothed in dark pants. One foot danced slightly against the carpet. He wasn't nearly as relaxed as he looked, she thought, and felt a little better.

"Is there anything you want to ask Nicole before we start?" Sutton asked, giving Luke a small frown.

"Yeah. What made you join the police force?"

The question took her by surprise. She glanced at Sutton, who looked disapproving but said nothing.

Turning her head, she said lightly, "I couldn't make it as a pilot."

A flicker of interest warmed his hard gaze. "Why not?"

She smiled. "I have a problem with my ears at high altitude." She waited until he nodded, then added, "And I'm afraid of heights."

A reluctant grin tugged at the corner of his mouth, unsettling her more than his scowl. "That'll do it," he murmured.

His voice was a lazy growl, the kind of voice that always sounded as if it had just woken up, Nicole thought. In fact,

Luke Jordan looked as if he'd just woken up. His light brown hair had a mind of its own, and his eyes were heavy lidded beneath the menacing brows.

The image disturbed her, and she looked back at Sutton, who was scowling at Luke in exasperation. "I meant something significant," he said.

Luke shrugged. "All right. How much have you told her?"

Sutton looked uncomfortable. A rare event, in Nicole's experience. "I told you. The basics."

"And what are the basics?"

Something almost lethal in the quiet tone made Nicole's flesh creep. "Shall I tell you what I know?" she said, beginning to feel annoyed at being left out of the conversation.

"It might be an idea," Luke said dryly.

Ignoring him, she fixed her gaze on the wall behind Sutton's head and concentrated. "Adrian Merrill was suspected of smuggling drugs under the cover of his export business. When his warehouse was raided, he was thought to have died in an explosion that followed the shoot-out.

"Opal Turner was his girlfriend, who betrayed him. A young officer was killed in the shoot-out...." Her voice faltered when she remembered what she'd been told about Luke's reaction to his partner's death. Resolving not to look at him she went on. "And Opal, who was not in the warehouse at the time, disappeared.

"Several months later, word was received from Opal that Merrill had not died in the explosion but had escaped. Opal disappeared because she knew Merrill wanted her dead. He's apparently disfigured and is using another name. A few weeks ago information was received that Adrian Merrill could be a man calling himself Morris Adams, who's currently running an export business in Honolulu."

Sutton nodded his approval. "Correct. Since you're the image of Opal Turner, or you will be once Luke gets through with you, we're sending you to Hawaii in the hopes that Merrill, if it is Merrill, will risk his cover to get at you. In which case we'll pick him up."

"Sounds nice and neat, doesn't it?" Sarcasm spiced his voice as Luke leaned forward. "Now, how about explaining just how you propose to do that? And how do you expect to protect this officer if something goes wrong?"

"She'll have you as bodyguard with her at all times," Sutton said, sounding defensive. "You'll be part of the cover. Honeymooners in Hawaii, what could be more natural than that?"

Nicole swallowed. She hadn't been told this part of the plan. Her fingers curled in her palms as she thought about it. She wasn't at all sure she liked the idea.

"Has it occurred to you," Luke asked harshly, "that all it would take is one shot from a high-powered rifle? How am I supposed to protect her from that?"

It was Sutton's turn to sound angry. "Aren't you forgetting something? What did Opal say to you in her letter? Merrill wouldn't let her die easy. He'd make sure she had a slow death. Does that sound like he'd use a high-powered rifle?"

Nicole glanced at Luke. So he was the one who'd received Opal's letter. For the first time, she wondered just how well Luke Jordan had known Opal Turner.

"You said yourself there were no guarantees," Luke said, pushing himself to his feet. Leaning his hands on the desk, he glared at Sutton. "You're taking too many chances, dammit. She'll be a sitting duck. Send me out there alone. Merrill wants me every bit as bad as he wants Opal. I'll be the bait."

"He'll figure it as a trap." Sutton picked up a pencil and started tapping it on his desk in a sharp staccato rhythm. "He could run, figuring you're not worth the risk. Now, Opal is a different matter altogether. When he sees the two of you out there together, and on honeymoon yet, that will be more than enough to light his fuse. The chance to get you both will be too much to resist.''

Sutton slid a sideways glance at Nicole before adding, ''Opal is right. He would want to see her die as slowly and as painfully as possible. And knowing him as we do, nothing would please him more than to have you watch him do it.''

Luke straightened. ''I'm not coaching a woman to walk into a death trap, not even to get Merrill. And not even for you.''

Both men looked startled when Nicole leaped to her feet, eyes blazing. ''Now just wait a damn minute. Don't I get a say in this? It's my life you two are bandying around with that charming, cavalier attitude. No one seems to care what I think.''

Neither man answered. Sutton looked a little sheepish, while Luke, she was unnerved to see, waited with a grim face that said clearly he'd already made up his mind.

''In the first place,'' Nicole said, addressing Luke, ''I'm *not* just a woman. I'm a qualified, experienced police officer. I don't need a bodyguard. I'm quite capable of taking care of myself. Just as capable as you are.''

She saw the cynicism in Luke's eyes and added, ''If not more so.''

He opened his mouth to speak but she forestalled him. ''Furthermore,'' she said, putting every ounce of confidence she possessed into her voice, ''I don't need you. There are pictures of Opal, and you can't be the only person to have known her. If you don't feel capable of doing this, then say so. I'm quite sure we can find someone else.''

She'd scored; she could see it in his face. Resentment flared in his eyes and he started to speak, but again she cut in swiftly and with deadly aim.

''After all, Mr. Jordan, you're no longer a policeman. It's quite understandable if you prefer not to be involved.''

This time his anger intimidated her. She knew then without a doubt that, with his temper aroused, Luke Jordan would make a formidable opponent.

He stepped toward her. Determined not to back down, she held her ground, but her entire body tingled when he stood close enough for his toes to touch hers. "Never," he said quietly, "and I mean never, underestimate what I'm capable of doing."

"That," she said just as quietly, "goes for both of us."

Sutton cleared his throat. "Do you think we can get back to business here?"

His gaze still locked with hers, Luke said nastily, "When does Officer Parker wish to begin her classes?"

"Anytime Mr. Jordan is ready." Her voice challenged him, and his eyebrow twitched.

"Come on, you two," Sutton said, "you'll have to get along if you're going to spend the next few days together."

Nicole drew a long breath and drew back. Sitting down, she ignored Luke and gave Sutton a tight smile. "So, what's the procedure?"

Sutton waited until Luke had slumped down in his chair before saying, "All right. Luke is security chief at the Royal King hotel. He has a suite there."

Nicole saw a flicker of apprehension cross Sutton's face, and knew she wasn't going to like what he was about to say. She watched him reach for some papers and begin shuffling them as he spoke.

"You will move into that suite, Nicole. You will eat, sleep and stay in that suite for as long as it takes for Luke to turn you into Opal Turner. No one must know you're there. You'll go into that suite as Nicole Parker, and you will not come out until you are Opal Turner."

He looked up, and her stomach jolted at the grave expression in his eyes. "Do I make myself clear?" he asked.

For the first time, she realized just how dangerous this setup could be. Up until now, she'd refused to consider the fact that she might not survive the assignment. Grant Sutton was giving her a chance to back out. For several seconds she thought about it.

Her temporary appointment as detective had been based on a stroke of luck. If she handled it right, her promotion would be assured. She knew that her future depended on her performance. The knowledge that her life depended on it, too, was sobering, but it was part of the deal. She'd known that when she'd accepted the assignment.

She looked up, aware that the man at her side was waiting for her answer just as anxiously as her boss. "When do I have to be there?" she asked, her voice calm.

"Now wait a minute," Luke said, rising to his feet again. "If she's going to live in my suite, where am I supposed to stay?"

Sutton smiled without humor. "In the suite with her. No one's supposed to know she's there, remember? You order room service and have them leave the food outside, and you tell the maid not to bother to clean your suite. You come and go as usual. Everything must look as normal as possible."

Nicole hoped her discomfort wasn't as obvious in her expression as it was in Luke's. His curse was loud and succulent. "I just hope," he said heavily, "that you know what you're doing."

"You'd better hope you know what you're doing." Sutton's face softened a little as he looked back at Nicole. "You'll have certain arrangements to make, of course. Perhaps you could tell your family and friends you're taking a vacation?"

Nicole nodded. "I'll take care of it. How long do I have?"

"By the end of the week?" Sutton glanced at the calendar. "Let's say Saturday. It's a holiday weekend—they should be busy at the hotel. There's less chance of you being noticed if you slip in then. Go straight up to Luke's suite—it's on the sixth floor. Number six-sixteen."

Again she nodded. "Right. Time?"

This time Luke answered. "Three-thirty. I'll take an afternoon break then."

She hoped the quivery feeling in her stomach wasn't an indication of her reaction to him as a man. It would be difficult enough to deal with the situation as it was. She didn't need to be aware of their biological differences at a time like this.

Steeling herself, she stood and gave him a gracious smile. "I'm sure we can handle this with professionalism and decorum," she said, not sure if she was warning him or assuring herself.

She didn't like the gleam in his eye when he murmured, "Really? I don't know how you can be sure of that."

Aware that he was baiting her, she refused to give in to the retort hovering on her lips. She'd deal with Luke Jordan when it became necessary, she decided. Until then, she would simply ignore his attitude.

She looked at her watch. "If that's it for now, I'd better get back. I've got a few things I want to clear up before the weekend."

Sutton nodded. "Go ahead. I can brief you later on any necessary details."

She made herself look at Luke. He was studying her with a thoughtful expression that unnerved her. Telling herself that he was merely deciding what she would need to work on to become Opal Turner, she said, "I guess I'll see you on Saturday, then."

He smiled. She could have done without that. It gave him a rakish look that was sexy as hell. "I'll be ready and waiting," he promised her.

Her legs displayed a decided weakness as she walked to the door. She could feel two pairs of eyes watching her as she pulled it open and walked through.

Luke waited until the door closed. Pounding his fist on the desk, he demanded, "Are you crazy? You can't send a woman like that out on a suicide mission."

Sutton sighed. "Are you going to start that again? When are you going to get it through your thick head that she wants to go? She has no illusions about the job. She knows what the score is. I made sure she knew. It didn't even faze her. She wants to make detective. She wants it bad enough that she's willing to try anything to prove she has what it takes."

Luke straightened, jamming his hands into the pockets of his jacket. "What about this honeymoon thing? Is that really necessary?"

Sutton looked up, a frown drawing his dark brows together. "You know it is. It's the only way I can be sure you'll be with her at all times. Besides, nothing will send Merrill off the deep end faster than to see what he thinks is his ex-girlfriend, who betrayed him, married to the cop who brought down his empire."

His frown softened. "Don't worry, Luke. She's qualified. She can take care of herself. I wouldn't have given her this assignment if I wasn't convinced of that."

"What if she isn't?" Luke started pacing around the room, his shoulders hunched. "Just because she's a good cop doesn't mean she's an actress. What if I can't turn her into Opal? What if she changes her mind and decides she can't do it?"

"She'll do it," Sutton said quietly. "I'm sure of it."

"Damn you, Sutton." Luke twisted away from the desk and moved to the window. "I know you want Merrill. I just didn't realize the lengths you would go to get him."

He heard Sutton's chair scrape back, and knew before he spoke that his former boss was furious. Grant Sutton didn't show his anger very often, but when he did, he could outstrip even Luke.

"Yes," Sutton said in a low, fierce voice. "I want Merrill. And you know why. I would like to tear him apart, limb by limb, with my bare hands. But I wouldn't risk anyone's life, man or woman, if I didn't feel confident in their ability and their willingness to put their lives on the line. If you're not comfortable with that, you'd better say so now. Because once the ball starts rolling, none of us will be able to stop it."

Luke stared down at the street below, unaware of the erratic flow of traffic. He was remembering a cold, wet night almost two years ago. He could still feel the hard pavement beneath his knees, could still see the incessant flashing blue light reflecting in the puddles around him while he watched a young life slowly ebb away.

Luke's fists curled as he remembered something else. The silhouette of a man, flames lighting the background behind him, his gun still pointed at the policeman on the ground.

Frozen in shock, it had taken Luke a moment longer than usual to raise his gun. Adrian Merrill had disappeared into the flames, but not before his second shot had killed Mark Wilson.

It seemed as if the explosion of the warehouse had come almost at once, but it was several minutes before Sutton had forced Luke away from the dead body of his partner and out of range of the deadly flare-up.

It was the only time in his adult life that Luke had cried. And Grant Sutton was the only man who had ever seen him do it. Neither of them had ever mentioned it.

Luke turned from the window and looked his former boss in the eye. "I promise you," he said evenly, "that Nicole Parker will come out of that room as Opal Turner. Her own mother won't know her. If that's what it's going to take to get Adrian Merrill, then so be it." He held out his hand. "I'll promise you something else. If it doesn't work out, if Merrill isn't fooled, it won't be because I didn't do my job."

Grant Sutton's smile was reflected in his eyes as he grasped Luke's hand. "I know. That's what I'm counting on. Thanks, Luke."

Luke nodded. "Sure. When do you want me to report back?"

"I'll call you and arrange a meeting. It'll be safer. Phones can have ears."

Luke frowned. "Do you really think he still has snoops around?"

"I'm not about to take any chances. Merrill had a powerful deal going, a lot of people working for him. It's possible someone still has his ear to the ground. For the same reason, you won't be able to use the phone in the Honolulu hotel. All calls will have to be made from outside."

"That's if Morris Adams is Adrian Merrill."

Sutton walked back to his desk. "I don't think there's any doubt about that. Our informant was certain he'd made a positive ID."

"And you can trust the snitch?"

"He's connected with us before." He sat down and picked up the pencil again. "One word, Luke. Go easy on her. She's a nice lady, and I don't want her hurt."

"Who, me?" Luke raised his hands in mock protest. "You know me, Captain. I'm a pussycat."

"Yeah, well, keep your claws sheathed, okay?"

A thought struck Luke, one he wasn't sure he cared for. "You, er, haven't got a personal interest in the lady, have you?"

Sutton laughed. "Cool it, tiger. Strictly professional, you know that. I steer clear of that scene."

Luke nodded, satisfied. "Well, don't worry about her on my account. Besides, I got the idea that Nicole Parker could hold her own in an arena full of hungry lions."

Sutton gave him a straight look from his piercing blue eyes. "Maybe, but we both know what we're dealing with here. I just want you to know that there's no one else I trust to carry this off."

If only he shared the captain's confidence, Luke thought as he stepped out into the cool, damp afternoon. He climbed into his car and closed the door, winding down the window in spite of the chilly wind. He needed some fresh air to blow the cobwebs from his mind.

The conversation that afternoon had disturbed too many memories he wanted to forget. He'd put them all behind him when he'd walked out of the station two years ago, and he wasn't happy about having them reinstated.

Sutton knew he would do it, of course. He could hardly refuse. And Sutton was right. Luke was the only person who'd known Opal well enough to coach Nicole Parker.

Luke switched on the engine and scowled at the rain streaking across the window. He still hated the idea. He hated the thought that he would be instrumental in putting someone in danger. That once more he'd been placed in the position of being responsible for someone's life.

But something else worried him almost as much. He pulled out of the parking lot and slipped into place behind a cab. There was Nicole Parker herself.

He'd felt it the second he'd turned and looked into her steady green gaze. No, he'd felt it the moment he'd first laid eyes on her picture.

It had been reinforced when he'd seen her in person. It had intensified potently when he'd faced her nose-to-nose and warned her not to underestimate him.

Call it chemistry, awareness, a natural instinct, whatever it was. There was not an atom of doubt that Nicole Parker affected him on a highly physical level.

That hadn't happened to him since he was a teenager. And his reaction then had been predictable. He couldn't afford that reaction this time.

He cursed as he came close to sideswiping a plumber's van. It wouldn't be easy to ignore that awareness. But ignore it he must. It had been two years since he'd had to use the kind of concentration it took to stay alive in a life-and-death situation.

They would be facing a formidable enemy. Neither one of them could afford to be distracted for one single second. The kind of show they would be forced to put on would entail close contact. Extremely close contact. Any personal interest, no matter how slight, could destroy their concentration.

All it would take would be a split second, a hairbreadth of misjudgment, and they could blow it. He would have to take steps to make sure that didn't happen. Even if it meant upsetting the cool, confident Officer Parker.

He pulled up at the light, his fingers drumming on the wheel. He just hoped he was up to the challenge. Failing that, there was one more card up his sleeve. He could do everything in his power to see that she changed her mind about doing the assignment.

The light changed, and he stepped on the accelerator, his brow creased in thought. If he had the slightest seed of doubt, he promised himself, then one way or another he'd see that she pulled out of the operation.

Feeling only slightly better, he headed down the windswept street to the hotel.

Chapter 2

Nicole entered the lobby of the Royal King on Saturday afternoon, hoping she looked calmer than she felt. She'd tried to keep her mind off the assignment over the past few days without much success, and now that the moment was finally at hand, the butterflies in her stomach felt more like sea gulls.

Keeping her head down to avoid eye contact with anyone milling around the reception desk, she crossed the dark red carpeting to the elevators.

A young couple waited by the doors, and a serious-looking man in spectacles stood studying the directory on the wall. Otherwise, she was alone. Nicole rested her suitcase on the floor and tried to relax the tension in her shoulders.

In an effort not to draw attention to herself, she'd dressed casually in jeans and had pulled a yellow sweatshirt over her white blouse. She'd fastened her dark hair with a yellow clasp and had used no more than a dash of coral lipstick.

Her wardrobe for Hawaii would be taken care of, Sutton had informed her. She'd written down her sizes and wondered if Luke Jordan would have a hand in the selection. Once more she wondered just how well Luke had known Opal Turner, then forgot about it as the elevator doors slid open in front of her.

The other three occupants got out at the third floor, leaving her to continue on up alone. Her apprehension was natural, she reassured herself as the elevator lifted her rapidly to the sixth floor. She was embarking on a difficult and dangerous assignment, and the fluttering in her stomach was a product of that concern.

As for the rest of it, she had to remember it was like being an actor in a play. It was all make-believe. If she kept concentrating on the fact that the slightest slipup could cost her life, she should be able to keep any personal feelings out of it. It was her job, she reminded herself as the elevator slowed to a stop. Though it might have helped if Luke Jordan wasn't quite so attractive.

She reached the door of his suite and glanced around to make sure the corridor was empty. Reassured, she rapped three times with her knuckles, hoping he'd managed to get there before her.

The door opened almost at once. His face appeared in the doorway, then before she could speak, he reached out to grab her arm and pulled her into the room.

"Did anyone see you come up here?" he demanded after closing the door.

"Only the people in the elevator."

He insisted on a detailed description of each person and questioned her two or three times before he was satisfied. All the time she talked, his eyes raked up and down her body with an air of someone assessing the features of a used car.

Nicole worked hard at controlling her resentment. He would have to change her entire appearance, she reminded herself. This kind of scrutiny was necessary, and she would have to get used to it.

A brief hello would have been nice, though. He was obviously establishing the boundaries right from the start. Which was just fine with her.

"Do you normally wear makeup?" Luke asked abruptly. "When you're partying, I mean."

"It depends who I'm partying with." She met his gaze with calm assurance. "And where I'm going, of course."

"Well, Opal used heavy makeup. I hope you know how to put it on. That's one thing I can't handle."

"I'll learn." She shifted her suitcase to her other hand. "Where did you want me to put this?"

"I'll put it in the bedroom." He leaned over and took the case from her. "It's through here."

Following him across the thick cream carpet, Nicole sent a sweeping glance around the room. Not a large living area, it appeared spacious from the lack of furniture.

Two reclining armchairs angled toward the middle of the room, facing a television set. A small, round coffee table sat between the chairs, and a square table holding a telephone and a lamp stood next to a couch against one wall.

Behind a narrow breakfast bar, she could see a stove and small refrigerator separated by a narrow sink. She caught a glimpse of a low bookcase and wondered what kind of books Luke Jordan read as she followed him through a door beyond the living room.

"You'll sleep in here," Luke said, dropping her suitcase on the floor by a queen-size bed. "The bathroom's next door. I'll be sleeping in the living room."

"I'm glad to hear that." She'd attempted a light tone and was dismayed to see his mouth harden.

"I know you're not any happier with this setup than I am," he said, resting his cool gaze on her face, "so I'll try to make it as easy as possible."

Obviously he didn't have a sense of humor about the assignment. "Don't put yourself out on my account," she said evenly. "I'm prepared to do a good job, and as long as you're reasonably patient, I don't foresee any problems." She felt a moment's discomfort when he flicked a glance over her that seemed to cut through her bones.

"Don't worry. You'll soon hear about it if I have any problems." He moved to the door, then glanced back at her over his shoulder. "I'll give you a few minutes to settle in, then we'll go over what information I have on Opal Turner."

Nicole nodded, letting out her breath in a rush when he left her alone. This was worse than she'd expected. He acted as if she was personally responsible for this arrangement.

Which wasn't fair, she thought, as she opened a dresser drawer as quietly as possible. He was right. She was no happier about the method of this operation than he was.

At least he'd anticipated her needs. He'd emptied the drawer. She investigated the one underneath and closed it quickly when she discovered an untidy pile of men's briefs, handkerchiefs and socks.

Her inspection of the closet revealed a half dozen empty hangers alongside a collection of pants, shirts and a couple of sports jackets. She grimaced and closed the door. They might not be sharing a room, but this cozy arrangement with the clothes could present some interesting complications.

Sitting on the side of the bed, Nicole contemplated her suitcase and sighed. The tension between them was thick enough to stop a freight train. He'd made no secret of his resentment, but she couldn't tell whether it was with her personally he had a problem, or simply the whole assignment.

She shook her head and slid off the bed. She had a distinct feeling that Luke Jordan's reluctance involved a little more than a concern for her well-being.

After all, she was a qualified police officer and responsible for her own safety. His job was to make sure she created an image as close to Opal's as possible, and then act out a charade to convince Adrian Merrill that she was the criminal's ex-girlfriend. She'd made it clear that she didn't expect Luke Jordan to act as her bodyguard, and that she neither wanted nor needed his protection.

Maybe, she mused, as she stored away the few items of clothing she'd brought, just maybe she hadn't made that point clear enough. In which case she'd reinforce it at the first opportunity. After all, the idea of a police officer needing a bodyguard was ludicrous. Especially when the bodyguard in question was no longer on the force. Surely even Mr. Macho Jordan would have to admit that.

When she could no longer find an excuse to stay in the bedroom, Nicole glanced in the mirror on the dresser for reassurance before leaving.

Without makeup and with her hair scraped back, she looked officious and capable, she decided. The uncomfortable feeling persisted that she'd deliberately played down her appearance, not so much to avoid drawing attention from a possible crony of Merrill's, but more to avoid any reaction from Luke Jordan.

She made a face at her reflection. She could forget about a reaction from him. Obviously he'd already formed an opinion of her, and it wasn't favorable. Which was perfectly all right with her, she told herself as she walked down the hallway to the living room. It would make things that much easier.

She found him sprawled on the couch when she entered the room, his legs spread out in front of him. The dark pants he wore seemed too formal for his casual posture, as did the crisp cream shirt, though he'd unbuttoned it at the neck.

His light brown hair also contradicted his businesslike clothes, springing in a thick, silky tangle above his square forehead, an apparent result of his habit of combing it back with his fingers. He repeated the gesture as she approached, and laid the pictures he'd been studying down on the arm of the couch.

"I have a folder of information on Opal Turner, but it isn't much. We'll have to rely on my memory for most of it." He handed her the file and she took it, moving over to one of the armchairs to sit down.

Nicole opened it and began skimming the typewritten notes. "Are those pictures of Opal?" she asked after she read the first page.

Most of the information was already familiar to her, but so far she hadn't seen any pictures of the woman she was supposed to impersonate. Sutton had told her that he'd given Luke the only ones available.

Luke picked up the photos and handed them to her. "They're not too recent," he warned, "but they'll give you an idea."

There were three of them altogether. One showed a skinny teenager, with eyes that looked too large in her pale, oval face, peering out from under thick bangs of reddish brown hair.

The second portrayed an older woman, and the difference was startling. While the younger Opal had revealed a somewhat pathetic vulnerability with her tightly braided hair and ill-fitting dress, the second picture depicted a harder, cynical attitude and an appearance that Nicole could describe only as common.

Her close-fitting dress reached to a point midway down her thighs, and the neckline plunged perilously close to her waist. Her hair was now a flame red and seemed to explode from her head like fuzzy tumbleweed.

On closer inspection, Nicole assumed the transformation had taken place over a short period of time. Opal didn't look that much older in the second picture, and in spite of the bravado of her outlandish image, vulnerability still showed through in the rather frightened expression in the light blue eyes.

The first misgivings crept into Nicole's mind as she stared at the picture. "We have different eyes," she said, without looking up. "Hers are blue, mine are green."

"I know. Sutton told me you wear contacts. Someone will contact your optometrist and order the kind that changes your eyes to blue."

"All right." He'd noticed the color of her eyes. Or had Sutton commented on the difference? Wondering why it mattered, she murmured, "Though I'm not sure I can look like Opal, even at a distance. We're not that much alike, despite what you and Sutton might think."

"You'll look enough like her by the time I'm through with you. It's much more than looks, anyway." He stood up and walked over to stand in front of her. "It's the walk, the gestures, the laugh, anything that can be seen or heard from a distance. Those are the things we have to begin with. Once you've got them down, the rest should be easy."

Nicole hid her shiver of apprehension. So much would depend on her doing the job right. She hoped he knew what he was doing.

"Take a look at the third one," Luke said. "It's the most recent."

She did so, wondering who had taken it. Though Opal's bushy hair still glowed a flame red, it had lost that wild, untamed look. She wore a sweater that emphasized her small breasts, and had smiled into the camera, softening the features made harsh by the heavy makeup.

But it was the expression in Opal's eyes that caught Nicole's attention, arousing her curiosity. Had Luke been the photographer? Despite her questions, Sutton had refused to comment on the relationship between Luke and Opal Turner, but the redhead was looking at the camera the way a woman looked at a man she wanted and intended to get.

Nicole felt compelled to ask. "Who took this?"

"I did." Luke leaned over and took the photograph from her. "Sutton wanted me to get a shot of her since she didn't have a record."

Nicole could tell nothing from his expression as he studied the picture, and after a moment or two he handed it back to her. She felt his cutting gaze on her and lifted her chin, steeling herself to meet his eyes.

"Stand up," he ordered abruptly.

She took her time returning everything to the folder, then closed it and laid it on the table next to her. Pushing herself up with her hands on the arms of the chair, she stood.

Luke hadn't moved, and the placement of the table made it necessary for her to stand close to him. Too close. She could feel his body heat, and the subtle, earthy cologne that he wore elicited an answering response that disturbed her.

Determined not to reveal the threat to her composure, she looked him full in the face and saw a tiny flicker warm his cool, gray eyes for a second before he masked it. She felt a moment's pleasure that he wasn't entirely unaffected by her, and immediately reproved herself. She couldn't afford those kinds of games.

"How tall are you?" he demanded, running another glance down her body.

"Five-four." She really wished he wouldn't do that.

"I thought so," Luke said, looking down at her sneakers. "You're a little shorter than Opal."

"Then I'll have to wear high-heeled shoes."

The grooves between his brows deepened. "Yeah. It'll help with the walk, anyway."

"The walk?"

"Opal always wore very high heels. She looked kind of like a turkey strutting around."

It had to be the cologne putting her off balance, Nicole thought, wishing she had space to edge away from him. He intimidated her, standing this close to her. She didn't like the feeling.

"Do you want me to try it?" Anything to get him to move away from her.

He studied her for a moment longer, and she would have given a month's salary to know what he was thinking. In an effort to regain some control, she returned the appraisal.

He really did have a sensuous mouth, she thought. His bottom lip jutted slightly, giving him an air of belligerence, while the deep groove in the center of his top lip added a touch of vulnerability. She could see the faint sheen of perspiration on his upper lip.

She raised her gaze back sharply to his eyes in time to see his eyebrow twitch. This time she couldn't miss the flicker of interest. It seemed a long time before he moved away and sat down on the couch.

"Yeah, take a walk up and down the room." He leaned forward, resting his forearms on his knees, his expression challenging her.

If he thought he was going to get a reaction from her, she thought, he was mistaken. Keeping her face a mask of unconcern, she took a few mincing steps across the carpet in front of him.

"Terrific. You look like you're dancing the minuet."

His dry tone annoyed her. She paused, standing as close to his knees as she could get without actually touching him. From the advantage of her height, she looked down at him, allowing just a hint of threat in her voice. "How about you showing me, then?"

He stared up at her for several nerve-racking seconds, then shrugged. Nicole took a seat on the armchair and prepared to enjoy the spectacle.

Luke got up slowly, walked to the edge of the carpet and turned. Sticking his hands in the pockets of his pants, he hunched his shoulders, thrust his chin forward and with an exaggerated swing of his hips, tottered forward on imaginary heels.

She made a valiant effort and failed. Her laugh exploded into the room before she could stop it. Clamping her lips together, she laid the tips of her fingers on her mouth and tried to straighten her face.

He looked offended. "All right, see if you can do any better."

"I doubt it. I think you looked charming." Her lips quivered. "Just don't try it in heels and a skirt."

She watched in fascination as his mouth tilted in a wry smile she found much too attractive. "How about an encore?" she suggested, grinning up at him.

"How about you giving it another try?" He leaned over and grabbed both her arms, pulling her to her feet.

"Like this?" Balancing on her toes, she executed a toned-down version of Luke's effort.

He frowned. "Have you ever worn high heels?"

"Not really. I prefer to be comfortable."

His eyes probed her face before he turned away to pick up the folder she'd left on the table. "Well, we'd better buy some shoes with heels so you can get practice walking in them."

"Okay." Taking advantage of the opening, she asked one of the questions bothering her. "Who's buying my wardrobe for this impersonation?"

"Someone on Sutton's staff, though I'll give final approval." He kept his eyes on the pages as he flicked them over. "You got a problem with that?"

"No." She wasn't being entirely honest. The thought of his picking out clothes for her to wear gave her a distinctly odd feeling. She wondered how he felt about it, since he was in essence selecting clothes for Opal.

Before she had time to speculate on that, Luke glanced at his watch. "I have to get back to work." He closed the file and handed it to her. "I should be through soon after six, so I'll order dinner when I get back. In the meantime, you can go over these notes."

He reached for a light gray jacket that lay on the back of the couch. "I'll bring some shoes back with me."

"Okay." She flicked open the file and looked at the pictures of Opal. "You know the size?"

She knew without looking at him that he'd sent another of his intense scrutinies over her body. "Yeah," he said softly. "I have all the measurements I need."

Her skin still tingled long after he'd closed the door behind him.

Luke picked out a pair of sandals in the department store two blocks from the hotel, then walked back, making the most of the opportunity to enjoy the fresh air.

For once the sun shone in a clear blue sky, and he could feel the warmth on his shoulders. The tropical heat of Hawaii was going to feel good after the cool wet Oregon spring, he thought, trying to drum up some enthusiasm at the prospect.

If he'd been going alone, he would have been looking forward to it with the utmost pleasure. Although he'd deny it if anyone asked, he'd missed the challenge and excitement of being on the force more than he'd thought possible.

But that wasn't all of it. He'd spent the past two years thinking about bringing Merrill down. In fact, if it hadn't been for Sutton's warning him to stay out of it, he'd have taken off to Hawaii when he'd first heard about the possibility that Merrill was living there under an alias.

Sutton had warned him that without the necessary authority, his chances of bringing in Merrill on his own were pretty slim. Luke's smile held no humor as he mounted the steps of the Royal King.

He had the authority now, thanks to Officer Nicole Parker. Sutton had sworn him in as a temporary officer of the law. If only there had been another way to carry out the assignment, Luke would have been a happy man.

And he was far from happy, Luke admitted as the elevator took him up to his office on the second floor. Not only had he been given the responsibility of protecting another officer, but the officer in question had to be a woman. And Officer Parker was on a temporary assignment, her first as a detective. Her lack of experience in that department made things all the more complicated.

Not that he had anything against women in the police force. Some of them, he had to admit, were every bit as capable as a man of hitting a target with a .38 or cuffing a struggling prisoner while reading him his rights.

Luke scowled as he stepped out of the elevator. Unfortunately he was the old-fashioned type. He couldn't get past the conviction that women needed to be protected in a crisis, qualified officers or not. It was a gut reaction, a built-in feature of his personality, and there was nothing he could do about it.

He opened the door of his office and dropped into his chair, running both his hands through his hair. He didn't want the responsibility for someone else's life. He especially didn't want the responsibility for a woman's life. And, in particular, he didn't want the responsibility for Nicole Parker's life.

She put him off guard. He couldn't seem to forget that she was a woman behind all that cool professionalism—an attractive woman, a woman who stimulated all the wrong responses that could take his mind off his job. And he had to keep his mind on his job. It was the only way he could ensure her safety.

Luke groaned and reached for the report he was supposed to be working on. Some niggling little foreboding in the back of his mind kept warning him that this time he just might have bitten off more than he could chew. It wasn't a comforting thought.

The time seemed to drag to Nicole, though it was only two hours since Luke had left her alone. The contents of the bookcase surprised her when she glanced through the titles. Several Westerns crowded the shelves, along with a couple of Jack London novels and a whole series on outdoor adventures.

She hadn't figured Luke Jordan as the outdoors type, Nicole thought, leafing through a copy of Mark Twain's *Life on the Mississippi.*

She went over the contents of the file a couple of times, but apart from an interesting description given by Luke, she didn't find much to help her.

The pictures provided her best source of information, and she studied them until she could see Opal's face clearly when she closed her eyes.

Standing in front of the mirror, she studied her own reflection, but the longer she looked, the less certain she became about her likeness to the woman.

She needed some makeup, Nicole decided as she paced restlessly around the room. It would take practice to put on the kind that Opal wore, and it would give her something to do while Luke worked at his job.

She was making out a list of what she needed when the sound of the key in the door announced Luke's return. She could have done without the sudden turmoil in her stomach, Nicole thought as she watched Luke's lean figure walk into the room.

He carried a plastic drawstring bag in his hand and waited until he was halfway across the room before throwing it on the couch next to her. "Try those," he said, tugging off his jacket. "They should fit."

Hadn't the man ever heard of a pleasant greeting? Nicole thought irritably, then in the next second reminded herself that officially they were on duty. He had no obligation to be pleasant to her. Even so, she sent him a reproachful frown before pulling open the bag.

The white sandals she drew out had skimpy straps and the highest heels she'd ever seen. Opal had to have strong ankles and well-developed calves, Nicole thought, staring at the shoes. No wonder she walked like a turkey.

She slipped out of her sneakers, slid her foot into one of the slender sandals and arranged the straps. Carefully she put her weight on it and stood. Her ankle caved in, and she transferred her weight hurriedly to the other foot.

"How the hell did she walk in these?" she muttered.

"Not too gracefully."

Nicole looked up when she thought she heard a trace of humor in his voice, but his face remained as passive as ever.

"Try the other one on," he said. Grimacing, she sat down again to remove her other sneaker and replace it with the sandal. She looked up at Luke, who stood a few feet away, watching her with his usual cool detachment.

"If I break my ankle on these things," she said grimly, "I'll sue."

"You can sue the department. I'm just a subordinate."

He'd sounded disgruntled, which didn't help. "Well," she warned him, "you'd better hope I don't break an ankle or there goes the entire operation."

"Not necessarily. You can always go on a honeymoon on crutches. I imagine it's been done before."

His unexpected reminder of their impending roles unnerved her completely. In an effort to control the sudden rush of color that flooded her cheeks, she shoved herself up with a muttered, "Here goes!"

Unfortunately her momentum carried her a little too far. She flung out her arms in a desperate attempt to steady herself. Her ankle gave way once more, and she felt herself toppling over.

She took two staggering steps in an effort to keep her balance, but her forward progress accelerated. With a sense of total humiliation, she made a grab for the nearest solid object, which happened to be Luke. Her hands connected with his shoulders as both her ankles turned out and her weight painfully distributed itself on the outer edges of her feet.

For a moment he looked as shocked as she felt. His arms hugged her as he supported a large percentage of her weight. His chest felt like solid rock jammed against her breasts, and his mouth parted in surprise.

The sensation that spiraled through her was anything but professional. "I think I've broken both my ankles," she said shakily.

His eyes seemed to have darkened. He made a visible effort to pull himself together and uttered a low curse. "I could have done it better myself."

Nicole had a mental vision of him wearing the sandals and doing that ridiculous strut across the room. The thought had her grinning as she clung to his shoulders and tried to climb back on the heels.

She heard his sharp intake of breath as her body slid up the length of his. Her amusement died when he muttered, "Dammit, Parker, this isn't funny. I knew this wouldn't work. I told Sutton you don't have the experience for a job like this."

Using his shoulders for leverage, she dug her fingers into solid muscle with a little more force than necessary to propel herself away from him. She stepped out of the shoes, waiting for her temper to cool before she delivered her speech.

"Okay, now let's get a few things straight." She saw his eyes narrow at her threatening tone, but she was too annoyed to care if she was trampling on his ego.

"I happen to be the cop here, in case you've forgotten. I'm fully qualified for the job and you know it. You've been out for almost two years. People can forget a lot in two years. If you value your pride, I suggest you quit treating me like an amateur, or I promise you, you'll live to regret it."

His lowered eyebrows reduced his eyes to slits. "I tell you what I regret. I regret being landed with this lousy setup. Period. I could do this job a whole lot better on my own."

"Really." She lifted a finger and pointed it accusingly at him. "You don't regret the setup, mister. What you regret is being landed with a police officer who just happens to be a woman. I've seen some macho resentment in my time, but you really—"

"It's got nothing to do with you being a woman."

"Oh, yeah?" She took a step closer to him so that her face was mere inches from his. "So why don't you tell me what it does have to do with? You made your prejudice pretty clear in the chief's office the other day. And you've been on my case ever since I got here this afternoon.

"And what's wrong with a little humor, for pity's sake? This situation could use some. I've got enough problems without having to deal with a moody, arrogant ex-cop sulking around like an overgrown adolescent who's lost his television privileges."

She turned to leave him, but he grasped her arm, twisting her back to face him. His harsh voice grated on her when he spoke.

"I may be an ex-cop, but I assure you I haven't forgotten one damn thing about the experience. And I suggest you cut the humor. It can get in the way of your concentration. If you knew Merrill the way I do, if you realized for one moment the danger you could be in, you wouldn't find it nearly so funny. You can take my word on that."

She struggled to pull away from him, but he held her fast, breathing hard. She knew a couple of moves she could use to free herself, but decided it might not be wise to utilize them.

Instead, she resorted to dignity. "You don't have to manhandle me," she said with just the right amount of scorn. "I get the picture. No laughs. If that's the way you want it, I'll be happy to oblige. But I don't think we're going to manage too convincing an image if we're clawing each other's eyes out on our honeymoon."

He deliberately dropped his gaze to her mouth. "Don't worry about our image. I'll make sure it's convincing. You can count on it."

He let her go, and she found herself trembling as she sat down to pull on her sneakers. She couldn't help wondering just how far he'd go to make it look convincing, and just how far she was willing to comply.

She refused to look at him when he retrieved the sandals and dropped them in front of her. "You'd better start practicing," he said quietly. "This operation depends on you doing a good job."

"I know that." She grabbed the sandals and stood. "You don't have to worry about me. Unlike you, I can have a sense of humor without sacrificing any of my professionalism. I'll have Opal Turner down so well even you won't be able to tell the difference."

She reached for the list of makeup she'd composed and handed it to him. "This is what I'll need. The sooner I get it, the more time I'll have to experiment. Now, if you'll excuse me, I'd like to have a shower."

His eyebrow twitched in the involuntary movement that she was beginning to recognize as exasperation. "Go ahead. I'll order dinner. Any preferences?"

"Something light," she said shortly, crossing the room. "I'm watching my cholesterol."

"Good idea." She had her back to him, so she couldn't see his face. But she heard the provocative note in his voice when he added, "And you're wrong, Officer Parker. I'll be able to tell the difference."

Wondering exactly what he meant by that, Nicole kept walking all the way into the bedroom.

She hadn't brought many clothes with her, since she'd be taking a new wardrobe to Hawaii. A pair of black pants and a turquoise blue shirt was the closest outfit she had to dressing for dinner. For some reason, she needed the security of looking her best if she was to get through an evening in the company of Luke Jordan, she decided after taking her shower.

"Strictly business," she muttered under her breath as she dragged a brush through her hair. As long as she kept that thought firmly in place, she'd keep everything in perspective.

She reached for a clasp, then gathered a handful of hair in her hand and paused, frowning at her reflection in the mirror. Slowly she let the thick strands fall back to settle lightly on her shoulders. She replaced the brush on the dresser, picked up her lipstick and placed a light film of coral on her lips.

For a long moment she stared into her own eyes, disturbed by the faint glow of expectancy she saw there. Then she gave herself a mental shake. "What are you trying to prove, Parker?" she muttered. "You know better than to play with fire."

With deft movements she pulled her hair back and fastened it, then walked out of the bedroom.

Luke sat on the couch watching the news on the television when she entered the living room. He glanced up, then down at his watch. "I've ordered room service for seven-thirty," he told her. "Sutton's supposed to have someone doubling up the meals I order. I hope he's got it covered down there, or we'll be losing some weight."

"Oh, well, it wouldn't hurt me to lose a few pounds." Nicole walked across to an armchair and sat down.

"Yeah. Opal's really skinny." Luke got to his feet and stretched his arms above his head. "I'll take my shower now. Don't answer the phone if it rings, or the door."

Was he deliberately trying to goad her, she wondered, or did he talk to everyone like that? She watched him saunter out of the room, wishing she knew what was bugging him. Sooner or later she'd have to find out, if only to clear the air.

She kept her eyes on the news report and her ears on the sound of water rushing from the faucet in the shower. Her mind was somewhere in between, striving not to dwell on the interesting images her ears provoked.

She relaxed when the sound ceased, and a few minutes later managed to look up casually when Luke walked back into the room. He'd shaved, she noticed, and the allure of his cologne beckoned to her from clear across the room.

Switching her gaze back to the magazine program in progress, she said lightly, "It's eighty-four in Honolulu. I hope Sutton's assistant knows how to pick out a lightweight wardrobe."

"I'll make sure of it."

An uncomfortable thought struck her. In one of the pictures, Opal had been wearing a skimpy dress. Skimpy dresses were one thing, but a skimpy bikini was something else entirely. Her tastes ran more toward the one-piece suit, Nicole thought, feeling prickles of apprehension creeping down her spine. She wasn't at all sure she could carry off an appearance of casual unconcern if she had to run around a beach half-naked.

The more she thought about it, the less happy she became with the prospect. She refused to admit that it wasn't so much the amount of skin she'd be displaying that bothered her as much as the person who'd be getting the closest look at it.

She jumped visibly when Luke asked quietly, "You got a problem?"

"Oh, no." She gave him a fairly indifferent glance before looking back at the television set. "I was just thinking about Hawaii."

His voice sounded brusque when he spoke again. "Look, this deal won't be any picnic for either of us, and I know better than most what Merrill is capable of doing. If you have the slightest doubt about it, if you want to back out, now's the time to say so. Nobody's going to hold you to an assignment you're not ready to handle."

This time her glance was pure disdain. "Sutton believes I'm capable, and I agree with him. I know that's what you want, but I'm not backing out, Luke, so forget it. I'm in this to the bitter end, so you might as well accept it. I'll do my part if you'll do yours, but I tell you now, I'm no Katherine Hepburn. I don't know if I can pretend to be madly in love with you if you're snarling at me at every opportunity. If this had been for real, I would have told you where to stuff your proposal."

She was close enough to see the corner of his mouth twitch. "If this had been for real," he said dryly, "I wouldn't have proposed in the first place."

"Well, I'm glad we got that much settled." She leaned back in her chair, determined not to let him see her chagrin.

"It's nothing personal," Luke said, sounding offhand. "You're just not my type."

"I figured that." She lifted Opal's picture from the folder and held it up. "I have a pretty good idea what *is* your type."

He opened his mouth to answer her, then closed it as a sharp rap sounded on the door. Placing a warning finger over his lips, he made a gesture with his hand toward the bedroom.

Nicole rose swiftly and trod quietly on bare feet across the carpet. She'd obeyed without question, her training making the response automatic.

In all likelihood, the visitor was simply bringing their dinner. The fact that Luke wasn't taking any chances emphasized the warning he'd given her earlier about the dangers they were facing. She tried not to think about that as she waited for him to open the door.

Chapter 3

Nicole waited out of sight but stayed within earshot while Luke opened the door. She heard a faint rattle of dishes, then waited until a loud click told her he'd closed the door before she ventured back into the room.

He greeted her with a hand raised in warning, and she watched him scrutinize the large tray he'd placed on the breakfast bar. He examined everything on it, even lifting it to look underneath. "It's clean," he announced, putting it back down on the bar.

The whole thing struck her as melodramatic. "Aren't you being a little overcautious? Merrill can't possibly know I'm here. Even if he did, it would've been a little hard for him to plant a bug."

She lifted the cover of a dish to look with appreciation at salmon bathed in a light cream sauce. The lemony aroma smelled wonderful, reminding her she hadn't eaten since breakfast.

"I'm not about to take any chances," Luke assured her. "If Morris Adams really is Adrian Merrill, it won't take him long to find out that Opal Turner is back in circulation. Once he bites, he'll move heaven and earth to get Opal. He has a big score to settle, and he'll make sure he gets the most out of his revenge."

"Then why do we have to go all the way to Hawaii? Why don't we just sit here and wait for him?"

"Because," Luke said, moving behind the bar, "Merrill wouldn't take the risk of coming himself. He'd send someone to pick up Opal and bring her back, or if that wasn't possible, he'd have her killed with as much mess as possible."

He opened a drawer and took out an assortment of cutlery, then reached in the cupboard for plates. "Merrill can be very inventive when dealing out punishment. And he hates cops. If he had you picked up by one of his thugs and found out you were a cop going to all that trouble to set a trap for him, he'd enjoy taking out his frustration on you. Believe me, you'd end up begging him to finish you off."

"Charming," Nicole murmured, trying to sound impassive. She wasn't about to let him know that his words had just given her a chill big enough to destroy her appetite. She would just have to make darn sure, she told herself, that Adrian Merrill never got his hands on her.

Luke's expression appeared unconcerned as he flipped a chunk of salmon onto a plate. "As long as we're on the subject, from now on you answer only to 'Opal.' The sooner you get used to being called by that name, the better."

"If we have to be this careful, wouldn't it be better to cook our own food instead of ordering it in?"

"I always order it from room service. It comes with the job. It would look odd if I didn't do it now. Everything's supposed to look normal, remember?"

Nicole hoped the rumors she'd heard about Luke losing his nerve were unfounded. So far, she'd seen or heard nothing to substantiate the stories. However, her conviction that she could take care of herself was beginning to lose weight. It was becoming clear that she would need a powerful ally in her corner.

She had to trust Sutton's judgment to a certain extent, but her life was on the line. She wanted to know exactly why Luke left the force, and something else that seemed equally important—just what the relationship had been between Luke and a deadly criminal's girlfriend. She made up her mind to have the answers to both questions before they left for Hawaii.

Luke seemed to be making an effort to be pleasant over dinner, and Nicole was quite happy to go along with him as she enjoyed the salmon and green salad.

She listened to him talk about the various aspects of hotel work, but when she tried to question him, he skillfully maneuvered the conversation back to more mundane topics.

After he'd avoided yet another of her casual attempts at subtlety, she decided it was time to get direct. "Do you ever miss being on the force?" she asked him, determined not to be sidetracked this time.

"I don't think about it." He helped himself to another slice of French bread and reached for the butter.

"You must really enjoy your job here, then."

"I wouldn't say that, either."

She looked up, surprised by his denial. "You'd rather be doing something else?"

"I'd rather be somewhere else. I'd like to get out of the city. I'd like to live in clean air, surrounded by country, some place where I could keep dogs and chickens, maybe a horse or two."

She looked at him, intrigued by this new insight. "You want to ranch?"

"I don't know what I want to do. I just don't want to do it here."

"So why do you stay?"

His glance skimmed her face, then flicked away. "I guess I don't believe in quitting. It smacks of failure."

And Luke Jordan wasn't a man who could accept failure, Nicole thought. Maybe he was more afraid of starting over again than of staying. "You quit the force," she pointed out gently.

She saw the bitterness distort his face for a moment before he erased it. "That was different." His expression clearly warned her not to pursue the subject.

She hadn't meant it that way. She'd simply wanted to illustrate the fact that if he'd done it once, he could do it again. Before she could explain, he added, "What made you decide on police work? I always wonder why a woman would want to be a cop."

The implied prejudice in that statement had her bristling. "The same reasons a man wants to, I guess. Actually it was my second choice. I wanted to be a pilot."

"Oh, yeah, I remember you mentioning it." His eyes regarded her with curiosity. "Not many women choose that occupation, either."

Nicole shrugged. "I'm not the type to sit behind a desk all day."

"I figured that."

She decided to ignore the dry comment. "I wanted to do something different. Both my brothers fly—they seemed to be having so much fun, I wanted to try it, too."

His smile made a brief appearance. "Do I detect a little sibling rivalry?"

"Not exactly. It was more a matter of wanting to prove I'm as capable as they are. I was tired of being reminded that I was a girl, as if that automatically precluded me from anything more strenuous than tennis or cycling. Ten years ago men were still relatively unenlightened."

Again his eyes studied her, as if he were trying to make up his mind about something. "I'm surprised you didn't try out to be an astronaut."

She picked up her coffee cup and held it in both hands. "Don't think I didn't consider it. I might even have made the attempt, if it hadn't been for my acrophobia."

"I guess a walk in space could be a little hairy if you're afraid of heights."

"It was enough to keep me grounded from flying." She shivered. "I did well in the training, until I got behind the controls of a plane. I'd see the earth coming up to meet me and I'd freeze. Even in the simulator, knowing I was flying a mock-up on the ground, I'd still shut my eyes on the landing."

He picked up his own coffee before asking casually, "So how do you feel about flying as a passenger?"

"I'm fine as long as I keep my eyes shut on landing." She deliberately closed her mind on the image as her stomach churned.

"Good. It would be a little difficult to drive to Hawaii."

"Don't worry," she assured him, "I'll be fine." She wondered how many times she'd have to say it before he was convinced of that.

"So why the police force?"

"I saw an ad in the paper. They were actively recruiting women for the force at the time, and the job appealed to me, so I applied." She took a sip of hot coffee, enjoying the smooth flavor. "I did think my acrophobia might keep me out of there, too," she added, "but apparently it wasn't a factor. I got through training **without any** problems, anyway."

"So now you want to make detective."

She looked up sharply when she detected an edge of skepticism in his voice. "Yes, I do. I enjoy a challenge, the complexities of solving puzzles, even though I know most of the work can be boring and routine. I happen to think the end results are worth it."

"Worth putting your life on the line?"

Although his expression remained passive, she had the feeling he was trying to goad her into admitting her vulnerability. She wasn't going to give him the satisfaction. "Isn't that what you're doing? And you're not even a cop anymore. Is it worth it to you?"

She was unprepared for his reaction. Shoving his chair back, he got to his feet. His voice was harsh when he said, "I wouldn't be doing it if it wasn't. Now, if you want to get through this assignment in one piece, we'd better start to work on your impersonation."

Aware that she'd pushed a button, she bit back the retort hovering on her lips. She stacked the dirty plates and cutlery and carried them to the kitchen, putting them into the sink before turning on the faucet.

"I'll take care of that later," Luke said, carrying the tray of empty dishes to the door.

"It'll take me two minutes."

She heard him open and close the door, apparently leaving the tray outside. The rush of water masked his footsteps, and she started when he spoke close to her shoulder.

"I'll dry." He picked up a damp coffee cup and added quietly, "You're a little jumpy, aren't you?"

She sent him a quick glance, but he appeared absorbed in polishing the cup. She decided there was no point in denying it. "I'll settle down once we're there. I never was very good at waiting."

"Yeah, I know the feeling." He placed the cup on the counter and reached for the second one.

Now was the time, she decided. The domestic scene seemed to have dispelled some of the tension between them. "You and Opal must have been very good friends," she said lightly.

"We spent quite a bit of time together." He put the cup next to its mate on the counter. "As soon as we get done here, we'll try the walk again."

If he'd told her to butt out, he couldn't have made it plainer. Nicole scowled as she let the water swirl down the drain. Obviously he didn't want to discuss it. Which only made her all the more curious. Since she was going to impersonate the woman, she thought in resentment, surely she was entitled to know? Sooner or later, she promised him silently.

Luke proved to be a tough coach. He made her walk up and down the living room in the awkward sandals, then, when he was satisfied, made her do the same thing in bare feet. He demonstrated Opal's hand gestures and the way she tossed her head in anger, then made Nicole copy them over and over until she was ready to swear at him.

After two hours of exhaustive practice, Nicole had had enough. Nothing she did seemed to please him. She was either too fast or too slow, too cautious or not aggressive enough, and finally, when he demanded for the tenth time in a row that she toss her head, the anger was real.

"Give me a break," she muttered when he'd lifted his hands in a negative gesture. "I'm not going to do this overnight."

"I'm aware of that." The strain was obviously telling on him, too. His commands had been curt and to the point, and he'd avoided looking at her as much as possible.

Apparently this was an intensely painful process for Luke Jordan, and Nicole longed to know why. Was she a potent reminder of a woman he'd once loved? she wondered. Or maybe still loved?

In spite of his imperious attitude, he looked exhausted. His hair lay tangled on his forehead, and weariness shadowed his eyes. He'd opened the top two buttons of his shirt earlier in a moment of frustration and had rolled his sleeves above his elbows.

If Nicole hadn't been so irritated with him, she might have found his disheveled appearance strangely appealing. It was just as well, she told herself, that she was mad at him.

"I'm doing my best," she announced, and flopped onto the empty couch. "If I have to do the turkey walk one more time tonight, I'm going to pull a muscle."

"Okay, we'll call it quits for now." He glanced at his watch. "We're both tired. We'll take it from here tomorrow."

Hungry for some word of encouragement, she asked, "Am I doing that bad?"

He seemed surprised and shot her a narrow glance. "No, actually you're doing pretty good. But pretty good won't cut it. You'll have to be perfect." He stretched, straining the fabric of his shirt across the muscles in his chest.

Nicole shifted her gaze, disturbed by the quickening of her pulse. "I'll be as near perfect as I can get. I'm tired now, but I'll give it another go tomorrow."

"Good. It's my day off, so we'll be able to get a whole day in."

Nicole wasn't sure how she felt about that. She could have done with a breathing space. "I'll make some coffee," she said, and headed for the stove. Aware that he couldn't go to bed until she did, she poured the coffee and took a cup over to him.

"I'll take mine to bed," she said as he took the coffee from her. "I need to study these reports some more." She felt unsettled for some reason and couldn't quite meet his gaze when he looked up at her.

"Good night," he said quietly. "I hope you sleep well."

"I usually do." She sent a rueful glance over at the couch. "I hope you do."

"Don't worry about me. I'm used to roughing it."

She meant to give him a polite smile and leave. Instead, some odd expression in his eyes held her, and she found it impossible to look away.

She couldn't breath properly. She watched his cool gray eyes darken and ran her tongue around lips that had suddenly gone dry. Her pulse leaped when his gaze shifted to her mouth.

A vivid memory of the moment her body had brushed intimately with his sent a shiver racing through her body. She cleared her throat, trying to break the almost tangible web that reached out for her.

"I ... good night," she muttered, and hurried across the room to the bedroom. After shutting the door behind her, she leaned against it and closed her eyes.

Maybe Luke was right. This wasn't going to work. How could she keep her concentration on her job if she was pretending to be in love with a man who could fire her blood just by looking at her?

She moved around the bed and glared at her image in the dresser mirror. She was thirty-one years old, for heaven's sake. She had to pull herself together before she made a complete fool of herself. Whatever the man had that affected her hormones, she told the worried face looking back at her, she'd better ignore it. Her life could well depend on it.

It was simply the novelty of the situation, she assured herself. Once she got used to sharing living space with a man, everything would be fine.

Her confidence fled as a light tap on the door froze her to the spot. Even as she wondered if she'd imagined it, she heard the tapping repeated, louder this time.

Her heart seemed to be trying to pound its way through her ribs as she crossed the carpet to the door. Opening it a fraction, she peered through the crack.

"It's only me," Luke said dryly. "You forgot your coffee."

"Oh." Feeling like a prize fool, Nicole opened the door and took the cup from his hand.

"And the report. I'd also like to get some clean underwear, if that's all right with you?"

Her breathing was malfunctioning again, but she managed a weak nod and stood back, letting him into the room. She made a big deal of drawing the drapes across the window so that she wouldn't have to watch him select his underwear, conscious all the time of the tingling feeling down her back. Her shoulders slumped with relief when he murmured a soft good-night and left the room.

Obviously, she thought grimly as she stared at the closed door, she would have to work on her resistance to Luke Jordan's doubtful charms. It shouldn't be all that hard. He'd told her bluntly that she wasn't his type.

She waited until all sound had ceased from outside before venturing into the bathroom. He'd turned out the lamps in the living room. Even so, she was glad that the couch was hidden from view as she came out of the bathroom and padded silently back to the bedroom on bare feet.

She had almost dozed off before the thought struck her that even if Nicole Parker was not his type, apparently Opal Turner was. She wondered how that would affect his attitude when she was playing the part of Opal.

Wishing she hadn't thought of that, she buried her face into the pillow and did her best to fall asleep.

Luke was having a great deal of trouble doing the same thing. He'd stretched his body out on the couch and had lain there, rigid as an iron pipe, listening to the sounds of Nicole moving around in the bathroom, and trying desperately not to visualize some kind of transparent, filmy fabric clinging to her ample curves.

It had become potently apparent in the past few hours that it had been way too long since he'd satisfied his needs with a woman. This was only the first night, and already he felt as if he were sitting on a smoking volcano.

Heaven help him when they got into the heavy stuff. He'd had his arms around the woman only for a brief moment or two, and his body had reacted without warning. He only hoped she hadn't noticed his predicament when she'd bumped into him.

He smothered a quiet groan and turned on his side. He'd noticed, all right. He'd been reminded of it every time he'd watched her hips swaying seductively across the room in a way Opal would have killed to emulate.

That was the problem. She was nothing like Opal. She had too much class, too much damn dignity. He didn't know if she would ever look like Opal. Maybe the wig and the cosmetics would help. He certainly hoped so.

He shifted onto his back and stared in the darkness at the shrouded ceiling. That was if he decided to carry on with this crazy plan at all. If it had been anyone else, he wouldn't have entertained the idea for one second. But Sutton had been right. This was probably their best shot at cornering that slippery bastard.

Even so, if he had any doubts at all, he'd have to call it off. He simply refused to take a chance with Nicole Parker's life unless he was reasonably sure they could pull it off.

And if by some miracle he could convince himself of that, he would just have to make sure that none of Merrill's men, or Merrill himself in particular, got too good a look at her.

As for his personal reactions, he'd just have to keep them under control. His breath came out in a quiet snort of derision. So far, he hadn't done too good a job on that score. He'd have to double his efforts if he was going to bring them both through this unscathed.

He turned onto his side again, tugging irritably at the blanket that half covered him. It should be easy. He just had to keep reminding himself of all the reasons why he didn't want to get involved in a relationship. He had the distinct impression that Nicole Parker wasn't the one-night-stand type. And that was the only type he was interested in. Period.

He'd just about given up hope of sleeping when he opened his eyes and saw daylight seeping through the gap in the drapes. Looking at his watch, he found he'd slept after all, but for all the good it had done him he might as well have been carousing the night away in the nearest bar.

He climbed off the couch and rubbed a hand across his scratchy jaw. It would have probably done him good to have done just that, he thought as he crossed the room to the bathroom. He might have worked a few powerful urges out of his system.

Nicole had been awake for hours, but hadn't wanted to leave the security of the bedroom and risk bumping into Luke in his underwear. She had enough problems with him fully clothed.

She listened to the sounds of the shower from the bathroom, doing her best to forget that this was Luke's bed she was lying on and that up until last night he'd slept on this very same mattress.

Where on earth did these adolescent thoughts come from? she thought irritably, then jumped nearly out of her skin when a sharp rap sounded on her door.

"Are you awake?" Luke's muffled voice demanded outside.

"Yes." She waited, heart thumping, praying he didn't want to come in.

"Are you decent? I'd like to get a clean shirt, if that's all right with you."

He sounded irritable. She looked around frantically, trying to decide whether she should get up and put on her robe or stay where she was.

He answered that for her by cracking open the door. "Did you hear me?"

"Yes, come on in." Did she look at him, she wondered, or pretend to be half-asleep? Before she could decide, he'd opened the door and walked in.

She found herself staring at him in helpless fascination. Luckily he had his back to her as he sorted through his shirts in the closet, or he would have seen her ogling his bare flesh.

He wore his dark pants and was naked from the waist up. She watched him lift a shirt from the rack and remove it from its hanger. His back was long and smooth, and with every movement, muscles rippled in his shoulders. Her fingers curled on the sheet.

"Oh, I forgot." He reached up and took a package down from the shelf above the rack. "Sutton sent this over for you." He turned toward her, holding his shirt in one hand while he offered her the package with the other.

Trying not to eyeball the dark wisps of hair covering his chest, she automatically reached for the package. "What is it?" She glanced up at him and caught the hot lick of his gaze on her partially exposed breasts.

Instinctively she pulled the sheet up to her chin. She wondered if he was as aware of the pulsing current between them as she was. The thought only intensified her discomfort.

After several agonizing seconds, he mumbled, "I'll put coffee on," and left the room a good deal faster than he'd come in.

She blew the air out of her lungs in an audible gasp as the door closed abruptly behind him. "Face it, Parker," she muttered, "you've got a problem."

Her usual method of dealing with a problem was to meet it head-on. Somehow, she didn't think that was going to work in this case. She couldn't just go marching in there and announce, I've got the hots for you so what are we going to do about it?

There had to be a more subtle way to handle things. They were both adults. Her mind shied away from the phrase consenting adults.

She pulled the covers over her head to muffle a groan, unable to believe she was having this ridiculous conversation with herself. She'd been attracted to men before, and it had always been so simple. Either they reciprocated or they didn't.

If they didn't, she accepted it with good grace and put it out of her mind. And if they did, well, then it was a place to start and she carried on from there. Most of the time the relationship ended before she became too involved.

She pulled the covers from her face and glared at the ceiling. That was what really bothered her, she realized. Somehow she had a niggling feeling that Luke Jordan might be a little harder to let go. She couldn't remember anyone affecting her as intensely as he seemed to do without any apparent effort.

This time her groan was audible. The prospect of how he would affect her when he was putting effort into it made her bones melt.

In a futile effort to forget the look in his eyes when she'd reached for the package, she opened the square box and pulled out something that resembled a large, flame red scouring pad. Grimacing at the wig, Nicole wondered how she was going to keep cool under a tropical sun wearing that thing.

A familiar smell filtered into the room, and she breathed in the warm aroma. Coffee. Exactly what she needed to clear the woolly feeling from her head and get her juices going again.

Poor choice of phrase, she warned herself as she climbed out of bed and reached for her robe. She'd better keep a lid on her juices. The last thing she needed was for him to find out how he affected her. She had problems enough without adding humiliation to them.

One thing she was certain of; the days ahead should be interesting, to say the least.

Damn, Luke thought, staring at the morning newspaper without seeing a word. He would have to do something about his clothes. He couldn't just go wandering into her room like that. He could end up embarrassing them both.

He should have waited until she was up and dressed. It was going to take him the best part of the day to forget what she looked like with her dark hair spread all over the pillow and her eyes still soft with night dreams. Not to mention the tantalizing glimpse of her softly rounded breasts.

If he could forget at all. He couldn't remember wanting to climb into bed with any woman that badly before. He hoped that his thoughts hadn't shown on his face. Hell, his hands were still shaking.

He turned the page with an angry crackle of paper. What was it about Nicole Parker that hit him so hard? He wished he knew, then maybe he could find a way to become immune to it.

He didn't want this. He didn't want to get involved. Not with Nicole Parker. Not with a cop. Not with any woman, but especially not with a cop.

She had so many strikes against her, yet every time he laid eyes on her he wanted her. And each time, he wanted her a little more badly. How in the hell was he supposed to put his hands on her in public and keep them off her in private? It was too damn much to expect of him.

He jumped guiltily when he heard the bedroom door open. Listening to her moving around in the bathroom, he viciously cursed Sutton under his breath. He cursed Nicole Parker for stirring up urges too powerful to ignore, and he cursed himself for not having the strength to resist the magnetism that vibrated between them.

He knew she was aware of the electricity between them. He also knew that she was fighting it just as hard as he was. He hoped she didn't stop fighting, because he wasn't sure just how long his willpower could hold out if his urges continued to escalate at the present rate.

His frustration did nothing to help the indifference he strived for throughout the long day, but manifested itself as a short temper that he couldn't seem to control.

He gave them both a break when he left to pick up the makeup she'd requested, hoping to ease the tension. But he'd been back only a short time before they were at it again.

* * *

The next few days showed little improvement in their personal relationship, though Luke could see definite results with his coaching efforts. For once, he was glad of the hours he had to work in the hotel, giving him time to brace himself for the tension-powered evenings he was forced to spend with Nicole.

Though he'd managed to keep his temper under reasonable control, the cool, almost disdainful way in which Nicole now accepted his tutoring got under his skin far worse than her spirited verbal sparring. He actually missed the battles.

The nights had been pure torture for him. Although she'd closed the door firmly between them, he seemed to hear every movement she made. There were times when he could swear he could hear her breathing. He'd even considered finding consolation at the local bar, but ten minutes after sitting there one night, he'd known it wasn't going to work.

It took him the best part of the week to admit what he'd been trying to avoid. Nicole was doing an excellent job with her impersonation of Opal. So far, he hadn't seen her in the makeup and wig, though he knew she'd been practicing with both in the privacy of the bedroom.

He hadn't seen her in the new outfits, either, since they hadn't arrived yet. But he didn't need the physical props to prove what he already knew. Nicole Parker could do the job. At least as far as the impersonation. Which meant that the operation was a go.

Luke lay in the darkened room and considered all the ramifications of his decision. He wasn't any happier about the situation, though he had to admit his estimation of Nicole had risen dramatically.

In spite of his abrupt treatment of her, she'd stuck with the regime he'd set for her, doggedly following his instructions with a determination he had to admire.

She was unlike any woman he'd met, either on the force or outside it. She had a casual attitude toward her appearance, as well as her image, that he found refreshing. She said what she thought, holding nothing back, meeting him on his own level with intelligent rejoinders and a dry wit. She was the first woman he'd met who could converse with him without using her femininity to sway him.

In fact, Luke admitted to himself in the quiet darkness, he respected her. As an officer of the law and as a woman. He'd never met a woman he really respected before. He'd never realized how important that was to him, until now. Which only compounded the problem. He didn't want to feel this way about her. He didn't want to feel anything for her at all.

His sleeplessness that night weakened his efforts to remain impartial. The next day was one of those days when everything seemed to go wrong. An elderly woman insisted her jewelry had been stolen from her room, and when Luke had finally tracked down the missing items in the hotel safe, the woman had accused him of lying about where he'd found them to save the name of the hotel.

That afternoon he'd been called down to a disturbance in the lobby and had roughly escorted one of the belligerent offenders outside, only to discover later that the man was a respected, long-time client and had not been responsible for the uproar.

Luke had been forced to apologize to the man, something he didn't do easily, and was further exasperated by the disdainful attitude with which his apology was accepted.

Well aware that his own bad humor had contributed to his problems, he was not looking forward to another tortuous evening with Nicole. He promised himself he would try to keep his irritation in check as he let himself into the suite.

Nicole heard him come in, and felt her stomach muscles contract with apprehension. So far, she had managed to hold her temper when Luke became too demanding and tyrannical, understanding the pressure he was under and the importance of perfecting every detail.

Her control weakened, however, as the long days dragged by, the monotony broken only by her difficult sessions with her short-tempered and sometimes unreasonable tutor.

She couldn't take much more of it, she thought as she braced herself to go out and greet him. Sooner or later all that resentment was going to explode. The strain of being cooped up day and night inside the small living space, without even the luxury of sticking her head out the window for a breath of badly needed fresh air, had tightened her nerves to breaking point.

He was a tough man to please, and she was getting sick and tired of Opal's walk, Opal's gestures, Opal's laugh, Opal's head-tossing. In fact, she was heartily sick of Opal Turner altogether. Every time he called her by that damn name, her fists curled.

She took a moment or two to compose herself, then opened the door of the bedroom and walked out into the living room. Luke was scanning the headlines of a newspaper, which he'd laid on the counter, and barely looked up when she spoke.

"So, how was your day?" she inquired, unable to keep the sarcasm out of her voice when he'd mumbled an answer to her greeting.

"Terrific." He flicked a scowling glance at her face. "How was yours?"

"Well, let's see." She laid a finger against her chin in one of Opal's gestures. "First I walked the poodle, then I popped into Magnin's to pick up a silver fox jacket, had lunch at Alexanders, then—"

"Okay, cut the comedy routine—I'm not in the mood for laughs."

"Are you ever?" She walked past him into the kitchen area and plugged in the coffee machine. "Why don't you order an early dinner? You're probably hungry."

"I'm not hungry." He picked up the paper and slumped down on the couch. "And I don't want coffee, either. My stomach feels like a burned-out percolator as it is."

Nicole snatched the plug from the socket. "Well, what would your majesty prefer? Champagne? Cognac?"

"A little peace and quiet." He rattled the pages. "I've had a bad day."

"Fine." She glared at him across the room. "I'll leave you alone. You can have all the peace and quiet you want. I'd like to leave, period, but since I can't, I'll be in my room."

God, she thought as she snapped the door shut behind her, she sounded like a teenager in a full-blown tantrum. Whatever had happened to her sense of humor?

Trampled, she answered herself, under a barrage of commands, insults and impossible demands. What did he want from her, for pity's sake? She was doing her best, only best wasn't good enough for Mr. Perfectionist. He wanted miracles.

Nicole sat on the bed and pulled her knees up to her chin. She couldn't give him miracles. He seemed to need a certified guarantee that they could pull off this assignment. And there were no guarantees. He'd said as much in Sutton's office that first day.

All they could do was their best. And unless he accepted that, she could never give him what he was asking from her. She lifted her head, her pulse leaping, when she heard a light tap on her door.

"Come in," she said warily, and waited while the door opened and Luke walked into the room.

His lopsided smile went a long way toward diluting her frustration. "Sorry. I really have had a bad day."

She nodded. "I can tell. Apology accepted."

"Do you want me to go out and try coming in again?"

Grinning, she slipped off the bed. "No. But I think we could both use a drink. Does that come with the job, too?"

"No, it's extra. But I guess I owe you that much. I'll order it with dinner. All I have is beer, and something tells me you want something stronger."

"Much stronger. How about bourbon?"

He lifted an eyebrow in mock surprise. "Straight?"

"On the rocks."

"Hard drinker, huh?"

She shrugged. "My brothers taught me some bad habits."

"Oh, yeah?"

"Don't let it throw you. I know how to be a lady."

He stood looking at her so long she could feel her face growing warm.

"Yeah," he murmured finally, and left.

She heard him ordering the dinner and waited until he'd replaced the receiver before she left the bedroom. He looked up as she walked into the living room.

"Drinks are on the way up."

"Good." She gestured at the newspaper. "Anything interesting in the news?"

"Not so far." He reached for the front-page section and handed it to her. "See for yourself."

"Thanks." Her hand shook slightly when she took it from him, though she wasn't sure why. Maybe it had something to do with the long look he'd given her in the bedroom.

Whatever it was, she was aware of a subtle difference in the relationship between them, though she couldn't put a finger on it. She knew by the way Luke fidgeted on the couch that he was aware of it, too.

The feeling persisted all through dinner, when even the bourbon failed to relax Nicole's tension. It was as if things were finally coming to a head, though what kinds of things she wasn't sure.

Luke subsided once more into terse remarks and brief answers to her questions, and she could have cried with frustration. For a little while she'd actually believed his attitude had improved.

She watched him take the tray of empty dishes and leave them outside the door, and wished she knew what was going on in his mind. He'd made it very plain that something was bothering him, something that had begun ever since she'd arrived. Whatever it was, it had gradually intensified as the week had slipped by.

If only he'd come out and tell her what the problem was, maybe they could solve it. But she knew him well enough now not to expect that to happen. Luke Jordan apparently did *not* buy into the adage that a problem shared was a problem halved.

Unless, of course, her guess had been right, and the problem was herself—the fact that she wasn't Opal Turner, but was a constant reminder to Luke of someone he'd cared for and lost.

The thought increased her frustration, and once more she found herself fighting her resentment as Luke resumed the endless commands and criticisms.

After an hour of answering his rapid-fire questions in the role of Opal, she desperately needed a break. Excusing herself, she got up from the armchair to head for the bathroom.

Luke waited until she'd taken a couple of steps, then called out sharply, "Nicole!"

She turned, frowning. "Can't it wait until I get back?"

He got slowly to his feet. "A week," he said, exasperation tightening his voice. "A whole week, and you're still not with it."

She stared at him in bewilderment. "With what?"

"You are not Nicole," he said, pronouncing every word with infinite care. "You don't answer to Nicole. You are Opal Turner. You understand? Opal!" His voice had risen on each word until he was practically shouting.

"All right!" She gritted her teeth. "Okay, I'm sorry. It won't happen again."

"Dammit, your life depends on it. When are you going to get that through your head?"

"Well, it's my life." She took a deep breath and exhaled it. "Don't worry, I won't hold you responsible if anything goes wrong, so you can hang on to your precious pride. But I tell you something, Jordan. I've had it. I'm sick of this suite, I'm sick of Opal Turner and I'm sick of you and your damn instructions. I'm calling Sutton myself to tell him I'm ready to leave for Hawaii, with or without you."

She marched across the room to the phone and started punching buttons. She didn't hear him coming and gasped when he snatched the phone from her fingers and slammed it back on the rest.

Grabbing her arm with his strong fingers, he said harshly, "You can't use the phone, Opal. You know better than that."

Maybe the slip was deliberate, to test her yet again. Or maybe, for a moment, he'd actually forgotten who she really was. It didn't matter. His use of the despised name destroyed the last of her control.

She tugged her arm from his grasp, muttering in a low, fierce voice, "Damn you, I am not Opal. Not until I get to Hawaii. I am Nicole Parker, police officer, so stick that—"

The rest of her words were lost when he swore, dragged her into his arms and smothered her shocked mouth with a hot, hungry kiss that wiped out every last thought from her mind.

Chapter 4

The kiss ended far too soon. For one wild moment she was caught up in the fire of his mouth hard on hers, then abruptly he let her go. He stepped back, breathing hard, his eyes alight with some intense emotion she couldn't analyze.

When he spoke, his voice betrayed none of the turmoil in his eyes. "Well, I guess it's going to take a little practice, but it's not bad for a start."

Anger erased all caution as she glared back at him. "If that's the best you can do, your acting talent could stand some improvement. That feeble attempt wouldn't fool anybody."

He stared at her in stony silence while the heated seconds ticked by, and she asked herself why she insisted on playing such a dangerous game. She was no match for his strength, if he ever decided to use it against her.

"Tomorrow," he said, lowering his voice, "I'll be happy to prove to you just how impressive my talent can be. Right now I'm going for a walk, before I do something we might both regret."

Nicole struggled to dampen the fire in her breathing as she glared at the closed door. She wasn't surprised to discover she was trembling. The man was intolerable.

She tried not to think about how his kiss had affected her. He'd probably done it to insult her, an attempt to prove who was in charge. A throaty growl rose from her throat as she turned her back on the door. Well, all he'd proved was that this was nothing more than a job for him, and an unpleasant one at that.

She should be happy to have it so clearly spelled out for her, she thought as she hunted in the fridge for a soft drink. At least his behavior had destroyed any stray fantasies that might have been lurking in the back of her mind. This was total war.

How that was going to reconcile with a picture of blissfully happy newlyweds, she had no idea, but she'd act her behind off if it meant getting the job done and finished with.

If she hadn't wanted that promotion so badly, she thought, viciously ripping open the can, she'd tell him and Sutton to go to hell. But she was in this for the long haul, and no smart-mouthed, arrogant dictator was going to take that away from her.

She dropped onto the couch and tilted her head to tip the cold liquid into her mouth. She'd seen too many men with less time and less experience than she had make detective. This was her chance, and she wasn't going to throw it away on an ex-cop carrying a giant-size chip on his shoulder.

She leaned forward and put the can down on the table. Had Opal Turner put that chip there, she wondered, or was there something else behind Luke Jordan's unreasonable attitude? Did it have something to do with the reason he'd left the force? Once and for all, she had to find out.

He was too clever at avoiding her questions. Every time she asked him something he didn't want to answer, he turned the conversation back to her. She would have to throw him off guard if she wanted to find out what she wanted to know. And, she thought, getting to her feet with a triumphant grin, she knew exactly how she was going to do it.

With the picture of Opal propped up against the mirror in the bedroom, she set to work. Although she'd had a few practice sessions, it took her the best part of an hour before she was entirely satisfied.

She didn't like the face that stared back at her in the mirror, but she had to admit she looked a lot closer to the picture of Opal Turner now than she had a week ago.

It was too bad, she thought, sorting through the few clothes she'd brought, that Sutton hadn't come through with the wardrobe yet. After a lot of consideration, she slipped out of her jeans and shirt and pulled on her peach satin wrap that matched the chemise she wore to bed.

The hem reached to several inches above her knee, and she tied the sash tight around her waist, leaving a slight gap to reveal the length of one thigh.

She studied the result in the mirror and almost lost her nerve. Then she reminded herself of the result she hoped to accomplish. After all, he'd see a good deal more of her than that if she had to wear a bikini. It took her only a minute to exchange her clear contact lenses for the colored ones, then she picked up the wig and pulled it on her head, tucking her own hair up underneath it. She wrestled with it for a few more minutes to get it right, but finally she was satisfied. After slipping her feet into the sandals, she took another long look in the mirror.

The image startled her. She really did look like Opal Turner. She stuck a hand on her hip and did a couple of steps, imitating Opal's turkey strut. The wrap gaped open and she clutched it with her fingers, her bravado evaporating.

Maybe this wasn't such a good idea, she thought, eyeing her reflection. There had to be a better way to catch him off guard. She was about to change again when the unmistakable sound of the key in the lock warned her that Luke was back.

She took another swift glance in the mirror. This was just too good an opportunity to miss, she decided. If nothing else, his reaction would tell her how closely she resembled Opal. Kind of a dress rehearsal.

Pulling in a deep breath, she opened the door of the bedroom and stepped out onto the square of carpet that separated the living room from the rest of the suite. With one hand resting on her hip and her ankles elegantly crossed, she leaned a shoulder against the wall and waited.

Luke had spent the past hour trying to clear the thoughts smoldering in his head. He'd known deep in his subconscious mind that sooner or later the tension between them would have to explode. He just hadn't expected it to materialize in quite that way.

He'd just about blown it. He'd wiped everything from his mind except for a single, burning purpose that he'd been powerless to resist. For days he'd ached to haul her into his arms and kiss that seductive mouth until she begged for mercy.

Two seconds after he'd surrendered to that relentless urge, he'd realized he'd made a mistake. He'd managed to end it before he'd embarrassed himself, but then he'd nearly grabbed her again when she'd thrown him that challenge.

He was going about this all wrong, Luke thought as he retraced his steps back to the hotel. He was trying so hard not to get close to her that he was adding to the tension instead of relieving it.

It would be necessary to get close to her if they were going to pull this mission off. He could hardly avoid it. She was right when she warned him that hurling insults at each other wasn't typical behavior for newlyweds.

He entered the lobby and walked to the elevators, punching the button in an automatic gesture when he reached the doors. He would have to change his attitude if he was going to make this convincing.

Just get in there and do it, he told himself as he stepped out on the sixth floor and walked slowly to the suite. Try not to think about it. She'd insisted again and again that she could take care of herself.

Surely they were both experienced enough to handle it without letting it take over their concentration? They both knew it was for the benefit of the assignment. After all, he'd managed it with Opal.

He fitted the key into the lock. He'd always prided himself on his control over his emotions. He had absolutely no reason to doubt it now. Even if a little voice in his head did keep warning that Nicole Parker was an entirely different proposition from Opal Turner.

Inside the room, Nicole held her breath as she watched Luke step through the doorway. He didn't see her at first, and she fought an urge to run back into the bedroom when he closed the door, slipping the key into his jacket pocket.

If she was going to do this, she reminded herself, it had to be all the way. While his back was still turned toward her, she uttered a low, throaty, "Hi, handsome."

He threw a startled glance over his shoulder and froze. His eyes widened, and he turned the rest of his body in slow motion while he continued to stare at her, apparently speechless.

Heady with her success, Nicole straightened, tossed her head, then strutted across the room toward him. She halted a few feet from him, put her hand back on her hip and murmured, "Aren't you going to say hello to Opal, baby?"

"I'll be damned." He shook his head. "If I wasn't seeing it with my own eyes, I wouldn't believe it."

Nicole relaxed, dropping her hand from her hip with a pleased laugh. "Not bad, huh? Think I'll pass?"

"Lady, you could've fooled Opal's mother if she was still alive."

His answering smile took all the wind out of her lungs. She saw it so rarely, she'd forgotten how dangerously attractive that smile could be. His apparent turnaround from the surly ogre who'd left earlier unsettled her.

She backed up a few steps, catching herself as she almost stumbled in the high heels. "Er... I'll go and change," she said in a vain attempt to sound offhand. "I just wanted to see your reaction."

He nodded, his eyes telegraphing a message that escalated her pulse. "I hope you weren't disappointed?"

She gave a breathless little laugh. "No...I mean..." Her voice trailed off, and she twisted awkwardly on the heels and fled to the bedroom.

Disappointed? More like blown away. What an idiot she was being. Nicole tore off the wrap and flung it on the bed. That look wasn't for her, she reminded herself; it was for Opal. Opal, damn her. The woman with whom Luke Jordan had apparently engaged in a hot-and-heavy affair.

Muttering under her breath, Nicole climbed into her jeans and shirt. Why couldn't she remember that? Why was she reading messages in every glance, every word, that simply weren't there?

She tugged off the wig and shook her hair loose before picking up the jar of cream on the dresser. Taking a large glob of it, she smeared it over her face and wiped off every trace of makeup.

She had to get this ridiculous infatuation out of her system. She dragged her hair back and fastened it with a clasp. Leaning on her hands, she stared at her scrubbed-clean image in the mirror. If she didn't, she was going to get burned. But good.

She puffed out her breath in exasperation. "You're in worse trouble than I thought," she muttered quietly. In fact, the worst was yet to come. Somehow, she had to pretend to be madly in love with this man.

Tomorrow I'll be happy to prove just how impressive my talent can be. That little charade was going to test her abilities in a way she had never imagined. If she valued her self-respect and her pride, she just couldn't let him know how he affected her.

Nicole straightened. This was a job, nothing more. And she would have to go on telling herself that until she got it firmly fixed in her mind. Bracing herself, she opened the door.

Luke looked up when she walked into the living room, but she could tell nothing from his expression. To her relief, he made no mention of her demonstration, but instead held out a long, white envelope. She took it from him, looking at it with curiosity. "What's this?"

"Our airline tickets to Hawaii. We leave the day after tomorrow."

"All right!" She sent him a dazzling smile of relief. The waiting was over. All the practices, the rehearsals and, she hoped, the arguments, were done with. She opened the envelope, her heart skipping when she saw the tickets. "I feel like celebrating," she said, tucking them back in the envelope.

"We're going to. I've ordered a special meal for two, for tomorrow night."

She fought to keep her expression neutral. "Sounds great." She searched in her mind for something else to say. Unfortunately what came out was the last thing she'd intended. "I hope this cover won't be too painful for you."

His look of surprise, mixed with humor, unnerved her. "Painful? I'm not expecting it to be. Is there something I should know?"

She could feel the heat spreading across her face. What on earth had possessed her to say that? "I only meant...I mean...well, you and Opal were..." Damn, she thought savagely. She sounded like a tongue-tied adolescent. Why couldn't she ask him straight-out?

He was watching her with a strange expression in his eyes, somewhere between bewilderment and intense interest. "Opal and I were what?"

Nicole shrugged with as much nonchalance as she could manage. "Involved."

Luke leaned back against the couch and studied her for several long, tension-filled seconds. "What has Sutton told you?" he asked at last, his voice ominously quiet.

"Nothing." She finally found her composure again. "But it's obvious you know her intimately. I wasn't sure if you still . . . felt the same way about her."

"And which way is that?"

"Dammit, Luke." Nicole swung around to leave. "I was just thinking about your feelings, that's all. Forget it."

She was halfway across the room when he said quietly, "Nicole."

Without breaking her stride, she kept going.

"Nicole!"

She heard him get up. Ignoring him, she reached for the handle of the bedroom door. She had it open when she felt his hands on her shoulders, turning her around to face him.

She was surprised by the look of appeal on his face. She responded to it immediately. "You told me not to answer to anything except 'Opal,'" she reminded him gently.

His hands still held her, and she could feel the heat from them through the fabric of her shirt. As his fingers tightened, she saw the telltale twitch of his eyebrow.

"So I did."

She saw a tiny muscle move high on his jaw. Then his mouth curved into his incredible smile, and she forgot she'd ever been annoyed at him.

"You want to give me a minute?" he asked softly. "I'll tell you the whole story about Opal and me."

She nodded, letting out her breath when he dropped his hands and moved back to the couch.

He waited for her to sit down on one of the armchairs, his fingers absently combing through his hair. When he spoke, his voice was devoid of emotion, as if he were reciting from a report.

"I met Opal when I was working undercover in Merrill's warehouse. We'd suspected for some time that he was involved in some big-time drug dealing. I must have slipped up somewhere, or someone tipped him off, because apparently Merrill got suspicious."

Luke leaned forward, resting his forearms on his thighs. "He tried to be subtle about it. He sent his girlfriend to find out if I was on the level."

Nicole shifted uncomfortably, not sure she wanted to know now that he was willing to tell her.

"Opal came on pretty strong," Luke continued, still in the same flat voice, "and it didn't take me long to figure it wasn't because of my formidable charm. Knowing Merrill as I did, I knew Opal wouldn't take the risk of upsetting him unless she had his blessing. So...I decided to go along with it."

He linked his fingers together and stared down at them. "I figured I could turn the tables on her and get her to give me the information I needed."

He paused for so long Nicole thought that was all he was going to tell her. "And you fell for her?" she prompted.

Luke shook his head. "No. I felt sorry for her. She was just a kid and scared half out of her wits. I don't know how she got mixed up with a creep like Merrill. She'd never tell me, but she was in way over her head."

"So why didn't she leave?"

Luke glanced up, and Nicole was shaken by the animosity in his eyes. "If you knew anything about Adrian Merrill, you wouldn't have to ask that. No one walks out on a man like that. He'd have hunted her down and made sure no one else ever looked at her again."

A shudder shook Nicole's body. "So what happened?"

"I persuaded her to give me the information. In return, I promised her that I would warn her when the warehouse would be raided. I swore to her that Merrill and his cronies would be put away where they could never hurt her again."

"And she trusted you?"

His smile held no humor. "Not at first. It took me a while, but I can be very persuasive when I want to be."

Nicole had no problem believing that. She waited for him to go on.

"Anyway, eventually she agreed. Only something went wrong. We figure Merrill had an informant on the force, or at least someone with access to information. Opal called me to warn me that Merrill knew about the raid and was moving out. We didn't have time to set it up, so we just took off for the warehouse."

Nicole's throat tightened when she saw Luke's hands suddenly curl into fists. She knew he was thinking about the partner he'd lost, the young detective on his first assignment.

She wanted to touch his shoulder, to offer a word of sympathy, but Luke began to speak again, in a hard, tight voice that chilled her.

"You know the rest. During the gun battle, the warehouse was set on fire. They must have had a stockpile of ammunition because the whole thing blew up, and we thought Merrill had gone with it. Only he hadn't. Apparently he was pretty messed up, but somehow they pulled him out of there and took him into hiding.

"Opal got word that he was alive, skipped the country and wrote to warn me. Merrill must have realized that Opal had tipped me off. I guess he wants us both pretty bad."

"Is that why you left the force? Because Merrill could come after you?"

Luke uttered a mirthless laugh. "If I'd worried about that, I would have left the country, too. There's only one way to stop a man like Adrian Merrill, and that's to make sure you get him first.''

"So why did you wait until now?'' Nicole asked, frustrated that one important question still hadn't been answered.

"We only found out a short while ago that Merrill could be Morris Adams. Sutton warned me about going to Hawaii on my own. There was too big a chance of blowing it. HPD—the Honolulu Police Department—did an investigation, but without a warrant, their hands are tied. They couldn't get too close in case they tipped him off, but so far, he's checked out clean.''

"So what makes you think it could be Merrill?''

"The informant. He was burglarizing a house and was surprised by the owner coming home. He heard the voice before he went out the window. He worked for Merrill once, and he swears it was him. Merrill has a very distinctive voice. You can change the way you look, but you can't change the voice.''

"I'll have to remember that if he gets too close,'' Nicole said soberly.

"We'd better make sure he doesn't get that close.'' Luke's voice lightened as he looked at her. "Though I'm not sure you couldn't fool him up close. You sure gave me a bad moment.''

"I thought . . .'' She let her voice trail off.

He smiled briefly. "I know what you thought. I promise you, my relationship with Opal was nothing more than my job. All in the line of duty. I just happened to be good at it.''

Yes, Nicole thought, feeling a response curl warm and deep inside her. *I just bet you were.* "Well, you're mistaken if you think that Opal doesn't care for you,'' she said, getting to her feet. "Just take a look at that picture you shot of her. I'd say there's a good deal more than the line of duty as far as she's concerned.''

She didn't look at his face as she crossed the room to the bedroom, but she knew without doubt that his eyes followed her all the way.

The wardrobe for Hawaii arrived the next day. Nicole opened each package with apprehension. Some of the dresses weren't too bad, though a little brief for her taste, but the shorts definitely lived up to their name.

All she had to do, Nicole thought holding up a pair, was remember not to bend over when she was wearing them. She found two swimsuits, both of which could have been tucked inside a regular business envelope and would still have left some space.

Luke was right about one thing, Nicole thought uneasily as she tried on one of the suits. There had never been a time in her life when she'd been as skinny as Opal Turner. She was relieved to discover that the bikini covered more of her than she'd feared, though it still left a large expanse of bare skin.

"All in the line of duty, Parker," she muttered as she studied herself in the mirror. At least her years of training exercises had kept her in shape. She'd pass in a crowd, she assured herself, and changed back into her jeans before the sight of her half-naked body thoroughly demoralized her.

The prospect of the coming evening was already making her nervous. She'd covered just about everything she could know about Opal. All that was left was her masquerade with Luke. And that, she admitted, was going to give her the most trouble.

She kept telling herself to relax as she waited through the long afternoon for him to get back to the room. She couldn't get her reaction to his kiss out of her mind, no matter how hard she tried. How did she go about kissing him enough to look convincing without letting him know she was enjoying it? she wondered.

She still hadn't resolved that question when Luke let himself into the suite later. She was in the bedroom, putting the finishing touches to her eyes when she heard him come in. Since this would be the last time she'd be with him as herself, she wanted to look her best.

Admitting that she wanted to give him something to remember when she was parading around in Opal's wig and flashy outfits, she'd selected a soft pink sweatshirt from her skimpy wardrobe, and her black pants.

She left her hair loose, letting it rest on her shoulders, and had used a much more subtle version of makeup than Opal's heavy-handed efforts. She'd slipped her favorite perfume into her purse when she'd packed for this mission, and used it now to dab the flowery fragrance on her wrists and throat.

Aware of the rapid beat of her pulse, she took a few moments to collect herself. After tonight she'd no longer be herself. She'd be Opal Turner. At least tonight would be hers, and she intended to make the most of it.

Luke was in the bathroom, apparently taking a shower. He'd hung most of his clothes in there so as not to disturb her, an arrangement she'd appreciated.

She sat on the couch to wait for him, pretending to read the paper, which he brought in every evening. At the sound of the bathroom door opening, the shiver that shook her body rustled the pages.

She looked up, her breath catching when she noticed his quick appraisal of her. He looked cool and relaxed in a gray-striped sports shirt he wore with stone-washed jeans.

"Did the clothes get here?" he asked as he walked into the kitchen area and opened the fridge.

"Yes." She wondered if he wanted her to wear Opal's clothes that evening, and hoped he wouldn't insist on it.

"Did you try them on?"

Thinking about the skimpy swimsuits, Nicole felt heat coloring her cheeks. "Yes, I did."

He pulled a bottle out of the fridge and held it up. "Wine?"

Remembering they were supposed to be celebrating, Nicole nodded. "That's fine."

His eyes met hers across the bar. "So, what did you think?"

"About what?"

"About the clothes. Did they fit all right?"

"They fit fine." Why were they talking in monosyllables? she wondered. After spending a week living together, in the basic sense of the word, they should at least be at ease with each other by now.

She'd never felt less at ease in her entire life. Nor apparently did Luke. She heard the lip of the bottle strike the glass as he poured wine into it. As usual, his face betrayed none of his feelings.

He finished pouring and handed her one of the glasses. "Here's to a safe and successful mission," he said, lifting his own glass.

"I'll drink to that." She took a long sip, trying to convince herself her jitters were due to the launch of the assignment. "Nice wine," she remarked in a voice that didn't quite hit the casual note she wanted.

Luke looked at his watch. "Dinner should be here in about ten minutes. I guess this is a good time to ask if you have any questions you need answering."

Yes, she had a question. But if she wanted an answer, she decided, she'd have to lead up to it. She walked over to the couch and sat down. "You've covered everything pretty thoroughly. I guess from here on we play it by ear."

He came around the end of the bar and walked toward her. To her surprise he sat down next to her on the couch. Her breath stilled when she wondered if he intended to begin practicing right then and there.

She tried not to move away from him as he leaned back and settled his cool, gray gaze on her face. Panic fluttered briefly in her chest before she had it under control. She'd come this far, she told herself—she could handle the rest. Besides, once they were in Hawaii, they'd be too busy watching out for crooks to give much attention to their actions.

Only that was tomorrow. Right now she was alone with him, in a private suite, with no crooks to worry about. And he'd never looked more appealing—or more dangerous—than he did right at that moment.

Nicole swallowed another gulp of wine and put her glass down on the table. "You never said why you joined the police force," she said a little desperately.

"No, I haven't."

"So why did you?"

A flicker of amusement crossed his face, and she wondered if he knew just how nervous she felt. To her relief, he settled back, hooking one knee over the other.

"I met a cop named Pete Walters when I was thirteen. He took the time to drag me off the path to self-destruction and set me straight."

He paused, and sensing there was more, Nicole waited in silence. When he spoke again, the amusement had given way to bitterness. "My father took off when I was eight years old. It didn't take my mother long to find me plenty of 'uncles,' but it was pretty obvious I was in the way."

He shrugged. "I guess I was always looking for my father, and I found one in Pete. If it hadn't been for him, I'd have probably ended up doing time. Or worse." He shook his head. "It was because of him I signed up on the force. I had some bright and shiny idea of helping other kids who looked like they were heading for trouble."

She liked that. Somehow it didn't come as a surprise. "And did you?"

"A couple." He drew his brows together. "The world is a lot different than the one I grew up in. They're tougher to reach now. I'm glad I met Pete when I did. That guy did me a hell of a favor.''

She was almost afraid to ask. "So what happened to him?''

"He died." Luke stirred restlessly. "Heart attack. I figure the stress killed him." He reached for his glass. "I guess you know all about the stress, if you've been on the force eight years.''

He sipped the wine and put it down without looking at her. "Like they say, if a bullet don't get you, the stress will.''

"That's pretty negative thinking," Nicole protested. "There are a lot of people I know who love the job.''

"I bet none of them are married.''

"Some of them are.''

His eyes challenged her when she looked at him. "So why aren't you?''

She wanted to tell him it was none of his business. "I just never met anyone I wanted to marry," she said instead.

"Or you never met anyone who wanted to marry a cop.''

He'd come uncomfortably close to the truth, and she felt resentment burn her face. There had been a few times when a date had failed to materialize after she'd admitted what she did for a living. Throwing the challenge back to him, she demanded, "Is that why you're single?''

His eyes flashed her a warning, but after a moment he said lightly, "I was married, once.''

While she was still wondering if she had the nerve to ask him about it, he went on, "It lasted three years. She couldn't handle the pressure of waiting up half the night wondering if I was still alive. She wanted kids, and she wanted them to grow up with a father to take care of them." He shrugged. "I was the last person to argue with that.''

Something twisted deep inside Nicole's body. "I'm sorry," she said quietly.

His wry smile dismissed her sympathy. "There aren't too many women out there who can handle that kind of pressure. Or men, for that matter. I learned the hard way that police work and marriages don't mix. You're better off if you have no one to worry about but yourself.''

''I don't believe that.'' Dismayed by his cynicism, she leaned toward him. ''Human beings are meant to have someone to care about. You're only half living if you don't. If two people love each other enough, they'll find a way to deal with anything. Including the pressures of a job, whatever they are.''

His gaze searched her face, as if trying to find something there to augment her words. ''You really believe that?''

It was there again, humming like a live wire between them. She wondered if he could sense it as acutely as she could, and if so, if it affected him as profoundly as it captured her.

''Yes,'' she said softly. ''I really believe that.'' She could have cried with frustration when a light tap on the door shattered the moment.

Luke sprang to his feet and, signaling her into the bedroom, waited for her to close the door before answering the summons. She waited, cursing the lousy timing of room service, until she heard Luke dismissing the waiter and the door closing behind him.

The usual tray had been replaced by a trolley, and she knew enough now to wait until Luke had thoroughly examined everything before she could speak.

To her intense disappointment, the distant expression had returned to Luke's eyes, and it seemed almost as if she'd imagined the warmth of a moment ago. She felt a deep sense of regret that they hadn't had a few more minutes.

Even the excellent steak and Caesar salad failed to revive her spirits. Luke didn't help matters when he asked her what perfume she was wearing. For a moment she thought he was paying her a compliment, until he informed her that Opal would never have used such a light fragrance.

"I'll get something a little closer to the stuff Opal wears," he told her as she stacked the empty dishes. She felt like telling him not to bother.

She watched Luke wheel the trolley through the door into the corridor. She'd spent most the day wondering when he was going to get around to practicing their supposedly loving relationship, and now she was getting to the point where she was past caring.

All she wanted now was to get it over and done with. The endless preparations had taken their toll. The waiting was always the worst, she reminded herself as Luke came back into the room. Once the assignment was actually underway, she'd feel a lot calmer about everything.

She watched without much interest as Luke walked over to the radio and switched it on. After a moment of fiddling with the tuner, the soft strains of a well-known melody floated across the room. Turning, he walked toward her and held out his hands.

She stared at him, uncertain of his intentions. He surprised her by reaching for her, pulling her into his arms. "You do dance, don't you?" he asked lightly.

She wasn't sure if she was more shaken by the feel of his arms around her or the sudden gleam that warmed his eyes.

She placed her hands on his shoulders. "Of course."

"Good. Since we have to get used to being close to each other, I figure this is a good way to start."

His hip nudged hers, and she stepped back quickly, unnerved by the contact.

He pulled her to a stop and looked down at her. "Relax. We're supposed to be married, remember?"

"Sorry. You just took me by surprise." She wished her heart would stop banging so hard. He was going to feel the vibration of it if he got any closer to her.

"I'm likely to be taking you by surprise a few times over the next few days. You'd better react better than that."

Her breathing had gone on the blink again. Struggling to sound natural, she said, "All right. Just give me a minute."

"You're standing too far away." He exerted pressure on the small of her back with his hands. She shuffled forward, catching her breath when her body came up against his.

"That's better." He reached up and grasped her hands, pulling them around the back of his neck.

She swallowed, aware of her upper body plastered against his firm chest. His arms folded around her again, pulling her closer. She clamped her lips together and tried to relax.

"Okay, now move."

This time, when his hip moved against hers, it stayed with her as she stepped back. His hand slid down, trapping her against him as he swayed to the rhythm of the music.

Gradually she felt her muscles slacken. The song finished, and another one began. She tightened her grasp around his neck, spreading her fingers into his soft hair.

After a moment he tightened his hold and rested his cheek against her forehead. His cologne seemed to surround her, drawing her into the magic of his body moving seductively against hers. She closed her eyes and gave herself up to the sheer pleasure of the dance.

The music finished again, and the hushed voice of the deejay filled the room. Luke halted, but when she tried to pull out of his arms, he resisted, holding her fast.

She looked up at him, her heart stopping when she saw the purposeful gleam in his gray eyes.

"Okay," he said softly. "Get ready for a demonstration of my talent." He lowered his head, fastening his lips to hers with a warm pressure that immediately exploded somewhere inside her.

She tried to tell her spinning senses that it was just an act, and the touch of his mouth on hers should have no meaning for her.

Her body refused to listen. Her fingers dug into his firm shoulders of their own accord. She leaned into him, fitting her body against the hard length of him, helpless to control the fire sizzling along her veins.

This was far more intense than anything she had imagined. She struggled to keep a moan from escaping when he nudged her lips apart, running the tip of his tongue along the sensitive inner edges of her mouth.

Driven by a need that shocked her, she edged out her tongue to meet his, and a red-hot thrill blazed through her when she heard his sharp intake of breath.

He closed his arms around her and opened his mouth, demanding that she give him access.

The last shreds of her resistance melted as she felt him stir against her lower body. She arched into him and felt the answering thrust of his hips against hers. She seemed to be drowning in liquid heat when his body proved his potent reaction to their contact.

She tipped her head back, murmuring her pleasure as his mouth left hers to brand burning kisses down her throat to the tender hollows at the base of her neck.

His hands moved on her back, sliding up to her armpits as his thumbs spread out tantalizingly close to her breasts. For a moment, sanity returned, and she tensed, only to melt again when his mouth returned to hers, fiercely demanding entry.

She was trembling violently when he finally lifted his head. She could hear his harsh breathing fill the room as he looked down at her. "I'd say that was pretty convincing, wouldn't you?"

His words brought her back to her senses, fast. She'd done the very thing she'd been most afraid of doing. She'd let herself forget that this was all an act. Or supposed to be. Mortified, she made a desperate attempt to save the situation.

Fighting for breath, she said unsteadily, "Enough to fool Merrill, anyway."

She thought she saw a brief glimpse of regret in his eyes, then knew she must have imagined it. His voice was smooth as polished glass when he answered lightly, "I guess this means you graduate with flying colors. Well done, Opal."

She pulled away from him, hiding her embarrassment behind a determined smile. "I owe it all to you," she said evenly. "Now, if you don't mind, I'm going to bed. We have to be up early in the morning, and I'd like a good night's sleep."

"Good idea. You'll find a suitcase under the bed for your clothes. Leave all your own stuff here. Someone will be by to pick it up for you after we leave. Don't take anything of yours. You'll find everything you need in the purse that came with the clothes."

She nodded, swallowing on the tight feeling in her throat. "I've already checked that out. Someone was pretty thorough."

"We have to be. As I've told you more than once, your life will depend on it."

She felt a momentary pang of apprehension. "And yours."

His gaze seemed to burn her skin when he rested it on her face. "We won't be on our own out there. We'll be shadowed all the way. As long as we keep our minds on our job, we'll be fine."

His warning couldn't have been more clear. She felt the warmth on her cheeks as her eyes met his. "Don't worry," she said shortly, "I won't forget."

Again, she added silently. She said a brief good-night and escaped to her room. The task of packing Opal's clothes kept her mind occupied for a short while, but soon she had everything taken care of, and there was nothing left to do but sleep. If she could.

So many concerns churned around in her mind. The dangers facing them in Hawaii were very real. She had enough experience to know that even with a constant shadow, all kinds of things could go wrong. Playing the bait in a game of bluff was always the most dangerous move in police work.

She didn't need Luke's constant warnings to remind her of that. Especially his last one. *As long as we keep our minds on our job.*

She groaned quietly in the darkness. That would be the most difficult part of the whole assignment. Even knowing the danger they were in, she knew it would be next to impossible to ignore the response Luke's kisses could arouse in her.

No man had ever created that kind of havoc in her body before. But then she'd never met a man like Luke Jordan before.

He put on a good show, but under all that tough cynicism was a man who'd joined the police force to help underprivileged kids. A man who longed for the solitude of country living. A sensitive man. A man a woman could love.

"Forget it, Parker," she whispered to the silent corners of the room. He might have responded to her physically, as any man might to a woman who offered no resistance.

But he'd made a few things clear that evening. The most significant of which was the firm statement he'd made when he'd talked about his broken marriage.

You're better off if you have no one to worry about but yourself. She had no doubt in her mind that Luke Jordan was convinced of that. It should have helped her determination to keep her feelings out of it, but it didn't.

In fact, if she wanted to be honest with herself, she was very much afraid that she was falling for the guy. And that was not only incredibly stupid, it could very well turn out to be suicidal.

She was almost asleep when it occurred to her that she still didn't know why Luke Jordan had left the force.

Chapter 5

Luke was grateful for the flurry of activities the next morning as he and Nicole prepared for their trip. It took his mind off the thoughts that had kept him awake for most of the night.

Nicole seemed jumpy, and she'd barely spoken to him on the way to the airport. Sitting next to her on the plane, he had to admit her likeness to Opal was more than uncanny. It was positively spooky.

Dressed in a slim white skirt and a low-cut blouse, and wearing that wild wig and heavy makeup, she gave him a jolt every time he looked at her. Even her eyes looked like Opal's with the new lenses.

She was doing an incredible job. Since he'd assured her that it was unlikely anyone connected to Merrill could be on the plane, she was using the plane ride for a dress rehearsal.

She had Opal's gestures down to perfection, and the Marilyn Monroe voice was as close to Opal's as anyone could get. He couldn't believe how much they'd achieved in one short week, considering that all they'd had to go on was a couple of pictures and his own memories.

She'd pass, he thought with satisfaction, as long as Merrill didn't get too close to her. He'd be the only one who would be able to tell the difference, since all the men who'd worked at the warehouse were either dead or were doing time.

Any other members of the group wouldn't have been around Opal enough to be able to detect any discrepancies after all these months.

He'd done a good job, Luke thought, congratulating himself, though he wished she were a little more relaxed. She was still inclined to tense up whenever he got too close to her.

He watched the flight attendant wheel the drinks trolley down the narrow aisle. He was more than a little tense himself. That clinch last night had been too real for comfort.

The pretty blond attendant smiled down at him when he ordered two bourbons on the rocks. It was the wrong time of day to be drinking, but he figured they could both use one. Maybe it would loosen up Nicole so that she didn't jump like a nervous rabbit every time he touched her.

He'd have to do better than this, he warned himself, or they could both be in trouble. She seemed wary of him now. He only hoped she wasn't worrying that he'd try to take advantage of their situation.

He handed one of the drinks to her, feeling again that odd sense of déjà vu when she grinned at him with Opal's red mouth. She'd done something with the lipstick, he realized, to make her lips look fuller and more pouty. He liked Nicole's mouth better, he decided.

She lifted an eyebrow at him in mock disapproval, but took the bourbon from him. Her hand shook as his fingers brushed hers. He gave her a reassuring smile and leaned back in his seat.

Her nervousness was natural under the circumstances, he told himself. After all, she was well aware of the dangers she faced. He was reading too much into her jitters. At least he hoped that was it.

He took a sip of his bourbon. His shoulder brushed against hers when he leaned back again, and he felt her flinch. It was slight but unmistakable.

Damn, he thought, he should never have told her about Opal. She probably thought he expected their little performance to end up the same way. Well, she couldn't be more wrong. He expected no such thing. It was the last thing he wanted. Even if his body did give out all the wrong signals when he got close to her. His head knew better.

He thought he'd done a pretty good job of explaining why he'd ended up in Opal's bed. After all, she'd been sent to seduce him. He'd had to make it look good. This setup was a whole different proposition.

Luke settled back in his seat. Nicole's face was buried behind a magazine. Obviously she wasn't in any mood to talk. He could understand that, especially if she had to use Opal's breathless voice all the time.

Once they were in their hotel room, they could both relax. He knew the boys from Honolulu PD would go over everything pretty thoroughly before they arrived to make sure it was clean, and from then on they'd have a couple of lookouts stationed either side of their suite.

Luke reached for his drink, taking care not to bump Nicole's shoulder this time. He hoped they'd covered everything. He'd checked it all out with Sutton over and over again, every minute detail, planning for every possible scenario.

As long as the HPD boys stayed with him, they'd be all right. If and when anything went down, there'd be enough muscle around to take care of it. He had nothing to worry about. Closing his eyes, he tried to convince himself of that.

Nicole stared at the print blurring in front of her and flicked a frizzy curl from her face. She should drink the bourbon, she told herself. It would help to relax her. Usually her tension eased off once the plane was in the air.

The wig felt strange on her head, and she longed to take it off. She concentrated on lowering her hunched shoulders. Ice tinkled against the glass when she lifted it to her lips.

Out of the corner of her eye, she noticed Luke's knee dancing. The knowledge that he shared her tension did nothing to relieve it. She took a cautious sip of the bourbon. The chill melted rapidly as the liquid burned her throat.

Of course she was nervous. After all, she was sitting there on her way to Hawaii, with a deadly criminal waiting at the other end to vent his rage on her. She took another gulp of bourbon. This time it burned all the way to her stomach.

"Take it easy," Luke murmured, leaning his shoulder against hers. "I don't want a drunk on my hands when we get to Honolulu."

"Opal can't handle her drink?" Nicole asked, too quietly for anyone else to hear.

Luke grinned. "She can drink me under the table."

Unable to stop herself, Nicole watched his mouth. The memory of his kiss sent a swirl of excitement up her body. "That shouldn't be too difficult." The magazine rustled as she lifted it.

"Are you casting doubts on my talents again?"

His voice teased her, and her fingers curled, crushing the edges of the pages.

"Heaven forbid," she muttered. "You're too anxious to prove me wrong."

"I didn't notice you raising any objections."

She managed a disdainful laugh. "You know what they say—practice makes perfect."

"Yeah." He settled back in his seat again, relieving the pressure on her shoulder. "Well, by the time we're through, we should both be perfect."

Don't let him get to you, she urged silently. She would have given a lot to know what had changed his attitude. She wasn't entirely sure it was an improvement. He was a lot easier to get along with this way, but her entire body seemed to react every time he touched her or looked at her. Every word he spoke in that husky growl seemed to coil like seductive smoke throughout her body.

But it was his smile that did the most damage. She just couldn't find any immunity to that sensual tug at the corners of his mouth. She would have to find some way to resist that formidable charisma of his, she thought, easing her back into a more comfortable position. Things would probably get a lot worse before they got better.

She relaxed her mouth in a rueful grin. Or the other way around, depending on how she looked at it. Either way, it was bound to be an interesting experience. If it hadn't been for the reason they were headed for this fake honeymoon, she admitted, she might have enjoyed the challenge immensely.

The captain announced that they were circling to land, and Nicole gave up all idea of relaxing. Luke leaned across her to look out the window, adding to her discomfort.

She closed her eyes when he said, "You can see all the islands from up here."

"Really." She hoped he would attribute her clamped lips to her dislike of landings, which was only partly the problem. If he tilted his head another inch, they would bump noses.

Then she forgot about him as the plane tipped gracefully sideways and began a series of bumps that had the sweat forming on her forehead.

"You okay?"

She nodded. "As long as I don't look down." She felt his fingers close over hers, and turning her palm up, she clung gratefully to his hand, then concentrated on her deep breathing. A slight jolt told her that the plane had landed, and she let out her breath.

"You can unhook your fingernails from my tender flesh now," Luke murmured.

"Sorry." She uncurled her fingers and let go. Opening her eyes, she saw him watching her, concern marked clearly on his face.

"Okay?"

She nodded, managing a smile. "Fine." Embarrassed that he'd seen her so vulnerable, she added, "Don't worry. It's not fatal."

"I'm glad to hear it."

She dragged her gaze from his before the turmoil in her body could unsettle her again.

"You weren't kidding," he remarked later as the cab raced down the crowded freeway toward Waikiki. "You really do have a problem with heights."

Nicole watched the sun-bleached buildings flash past the window in a glittering blur. "I don't have to deal with it very often. Sometimes it's unavoidable." Now that the flight was over, she had time to dwell on other problems. The thought that she could be in the same city as her potential murderer gave her chills.

"Have you ever thought of trying hypnosis?"

"Yes." She leaned back with a sigh. "Unfortunately I can't go under."

"That's a sign of insecurity."

She sent him a swift glance, but his expression held only concerned interest. "That's what comes of trying to keep up with two brothers," she said. "It can be very demoralizing."

"I wouldn't have thought you'd be that easy to demoralize."

Smiling, she asked, "Not even on the plane?"

She wished she could read the expression in his eyes when he said, "Most people hide an irrational fear of some kind or other."

She wondered what it was he wanted to hide, then her thoughts were interrupted as the cab drew up in front of the hotel.

The next few minutes took all her concentration as she tried to remember the turkey strut, the breathy voice and the expressive gestures with her hands, while Luke booked them into the hotel.

"The honeymoon suite is on the twenty-third floor," the desk clerk announced in a voice that carried across the crowded lobby. "Someone will help you with your bags."

Nicole winced and tucked her hand into Luke's arm with one of Opal's throaty laughs. "Oh, honey," she exclaimed for the benefit of anyone interested, "I just love this place. It's so romantic."

Luke gazed down at her and winked. "I'm glad you approve."

She hugged his arm to her breast, pressing her hips up against him. She saw the startled look in his eyes and gave him a provocative smile. "I can't wait to see the room."

To her immense satisfaction, she saw his eyebrow twitch. Revenge was sweet. It was nice to see him unsettled for a change. She was tempted to capitalize on her advantage in return for all the bad moments he'd given her, but the bellboy had already swept off with their luggage and she followed him into the elevator with Luke close behind her.

On the twenty-third floor, neither of them spoke as the solemn-faced man led them down a thickly carpeted hallway to a door at the far end. Nicole's unobtrusive glance around registered the emergency exit several yards away at the very end of the hallway.

A single door sat between their suite and the exit, and they had passed two doors on the way from the elevator. That meant only four rooms, or suites, in all. The opposite wall held only one door, with a sign over it that read Staff Only.

She just had time to locate the sprinklers near the emergency exit and a glass box holding the fire alarm before the bellboy pushed open the door to the suite and stood back for them to enter.

Nicole walked in first, and for a few breathless moments forgot why she was there. The entire suite was decorated in shades of lavender and pink. Long, low couches in dark gray velvet lined the walls, facing a glass-topped coffee table.

Her gaze skimmed over the lighted cocktail bar, the huge television screen and gold-veined mirror that covered one wall. The window caught her attention, where a huge bed, swathed in pink lace, sat raised on a platform.

Stepping up to the floor-to-ceiling glass, Nicole looked out onto a view that epitomized everything she'd ever heard or imagined about Honolulu. Graceful palm trees cast shadows across a smooth stretch of sand, where seminude bodies basked in the late-afternoon sun. Colorful sails of sailboards raced back and forth across an incredible blue-green ocean, while overhead, white clouds drifted across a warm, blue sky.

She choked back the exclamation that came to mind and instead let out her breath on a delighted gasp. "Oh, Luke, honey." She whirled around, balancing carefully on her thin heels. "It's so beautiful."

"Only the best for my beautiful wife." Luke beamed at the uninterested bellboy and crushed a bill into his outstretched hand.

The man murmured a polite thanks and backed out the door. Nicole watched as Luke tested the handle, making sure it was securely fastened. He lifted a finger at her in warning and said, "Come here, sweetheart. I've been waiting for this all day."

She rolled her eyes skyward in mock disgust and said huskily, "So have I, honey. More than you'll ever know."

Luke sent her a dubious look and moved around the room, examining the phone, the television set and the light fixtures.

Nicole wondered if she should make some kind of noise. From what she'd heard about Opal, she didn't think the enthusiastic redhead would neck in silence.

Luke opened closets and looked in every one of the drawers, then moved back to the phone. Lifting the receiver, he punched the buttons and waited.

After a moment he said, "Room service? I'd like a bottle of champagne on ice, please. Yes, and macadamia nuts. The ones with the coffee glaze. Thank you."

Nicole raised questioning eyebrows at him, but he shook his head. "Why don't you get unpacked, honey?" he suggested. "Then we can get into something more comfortable."

She grimaced at the cliché and said breathlessly, "That sounds wonderful." She pointed at her head with an urgent finger, pleased when he caught on right away.

He nodded, and she fluttered her hand at her heart in a comic gesture of relief. Dragging off the wig, she shook her hair free and pulled in a breath of pure pleasure. She'd felt as if she'd been wearing a wool cap on her head.

"Which side of the dresser do you want, darling?" She pointed at the drawers.

"Doesn't matter, sweetheart. We won't be wearing clothes much, anyway."

He grinned when she glared at him. "I'll just go ahead and put them in here, then." She froze as a sharp rap came on the door, then relaxed again as a voice called out, "Room service."

She pointed at the door to the bathroom and Luke nodded. "You answer it, honey," she said, crossing the room. "I have to powder my nose."

Stepping into the bathroom, she pulled the door, leaving it open just wide enough to hear what was going on. She heard Luke mutter something, then a deep voice answered him. The door closed, and a moment later Luke called out, "It's all right. You can come out now."

She did so and stopped short when she saw a dark-haired man seated on one of the couches. He wore the white jacket and dark pants of the hotel staff, and looked up at her with curious dark brown eyes as she advanced into the room. Pausing, she shot a startled glance at Luke, who was standing by the window.

"Relax," Luke said, "he's on our side. Tony Lopaka, Honolulu Police Department." He introduced her, and the officer stood, holding out his hand. Around mid-forties, Nicole gauged as he swallowed her fingers in his chunky hand.

His pleasant round face smiled at her. "Aloha. Pleased to know you, Officer Parker. Welcome to the islands."

"Nicole. And thank you." She smiled back, taking an instant liking to the friendly man. "I'm happy to be here."

"Tony is one of our tails. His partner's checking out the lobby. He'll be up in a minute." Luke waved a hand at the champagne sticking out of an ice bucket on the coffee table. "Want a drink?"

For the first time, Nicole realized that the room service call had been a code to the police officers assigned to them. Obviously Luke was taking no chances on the switchboard being monitored. She hesitated. "Champagne tends to go straight to my head."

Tony laughed. "Don't worry. It's nonalcoholic."

"Then in that case, I'll have some." She glanced back at Luke. "I take it we can talk now?"

"Yeah." Luke sat down on the bed and ran his fingers through his hair. "Tony and his partner have checked for bugs. At the moment, we're secure."

"Good. Then I'm going to get this junk off my face." Nicole pulled off her sandals. "If you'll excuse me, gentlemen?"

Tony beamed at her. "Sure!"

Without looking at Luke, she picked up the tote bag she'd carried with her on the plane and returned to the bathroom. She closed the door with a sense of relief.

It felt wonderful to have a few moments to herself after the stress of the long day. After opening her tote bag, she rummaged for her jar of cleansing cream. She couldn't wait to have clean skin again.

She heard the two men murmuring as she worked on her face, their voices too low to hear what was being said. At this point, she didn't much care. This was only the beginning, and already she felt the strain of trying to be someone else.

If this man really were Adrian Merrill, she thought, wiping cream off her face, she hoped he would make a move soon. She didn't want to think about spending days in this romantic tropical paradise with Luke Jordan. Not under these circumstances, anyway. And the chance of her being here with him under different circumstances was as remote as an unnamed planet.

Luke Jordan had made it very clear where they stood. Strictly in the line of duty. Nothing more. She'd have to take care not to put anything more to it than that.

Nicole carefully wiped the last traces of eye shadow from her brow. Now all she had to do was convince her heart.

Out in the living room, Tony poured the sparkling grape juice into long-stemmed glasses. "Does she understand the danger she's in?" he asked, offering one of the glasses to Luke.

Luke shook his head. "Thanks, I'll make do with fruit juice." He got up and walked over to the cocktail bar. Deciding on a can of papaya and pineapple juice, he added,

"She knows all the facts. I'm not sure she realizes what she's up against."

Tony took a sip of his drink. "You know, if Merrill sends a hit man, there won't be much we can do. She'll be right out in the open. We can't stay too close to her, or he'll smell a rat."

"I know that." Luke snapped the lid open and walked back to the bed. "We're betting on his famous streak of cruelty. Merrill won't miss the opportunity to make both Opal and me suffer before he puts us away."

"I hope you're right." Tony shook his head. "You know he won't grab you himself. He'll send his thugs to pick you up."

"I know." Luke tipped up the can and held it to his lips. The juice tasted sweet and tangy but failed to rinse the bitterness from his mouth. He hadn't felt this way since his rookie days—nervous, uptight, unsure of himself. He hated the feeling and made a conscious effort to ease the tension gripping him.

"But all we need is for someone to make the attempt," he added. "It doesn't matter who. They'll lead us to Merrill. We'll have what we need to pick him up. He won't find it easy to get off the island. By the time he finds out what's going on, we'll be closing in."

Tony nodded. "Sounds okay. I just hope it works out that way. I'd hate to see a woman like that get hurt."

A memory flashed through Luke's mind, a vision of a rainy night, blue lights flashing and a young man lying in a pool of blood. His fingers clenched on the can, putting a dent in it.

"No one's going to get hurt if we all do our job right," he said harshly. He finished the last of the juice, wishing he could be as sure as he'd sounded.

"Don't worry. We won't let you down." Tony put down his glass, and Luke could read the curiosity in his eyes when he looked across the room at him. "You must want this guy pretty bad," he said, "to take a risk like this."

"I want him pretty bad."

Tony opened his mouth to answer, then closed it again as someone rapped on the door. Getting silently to his feet, he moved out of sight behind the wall as Luke crossed the room to the door.

Drawing it open, Luke saw a thin-faced man with a droopy mustache and tired eyes standing outside, holding a paper sack. He was dressed like Tony, in a white jacket and dark pants.

"The waiter forgot your macadamia nuts, sir," he said, handing the bag to Luke. "Coffee glazed, right?"

"Right," said Luke, stepping back. "Do you want to pick up the glasses?"

"Yes, sir." The man walked past him into the room, and waited for Luke to close the door before holding out his hand. "Neil Clements. HPD."

Luke shook his hand. "Is all this necessary?" He held up the bag. "I thought you guys had eyeballed the place."

"We did." Neil sat down next to his partner. "But the word is not to take any chances. We're supposed to have this end of the floor covered, but mistakes can be made. If this guy is who we think he is, he can get a man past us without us ever knowing it."

"For instance," Tony put in, "the guy who brought up your bags. Notice anything unusual about him?"

Luke frowned. "Now you mention it, he wasn't exactly holding out the welcome mat with the usual friendly smile."

Neil nodded. "Yeah. We noticed. He signed on a few days ago, right after your man in Portland booked your suite. So far, he's checked out, but we don't feel comfortable about him."

"That doesn't make me feel too secure," Nicole said from the bathroom doorway.

In spite of his efforts to remain impartial, Luke's breath stilled when he looked at her. The transformation back to the woman with whom he'd spent the past few days was almost complete. Only the clothes and the blue eyes remained of Opal's presence.

He'd forgotten how she could affect him. He'd also forgotten that without the disguise, Nicole Parker was as far removed from Opal Turner as a hula dancer from an Eskimo.

The reminder shook him, and it was a moment before he realized that Tony was watching his face with undisguised speculation, while Neil waited to be introduced.

"Nicole Parker, Neil Clements," Luke murmured, stepping off the raised floor. "He's Tony's partner."

Nicole held out her hand, returning Neil's strong grasp. "So what's this about our friendly porter?"

"Just being careful, that's all," Neil said smoothly. "I'm sure there's nothing to worry about."

"I hope you're right." Nicole glanced at Luke for reassurance, and felt a pang of apprehension when she saw the swift glance he exchanged with Neil.

"If there's anything I should know," she said evenly, "I'd appreciate hearing it. After all, it is my life at stake here."

"She's right," Luke said gruffly. "If you've got anything at all, we'd better hear it."

He stepped back onto the platform and sat on the edge of the bed. Beckoning at Nicole with his head, he patted the spot next to him.

After a moment's hesitation, she crossed the room and sat down, grabbing the bedspread with both hands as the mattress undulated beneath her. She hadn't realized it was a water bed. Luke's swift glance unnerved her, though she wasn't sure why.

She waited, feeling little prickles of apprehension creeping down her spine, while Tony and Neil settled themselves on the couch.

"We haven't got much," Neil began. "Just what you probably know already about the informant who fingered Morris Adams."

"He was certain the man was Merrill?" Luke leaned forward, and Nicole saw his fists clenched on his knees. Again she felt that stir of anxiety. His partner had been killed in the raid on Merrill's warehouse. Obviously Luke had good reason to want Merrill. Yet she couldn't dismiss the feeling that there was more to it than Luke was telling her.

"Yeah." Neil reached for Tony's glass. He tasted the grape juice, and Tony grinned when Neil pulled a face and set the glass down again. "At least, he said it sounded like Merrill."

Something in his voice put a chill into Nicole's bones. "The informant didn't get a look at him?" she asked. She saw Luke's knee begin its dance again.

"Oh, he saw him all right," Neil said softly. "He caught a glimpse of him as he went out the window. He told his lawyer he would see that face in his nightmares for the rest of his life."

"Yeah," Tony said, his voice hushed. "I guess fire can do some pretty ghastly things to your face."

Nicole shuddered, and Luke moved impatiently on the bed, bouncing her up and down. "Can I see this guy?"

Neil shrugged. "Bill Foster's under protection. You can see him, but he won't talk. He's too scared. See, Merrill, if it is Merrill, got a good look at him as he took off. Merrill couldn't afford to let anyone run around loose who can identify him. Foster will only talk to the cops who picked him up. He doesn't trust anyone else near him."

"I can't say I blame him," Luke murmured. "Adrian Merrill is not someone you cross and live to talk about it."

"But surely," Nicole protested, "you must be able to check this man out? There has to be something that will tie him in with Merrill. What about fingerprints? And the warehouse? Can't you find something there you can use?"

Tony shook his head. "It isn't that easy. According to what we learned so far, everything about this guy checks out. He's supposedly a man called Morris Adams. He's badly disfigured. His face is a mess. His fingers were burned. No fingerprints."

"The business is legit as far as we can see," Neil added, "and we can't go over it without a warrant. Adams runs it from his house. He goes out only at night for a walk along his private beach. You can't arrest a man for walking on a beach."

"And you can't pick him up just because he's been disfigured in a fire," Luke said slowly.

"Yeah." Tony uttered a short laugh. "Can you imagine what the lawyers would do with that one?"

"So what do we have?" Luke shoved himself off the bed and moved to the window, turning his back on the people in the room. "A small-time crook who says he recognized a voice."

Nicole dug her feet into the floor and waited for the bed to stop heaving.

"And," Neil said, "an import/export business. Apparently dealing in souvenirs."

"And Adrian Merrill ran an export business in Oregon. Only he was dealing in furniture."

"Yeah. Oriental furniture, right? And guess where Adams Imports' supplies come from."

Luke turned. "The Orient."

Neil nodded. "Give the man an A."

"Then," Tony said, lifting the champagne glass to his lips, "there's the initials. M.A.—Morris Adams. A.M.—Adrian Merrill."

"That's what convinced me." Luke sat down on the bed again, and once more Nicole gripped the covers. "Merrill had more than his share of vanity. He would want to hang on to at least some small part of his identity. The initials would be it."

"A little too much for coincidence, right?" Neil asked smugly.

"Yeah." Luke sighed. "Too bad we couldn't have proved it."

"Well, hopefully we will now." Tony finished his grape juice and stood. "I guess it's up to you two."

Neil got to his feet and glanced down at his watch. "Time for chow." He nodded at Nicole across the room. "Nice to meet you, Nicole. We'll be in the rooms on either side of you, but we won't be in contact again unless it's an emergency. Safer that way."

She slipped off the bed as Tony crossed the room toward her and held out his hand. "Don't worry," he said, displaying his gleaming white teeth. "We'll be with you all the way. And this guy has a reputation." He nodded his head at Luke. "From what I hear, you're in good hands."

Nicole smiled. "How can I go wrong, with all this protection around me?" She looked up at Luke, her smile fading when she saw his expression.

"Don't take your eyes off her for a second," he said, gripping Tony's hand.

Tony slapped him on the shoulder. "You got it." He strode across the room and turned at the door, where Neil waited for him. His teeth flashed against his dark skin again as he grinned. "Good luck, and aloha." He lifted his hand, curling his fingers and spreading out his little finger and thumb as he wiggled it in the traditional Hawaiian greeting.

Neil lifted his hand in a more conservative gesture. "See ya around." He opened the door cautiously and looked out, then slipped outside with Tony on his heels.

Nicole felt sorry to see them leave. Now that she was alone with Luke again, she felt more than a little jumpy. The more she heard about Adrian Merrill, the more formidable he appeared.

This had started off as a job, maybe a more ambitious job than anything she'd tackled so far, but just a job nonetheless. But as all the implications were revealed, she was getting a clearer picture of what that job involved. She glanced at Luke, who was staring out the window. And his grim profile did nothing to relieve her anxieties.

A few miles away, a thickset man sat at a desk, a phone propped awkwardly between his shapeless chin and disfigured fingers. He listened to the voice on the other end for several seconds, grunting now and again when the voice paused.

At last he braced for the painful process of moving his mouth. Despite the mutilation of his lips, his voice sounded remarkably clear when he spoke.

"Stay with them. I'll let you know if and when to move. Once I have absolute proof, I'll give the order." The line went dead, and he leaned forward, letting the receiver drop before maneuvering it into its proper place.

Revenge. He had waited so long. Now it was in his grasp. As for the woman, once he'd confirmed her identity, he wouldn't waste his time on her. He'd order them to pick her off with a silencer. She'd be dead before she hit the ground. Long before her lover-boy realized what was happening.

Leather creaked as he leaned back in his chair. She was expendable. It was Jordan he wanted. Jordan who had set fire to his warehouse. Jordan who had caused the excruciating agony and the nightmare of pain that had been with him ever since.

He'd always known that one day they would face each other again. He hadn't expected it this soon. He hadn't expected Jordan to track him down and come looking for him.

He'd been prepared to wait until the time was right to pick him up. Jordan had saved him the trouble. He'd left the security of home quarters and invaded enemy territory, where he was vulnerable.

It had been a long time coming, and now he could afford to wait a little longer. The anticipation was sweet. Soon the adversary would be in his hands, and he'd make damn sure that Jordan stayed conscious long enough to realize what was happening to him.

A sound rattled in his throat. A sound that could have resembled the laugh of Satan.

Chapter 6

"I guess we'd better find somewhere to eat," Luke said, glancing at his watch. "I don't know about you, but I'm hungry."

Nicole sighed. "I suppose that means I have to put my clown's face back on again?"

"Sorry." He held up his hands in an apologetic gesture. "Opal wouldn't be caught dead without her makeup."

"Well, I wish she'd had hair closer to mine," Nicole muttered as she picked up the wig.

"You could have dyed your hair, then you wouldn't have had to wear a wig."

She shuddered. "I just couldn't bear the thought of looking at hair that color first thing in the morning."

Luke grinned. "I guess it is a little wild."

"Little?" She snorted in disgust. "I look like a tumbleweed on fire."

Laughter rumbled in his chest. "Come on, it's not that bad. Opal used to think it was trendy."

"Yeah?" Nicole walked to the bathroom, swinging the wig in her hand. "Well, we all know Opal's taste is more than a little tacky." She would have given a lot to have seen his face as she walked into the bathroom and closed the door.

"So where's your girlfriend now?" she asked him as she faced him across a pink tablecloth an hour later. From where she sat in a dark corner of the Chinese restaurant, the other occupants of the room seemed innocuous enough.

A young couple sat in another corner, oblivious to anyone but each other. Nicole's gaze kept straying to them in spite of her best efforts to ignore them.

The brand-new rings gleaming on their fingers suggested newlyweds. Glimpsing their whispered exchanges, the hand-holding and the almost-dazed expression on the young man's face, she was constantly reminded that this was what she and Luke were supposed to look like. The contrast between the happy couple and her own rather stilted conversation with Luke was a stark example of the difference in their situations.

Apparently Luke felt no need to emphasize their pretend relationship. The only other customer in the place was Tony, who sat unobtrusively by the door, eating alone.

She could see no sign of Neil and assumed he was probably close by on the street somewhere. She jumped when Luke answered her question. She'd almost forgotten she'd asked it.

"If you mean Opal, she's in South America," he said, manipulating his chopsticks with surprising dexterity. "Her letter was mailed in Rio."

"I wonder if she likes it." Nicole managed to balance a tiny portion of rice on the end of her chopsticks.

"I imagine it's better than what she has waiting for her here."

The rice fell between the slender sticks onto her plate. Grimacing, Nicole tried again.

"You know you could ask for a fork."

He'd sounded amused and she looked up, her pulse zinging when she saw his smile. "I'm getting the hang of it now." This time she managed to get some of the rice into her mouth.

"Well, as long as you finish before midnight. I'm beginning to suffer from jet lag."

"That's right." Nicole glanced at her watch. "It's nearly morning in Portland. I keep forgetting we're two hours behind."

Luke yawned. "Well, my body's doing a pretty good job of remembering. I'm looking forward to getting my head down."

Nicole had her cup of tea halfway to her lips when the next thought occurred to her. The couches in the suite were nowhere near as wide as the one in Luke's suite in Portland.

In fact, for a man of Luke's size, it would be near impossible to be comfortable on those couches. Once more her gaze moved to the couple in the corner. She saw the young man lean forward and kiss his radiant wife. Nicole's hand jerked.

"You're spilling your tea."

Her eyes shot back to Luke's face, and she lowered the cup.

"Something the matter?" She saw the sudden tension in his face as he swept his gaze around the room.

"No," she said quickly. "I guess I'm tired, that's all."

He nodded. "Ready to go?"

"Sure." Her stomach performed a somersault as she watched him pull his wallet from the back pocket of his pants. She'd never noticed his long fingers until now. His knuckles were pronounced, his nails cut short and square. Strong hands. Capable hands.

Again her stomach reacted, and she pushed her chair back. Holding the edge of the table, she adjusted her balance on the heels. She walked carefully past Tony's table without so much as a glance at him, and waited at the door for Luke to join her.

Outside the restaurant the humidity seemed to cling to her skin. The warm night air swirled around her in an exotic, fragrant cloud, heightening the strange feeling of unreality that had plagued her ever since they'd left the hotel.

Breakers washed onto smooth sand as they walked along the edge of the beach in the warm, sultry darkness. Somehow she couldn't dismiss the sensation of acting out a long, complicated dream.

As if to reinforce the notion, Luke put his arm around her and drew her close. "Just in case anyone's watching," he murmured close to her ear, and before she could prepare herself, he caught her to him and pressed a warm kiss on her mouth.

She automatically parted her lips and felt him tense as she pressed her body against him. Immediately she pulled back, striving for Opal's throaty laugh.

It came out a little high-pitched, and Luke pulled her closer, his arm clamping her to his side as they continued to walk. His fingers slid down her bare arm, and she shivered.

"You okay?" he asked softly.

She tilted her head back to look up at him, and this time the laugh was perfect. "So long as I'm with you, I am," she said in Opal's voice.

He smiled down at her, and she wondered what he'd say if he knew the words had echoed in her heart.

Reaching the hotel, Luke warned her with a finger on his lips as he opened the door to the suite. He went straight to the phone and dialed a number. "Room service? This is the honeymoon suite."

Nicole waited, worrying her bottom lip with her teeth as he listened for a moment, then added, "Fine. We'll wait till tomorrow."

He hung up and smiled at her across the room. "All clear. We can relax for the night, at least."

"Good. I can't wait to get out of this thing." She dragged the wig off her head.

"I bet it's hot," Luke said, surprising her with a note of sympathy in his voice.

"Actually it's not too bad." She kicked off her sandals, breathing out a sigh as she curled her toes into the thick carpet. "I'm getting used to it. I just wish I could wear it in the water. I would have loved a swim in that ocean."

His gray eyes rested on her with a look of speculation. "Well, maybe when this is over you can have your swim before we leave."

She smiled at him. "I'd like that. It will give me something to look forward to."

She could almost hear her heart beating as he continued to look at her. Now seemed as good a time as any to ask the question burning in her mind. "Er, are you going to be comfortable on that couch?"

His gaze remained steadfast on her face. "What makes you think I'm sleeping on the couch?"

Her stomach plummeted, then rose so quickly she couldn't breathe. "Then . . . where are you going to sleep?"

Still with his gaze holding hers, he gestured at the couch. "I think it's fairly obvious that a cat wouldn't be comfortable on that thing. I'd roll over once and end up on the floor."

"Oh," she said faintly. There didn't seem to be anything else to say.

"So," Luke said quietly, "I might as well start off on the floor and save myself some bruises."

She hoped her relief didn't show on her face. She was about to turn away when he added, "Unless you have a better suggestion?"

She seemed to have trouble swallowing. She knew what he was asking. The last thing she wanted was to come across like a naive little prude. At thirty-one, that would be a tad hard to pull off.

At the same time, sharing a bed with any man, let alone one who stirred up her hormones the way he did, was not a decision to be made lightly.

Putting all her effort into sounding uninterested, she murmured, "Please yourself. Wherever you'll be most comfortable. It makes no difference to me."

"We both know I'll be more comfortable in the bed," Luke said, watching her with a certain wariness in his eyes. "But if it bothers you—"

"Why should it bother me?"

He didn't answer, and she stared at him across the room, feeling a pulse beating furiously in her throat. She knew what he was thinking. He was remembering their last night in Portland when he'd kissed her and she'd practically attacked him. He was probably wondering if she expected . . . She pulled in a sharp breath.

She'd made a fool of herself that night and she had no intention of doing that again. This was as good a way as any of proving to him she was in control of the situation.

She tossed a casual glance at the bed. "It looks big enough that we won't get in each other's way. If you can handle it, then so can I."

She made herself walk slowly to the bathroom and carefully closed the door behind her. Slumping against the wall, she put a hand over her pounding heart and muttered under her breath, "Please, let me handle this like an adult."

Luke swore under his breath and kicked at the couch with the toe of his shoe. Damn Sutton. Surely he could have arranged things better than this? Admittedly they were supposed to make it look real, but this was asking a bit much.

He'd known ever since they'd arrived that the couch was out, as far as sleeping went. He'd spent the entire evening trying to think of an alternative, but it was either the floor or the bed.

And if he had a choice, it was going to be the bed. He doubted he'd get much sleep either way, but at least his body would be rested.

And he needed all of his energy to stay on the alert. Talking to the guys earlier had reminded him just how deadly Merrill could be. He couldn't afford to let down his guard for one second.

He paced around the room, waiting for Nicole to get through in the bathroom. She'd unpacked earlier, before they went out to eat. He paused in front of the dresser, then opened a drawer and hooked out a pair of briefs.

Normally he slept in the buff, but he didn't think that would go down well with Officer Parker. He couldn't stop the wry grin that curved at his mouth. None of this was going down well with her.

He wished he could give her the consolation of knowing that he was every bit as uncomfortable as she was. But he couldn't afford the luxury. Indifference was the key. As long as she thought he wasn't interested in her that way, there'd be no chance of a misunderstanding.

His grin faded. He dropped the briefs on the bed and walked to the window. After sliding it open, he stepped through onto the tiny *lanai*. The warm breeze ruffled his hair as he stood listening to the breakers smash onto the sand in a never-ending rhythm of pulsing sound. Somewhere on the darkened beach a radio played, and soft laughter joined the distinctive island music.

He could feel his body tightening in an almost-forgotten ache, and he lifted his face to the starlit sky. If there was ever a perfect place for romance, this had to be it. He felt a sudden, intense longing for something that he knew was out of reach. He couldn't do that to her. He couldn't do that to himself.

"Cool it, you idiot," he muttered, "before you get yourself in more trouble than you can handle." For the first time in years, he wished he still smoked.

A sound from inside warned him, and he stepped back into the room. Wearing a sleeveless cotton shift, Nicole crossed the room toward the bed.

She avoided his gaze when she asked, "Which side do you prefer?"

His fists clenched at his sides. "Doesn't matter. It's up to you." He almost added that he'd changed his mind and would sleep on the floor. But that would let her know how susceptible he was feeling. That would be a mistake. He'd initiated this latest dilemma, and he wasn't going to back down now.

He picked up the briefs from the bed and walked quickly to the bathroom, hoping that she'd be asleep by the time he came out again.

Relax, Nicole told herself fiercely as her rigid body settled on the unstable bed. Any slight movement rocked her, not an unpleasant experience, even if it was unfamiliar.

She experimented by rolling onto her side, feeling the mattress settle beneath her. Actually, she decided, it was really comfortable, once she got used to the gentle motion.

One thing—if Luke made any sudden moves, she'd be warned. Her nerves got the better of her, and she dissolved in a fit of silent giggles. She was still struggling to control them when she heard the bathroom door open.

Squeezing her eyes shut, she kept as still as possible and tensed for the moment when he climbed in next to her. He must think I'm asleep, she thought with relief as he edged carefully onto the bed, causing only a slight fluctuation of the mattress.

She was just beginning to relax again when he said, "Good night. I'll try not to toss in my sleep."

"Do that," she murmured when she'd recovered her breath. "Or you'll be sleeping on the floor tomorrow night."

He didn't answer, and after a while, much to her surprise, she actually fell asleep. She woke up several times during the night, but after the first shock of remembrance, managed to drift off again. When she finally awoke to see the sun pooling at the foot of the drapes, she was alone.

She'd done it, she thought as she turned over and saw the empty space next to her. She'd actually managed to sleep and had survived the night with her pride intact. In fact, she realized as she waited for the rocking motion to settle, she'd hardly known he was there. Except for his steady breathing and the occasional movement of the mattress, she might as well have been alone in the bed.

By the time he came out of the bathroom, she'd wandered out onto the *lanai,* enjoying the warmth of the early-morning sunshine. He stepped out to join her, bringing a faint breath of his cologne to disturb her senses as he leaned on the balcony to look down.

He wore a pair of white shorts and hadn't yet buttoned his sand-colored shirt. "Sleep well?" he inquired without looking at her.

She decided to take his question at face value and ignore the hint of irony in his voice. "Very well. And you?"

"Like a log." He straightened, and when he looked at her, the expression in his eyes told her nothing. "We should pick up some suntan lotion this morning. I think we should spend some time on the beach, and I'll book us into a luau this evening. Since we have to be as visible as possible, we might as well make the most of it."

She managed a casual grin. "Sounds good to me. I'll get dressed."

He nodded. "I'll order room service for breakfast."

"Just cereal and fruit for me." She stepped through the French window. "And coffee," she added before crossing the room to the dresser.

After a moment's hesitation, she picked out the bright blue bikini and added blue shorts and a white halter-neck sun top. She'd need suntan lotion, she thought grimly as she made for the bathroom. She'd be baring skin that hadn't seen sunlight in years. At least, not since she was a teenager.

She was reminded of that thought later as she spread out a towel on the hot sand. Luke had picked out a spot that gave them some space between the sunbathers and the more energetic types playing volleyball.

Her olive complexion rarely burned, Nicole thought, but it had been a long time since she'd subjected herself to a tanning marathon.

She slipped off the shorts and top, then sat down. She'd dropped the suntan lotion she'd bought into her tote bag and she hunted for it while Luke laid down his towel next to her.

Her fingers brushed against the revolver she always carried, giving her a chilling reminder of why she was there. It suddenly occurred to her that she'd seen no sign of Luke's gun. He had to be carrying one, yet she didn't remember ever seeing it.

Wondering where he kept it, she glanced up at him. She watched him take off his shirt and drop it on the towel. He didn't wear a shoulder holster, she thought, or she would have seen it. Dismissing the thought, she searched the tote bag and found the suntan lotion.

"I'll do yours first, then you can do mine," Luke said as she unscrewed the cap.

Puzzled, she looked up at him. "Do my what?"

He grinned, sending her pulse scrambling for control. "Your back." He leaned down and took the lotion from her nerveless fingers. "Lie on your stomach," he ordered.

"Oh, I don't think—"

"Do you want a burned back?" He sat down next to her. "You can't reach it yourself." When she still hesitated, he added quietly, "We're supposed to be married, remember?"

She flipped over onto her stomach, thankful for the sunglasses that hid a large portion of her face. Turning her face away from him, she rested her cheek on her folded arms while he poured lotion into his hands. In spite of her determined effort not to, she flinched when his fingers smoothed over her shoulders.

He leaned over her and murmured, "Cold?"

Not trusting her voice to speak, she gave a quick shake of her head. His fingers felt slightly rough on her smooth skin as he slid them over her back. He maintained a light pressure, but she felt as if his touch burned into her flesh.

She captured her bottom lip with her teeth and closed her eyes as his hands slid lower to the small of her back. Conscious now of her brief bikini, she tried not to think about it as he spread lotion across her hips.

"Do you want me to do your legs, or can you manage that yourself?"

She rolled over, catching a spark of satisfaction in his eyes that made her teeth clench. "I'll manage." She cleared her throat, realizing she'd been using her own voice. Almost snatching the lotion from him, she uttered Opal's husky laugh.

"Okay, honey," she purred, "it's your turn now."

The gleam in his eye unsettled her further as he stretched out on his stomach. If she'd been hoping to retaliate in kind, she was disappointed. His murmurs of contentment as she skimmed the smooth contours of his back added to her confusion, until she was feeling a warmth under her skin that she couldn't blame on the hot sun.

She was glad when she could recap the lotion and hide behind the magazine she'd brought with her. To her relief,

Luke seemed content to lie there on his stomach, though she knew he wasn't nearly as relaxed as he looked.

She could see the knotted muscles in his shoulders and neck when she glanced at him, and she knew he was scanning the beach without appearing to do so.

More couples joined them on the sand, taking up the available space, until several people rested within earshot.

After a while, Luke turned onto his back, saying lazily, "We'll have to move into the shade if we stay here much longer."

"I know." She shifted onto her stomach and glanced at him. His smile seemed tense, and she frowned. "You okay?" she asked quietly. "You're not getting burned, are you?"

"Not yet." Raising himself on one elbow, he leaned over and kissed her ear. "I thought I saw the porter who took up our bags yesterday," he whispered, his mouth still on her ear. "Over by that clump of palm trees. Take a look in a minute and see if you can spot him."

She nodded, her heart skipping a beat. Moving slowly, she planted a brief kiss on Luke's mouth, then sat up, stretching her arms above her head in a lazy gesture.

Casually she turned her head and scanned the beach. Narrowing her eyes, she rested her gaze on the palm trees clustered at the edge of the path that separated the hotel from the beach.

Several people lay in the sparse shade of the trees, but none of them looked like the solemn-faced porter. Then she saw a figure detach itself from behind one of the trees and hurry off in the opposite direction.

She caught her breath and turned back to Luke. Smiling at him, she leaned over him and rested her arms on his chest. Tracing his mouth with one finger, she said softly, "I think you're right."

His eyes glinted with some suppressed emotion as he murmured, "Yeah. I thought so." He raised his arms and, wrapping them around her shoulders, pulled her head down to his. "Where is he now?"

She felt as if she were suffocating. The presence of the porter had unsettled her, and now a large expanse of her bare skin was in direct contact with Luke's naked chest. With her mouth brushing his, she whispered, "He's gone."

"Which direction?"

"Away from the hotel. Do you think he's one of Merrill's men?"

"At this point we're not even sure if Adams is Merrill. Our porter could simply be on a lunch break."

She turned her head sideways and glanced down the beach. "Well, he's disappeared now."

"Good." The kiss he gave her reflected his release of tension, but intensified hers. Desire sliced a path all the way up her body, and she felt the response as her breasts tingled.

She jerked away from him and sat up, straightening her sunglasses. Praying he hadn't detected the subtle change in her body, she said unsteadily, "If you want to go in for a swim, I'll be fine." As an afterthought, she added, "Honey."

He sat up, too, and wound an arm around her shoulders. "I'm not going in without you, sweetheart."

She sent him a warning frown. He must remember she couldn't swim wearing the wig. "You know I can't. You go ahead."

"We're joined at the hip, remember?" He leaned forward and brushed her cheek with his lips. "Where you go, I go."

"Then I'll come down and paddle at the edge."

He grinned. "Good thinking. I need to cool off, anyway."

He's so damn casual about it all, Nicole thought, trying not to stare at his body as he stripped off his shorts to reveal a brief swimsuit. He was so unaffected himself, it didn't occur to him that he could be making her uncomfortable.

And there was no way she was going to let him know that, she promised herself when he caught her hand and pulled her down to the water.

She had to be content with a few odd breaststrokes, making sure to keep her head out of the water, while Luke swam lazily on his back a few yards away.

Out of the corner of her eye, she saw a familiar head bobbing in the ocean, and realized with a shock that it was Tony Lopaka. She'd almost forgotten about the officers assigned to tail them.

It would be so easy to let the leisurely ambience of this wonderful place overcome her vigilance, she thought uneasily. She would have to guard against that, just as she would have to guard against the effect Luke Jordan had on her every time he came near her.

The water felt wonderful, warm and buoyant and incredibly clear. She could see her feet sinking into the sandy bottom and the shifting shells around her toes.

Her body began to relax under the tranquil effect of the sea and hot sun. For a while, she forgot her tension in the sheer enjoyment of her surroundings.

She was sorry when Luke broke the spell by coming up behind her to put his hands on her waist. "Fancy walking along the beach to the Royal Hawaiian for lunch?" he asked, smiling at her when she looked up at him.

"I'd love it." She followed him out of the water, back to the towels, where he flung himself down to dry off. Lowering herself beside him, she caught herself wishing that all this was for real—warm, sultry days spent lazing on the beach, cozy dinners to look forward to and a man like Luke Jordan to love.

Panic swept through her like a tidal wave when she realized what was in her heart. She couldn't do this, she told herself. She knew all the consequences of falling for a man like Luke. He made no commitments. He was a loner, a man who valued his independence, a man determined not to give his heart to anyone.

You're better off if you have no one to worry about but yourself. He'd been talking about police officers when he'd said that. But somehow she knew that it was his own philosophy. Luke Jordan didn't want to worry about anyone else. And, Nicole thought, she would give a great deal to know why.

She dressed for the luau that night with mixed feelings. On the one hand, everything she'd read about the proceedings fascinated her, and she couldn't wait to experience it all for herself.

On the other hand, being with Luke in that environment would not be easy. She could hardly look at him now without feeling an intense longing that took all her attention to hide from his penetrating gaze.

Whenever he smiled at her, each time he brushed a casual kiss across her mouth, touched her bare skin with his roughened fingers or teased her in that low husky voice that fired her blood, she wanted to respond the way a woman responded to the man she loved.

Why had she let this happen? she asked herself as the tour bus carried them alongside palm-fringed beaches. He had given her no encouragement. In fact, a number of times he'd made it clear that everything he did was in the line of duty.

I'm beginning to hate that phrase, Nicole thought as she walked across the sand with Luke to where a large crowd stood around in a circle.

She looked up at him as they waited for the ceremony to begin. He looked casual and quite devastating in white slacks and a blue Hawaiian print shirt. She'd made him buy the shirt that afternoon when she'd bought her muumuu. She had to admit the sleeveless dress with its long flowing skirt was extremely cool and comfortable.

He must have felt her gaze, since he looked down at her and smiled, catching her hand in his. She smiled back, hiding the sudden ache that was becoming all too familiar. She was glad when a stir from the crowd signaled the arrival of the royal court.

Several Hawaiians in grass skirts and colorful headdress walked around a large pit in which, so Nicole had read in a brochure, a pig had been slowly cooking all day. After a young man had blown three mournful notes into a large shell, the Hawaiians chanted a prayer of thanksgiving.

Conscious all the time of Luke's warm grasp on her fingers, Nicole watched the men dig up the pig from the pit. They carried it in a net across to the tables, where they began carving it into small pieces. It didn't look all that hygienic to her, but everyone seemed prepared to eat it.

Deciding to take the chance, she piled small portions of teriyaki beef, fried chicken, mahimahi, salmon and the pork on her plate, adding salad, sweet potato and poi before following Luke to one of the long tables set up on the sand.

She tucked her sunglasses into her purse, then prepared to tackle the exotic food. The rapidly sinking sun turned the horizon a fiery orange, then red, and finally peach as it disappeared into the sea. The leaves of the palms swayed in the night breeze, like huge black feathers against the purple sky.

Smiling women in grass skirts quickly cleared the tables, and a Hawaiian band began to play the soft, haunting music of the islands. Everyone twisted on the long benches to face the stage.

Luke swung a leg astride the seat and pulled Nicole toward him until her back rested against his chest. Folding his arms around her, he dropped a kiss on the back of her neck. She felt the effect of it shiver deliciously down her body.

The fragrance of gardenias and ginger blooms blended with the aromatic spices from the barbecues, bringing with it a bittersweet pain. She knew in that moment that she would never forget this night.

Suppressing a sigh, she watched a tall man walk onto the stage. The handsome host looked quite dramatic in white slacks and a bright red sash around his waist. He greeted the crowd with a shout of "Aloha!" and the crowd roared back.

After a few jokes he asked for all the honeymoon couples to stand. Nicole was startled when Luke tugged her to her feet. "Visible, remember?" he murmured when she shot him a look of dismay.

The host's voice echoed from the speakers as he ordered all the brand-new husbands to kiss their wives. The fact that the vast majority of the crowd appeared to be on honeymoon and were all obeying the command did nothing to ease Nicole's swift panic.

Helplessly she allowed Luke to draw her into his arms. "Let's make it look good," he murmured, and covered her mouth with his. She fought her swimming senses with every ounce of willpower she possessed.

She tried to think about the rest of the people applauding at the tables. She tried to think about Tony and Neil, who surely must be witnessing the whole performance.

Nothing worked. All she could think about was Luke's mouth on hers, warm and demanding, and the hard contours of his body as he closed his arms around her. The memory of him lying in the bed next to her all night ignited the inevitable fires.

He tightened his hold, and she gave in to the demands of her body. She melted against him, returning his kiss with an urgency that blotted out everyone and everything. There were only the two of them, locked in each other's arms in a world of soft scents and music.

When he lifted his head, she could feel herself trembling, and knew he was aware of her reaction. For a long moment, he looked deep into her eyes, while her constricted lungs struggled to breathe. Then, with a lopsided grin, he whispered, "If I say so myself, practice does make perfect."

She jerked away from him, more angry with herself than with him. She sat down quickly before the words she was tempted to say forced their way past her lips. When he sat down behind her and tried to pull her close again, she resisted, pretending to reach for the mai tai she'd been playing with all evening.

Sipping the fruity drink, she tried to reason with herself. She had no right to be mad, she told herself fiercely. Her unprofessional reactions to him were out of line. He was simply doing his job. And he was right. He was good at it. He was damn good at it.

She put the glass down and tried to concentrate on the jovial host. She watched him stride across the stage, urging all the women to come up and join him.

Several women obeyed, laughing and giggling as a group of men wearing grass skirts and leis helped them up onto the floodlit stage. The host begged for more ladies to join him, promising to give them all a free hula lesson.

Nicole jumped as Luke's fingers brushed down her bare arm. He leaned forward and pressed another kiss into the back of her neck. "Relax," he whispered.

In spite of her valiant endeavor to soften her voice, the words snapped out. "I *am* relaxed." Suddenly she'd had enough. She couldn't take any more romantic music, sensuous aromas and soft, warm breezes. And she couldn't take the pain of being so close to him and yet so impossibly far.

With a swift movement she grabbed her purse and swung her legs over the bench. As she started forward, Luke caught her wrist, pulling her around to face him.

"Where are you going?" His voice sounded light and teasing, but his eyes glinted like steel in the reflection of the colored lights.

She leaned forward and pretended to kiss him. With her mouth close to his, she muttered, "You wanted visible. I'm going to give you visible."

"No." Alarm flashed across his face, but she ignored it. She just wanted it over with. If Adams were Merrill, she wanted to know, and if he wanted her, she was going to make damn sure he found her.

She snatched her arm from Luke's grasp and pushed her way down the narrow aisle between the tables to the stage. She heard Luke call out "Opal!" in a command that only made her all the more determined.

Strong arms reached down to help her as she clambered up the steps, and she found herself high above the audience, staring down at Luke's grim face.

He started toward the steps, then stopped when the host jokingly warned him that this was for ladies only. Two of the men stood at the top of the steps barring his way, while the host made an off-color remark about the impatience of newlyweds.

Nicole caught a glimpse of pure fury in Luke's eyes before he allowed himself to be led to the side of the stage to wait for her. For a moment, her bravado faltered, and she took a tentative step back to the stairs. Then the music began, and one of the dancers on the stage caught her hand.

Nicole had seen signs of Luke's temper during the long week in his hotel suite in Portland. Nothing had come close to the look in his eyes now. She tried not to think about it as she halfheartedly followed the steps of the dancer, trying to swivel her belly the way he was doing without losing her balance on her heels.

If she'd wanted to draw attention to herself, she couldn't have picked a better way to do it. People laughed and whistled, and Nicole gritted her teeth as she continued to make a perfect ass of herself. If this ever got back to Sutton and the precinct, she swore inwardly, she'd have Jordan's guts for garters.

The fact that she alone was responsible for her predicament did nothing to cool her own temper. She could have cried with relief when the band played the final chords and the audience burst into noisy applause.

She was forced to take a bow along with the rest of the women, and as she faced out to the audience, she saw Neil moving swiftly down one side of the tables. Luke still stood fuming at the edge of the stage.

She didn't care what he thought, Nicole assured herself as she waited for her turn to descend the steps. He was doing his job and she was doing hers. It was up to her to draw Merrill out into the open and that was exactly what she was going to do.

No more hiding behind Luke's broad back. It was time he allowed her to be what she was—a qualified officer of the law, not some dumb amateur along for the ride.

She'd never be able to prove her competence if he hovered over her like some fussy mother hen. She was here to carry out an assignment, and no one was going to get in her way. Including Mr. Practice-Makes-Perfect Jordan.

She reached the bottom step and was nearly hustled off her feet by Luke's grip on her arm. "We're going back to the hotel," he said quietly, pretending to smile as he curled an arm tightly around her shoulders.

"The hell we are," Nicole muttered, baring her teeth in a false grin. "I'm just beginning to enjoy myself."

Ignoring her, he forced her to walk alongside him as he skirted the tables and made for the parking lot.

Checking around to make sure no one was in earshot, she said in a low, furious voice, "You're making a mistake. Anyone can tell you're mad. What are you trying to do? Blow the whole cover?"

"Shut up," Luke warned, "before I do something really drastic."

"We came by bus," Nicole went on recklessly. "How do you propose to get back to the hotel?"

"There'll be a cab here in a few minutes to pick us up."

Realizing that Tony or Neil must have radioed for one, she demanded, "And if anyone is watching, what are they going to think?"

"They'll think I'm a jealous newlywed with a problem."

They reached the bare stretch of ground that served as the parking lot just as a cab swung in off the highway and rocketed toward them.

Luke held her back until the cab stopped and the driver stuck his head out the window. "Mr. Jordan?"

"That's me." Grim-faced, Luke hauled the door open and shoved Nicole none too gently inside.

She sat with a stiff spine all the way back to the hotel, rehearsing everything she was going to say once they were in their suite.

Luke didn't speak as he propelled her into the elevator, and they rode up to the twenty-third floor in stony silence.

Nicole grimaced as a ridiculous thought popped into her mind—something her mother had told her. Never go to bed angry. She couldn't let that stop her. She had a few things to get straight with Luke Jordan, even if it infuriated him further.

She let him unlock the door and open it, and followed him into the room. He stopped so suddenly she bumped into him. Swinging around to face her, he held both her arms, his fingers biting into her bare flesh.

"Okay, Officer Parker, just what are you trying to prove?"

He'd hit home with the first shot. Refusing to struggle with him, she stood there in his grasp and met his furious gaze.

"I don't know what you're getting so damn excited about," she declared. "I was doing my job. I'm supposed to be visible. I was being visible."

"Not without me, you're not." He glared at her for a moment longer, then, with a low curse, let her go. Moving a couple of steps away from her, he ran both hands through his hair in a gesture of exasperation. "How the hell am I supposed to protect you if you pull some damn-fool stunt like that?"

"Maybe," Nicole said quietly, "I don't need your protection. Just maybe I can take care of myself."

He swung around again, his eyes glinting fire. "Have you forgotten what you're up against here? Haven't you heard enough already to convince you? Adrian Merrill is the most dangerous type of criminal. He is malicious. He is clever. And he wants Opal Turner very badly."

"I know all that." Why wouldn't he let it go? she thought, her resentment burning. "You're not even sure it *is* Merrill—you said so yourself. And I resent the implication that I'm not capable of handling this job. No one was going to grab me while I was on a stage in full view of an audience. And if they had tried it, I was armed. I had my gun with me."

"If you'd had a chance to use it."

She flung out her hand in a gesture of contempt. "At least I had one. Where's your gun, Luke?"

His face went white, and a muscle ticked furiously in his cheek. Lifting up his shirt to reveal a revolver tucked in his belt, he said harshly, "Right here."

Intrigued by the expression on his face, she kept silent.

"I'll tell you one thing. If you ever pull something like this on me again I'll . . ." His voice trailed off as he apparently searched for an appropriate threat.

Nicole curved her mouth in a disdainful smile. "You'll what? Fire me? You seem to forget who's the official law officer around here. I'm sorry to blow your ego, Jordan, but you're only a temp. You have no damn authority to order me around."

He took a step toward her and she backed up, unnerved by the gleam in his eyes. His voice dropped to a near whisper. "I'm going to check with HPD on an outside phone. When I get back, I suggest you be asleep, Parker. Or I'll really give you something to complain about."

Before she could respond, he spun on his heel and strode to the door. He'd barely closed it behind him before the sandal she'd snatched off hit it square in the middle. She stood breathing fire and wished it had been his head.

Chapter 7

Nicole pretended to be asleep when she heard Luke's key in the door an hour later. She lay rock still, listening to him moving around, and did her best to relax her tense muscles when he slid into the bed beside her.

Something told her that in spite of her efforts, he was aware of her restlessness. Much later, when sleep still eluded her, she slipped out of bed and quietly slid open the French window.

The moonlit night greeted her, and soft laughter floated on the breezes from the ocean, together with the heady fragrance that consistently pervaded the air.

If only she were there under different circumstances, she thought, leaning on the balcony to look up at the distant stars. Would he still treat her with that maddening unconcern? Was he so unaffected by her that he could kiss her so convincingly without feeling an atom of emotion?

She let out a long, rueful sigh. Face it, Parker, she thought with an ache of regret. If they were there under different circumstances, he wouldn't be kissing her at all.

She folded her arms as the cool breeze penetrated the thin cotton of her shift. Yet there had been times, she thought wistfully, when she thought she'd detected a spark of interest, a gleam of awareness in the depths of those cool gray eyes. Obviously she'd been mistaken.

Suddenly she straightened as a slight movement caught her eye. From where she stood, she could see the row of balconies belonging to an adjacent hotel. It appeared that someone else was having trouble sleeping on this sultry night.

A shadow moved on one of the balconies, and she thought she saw the glowing tip of a cigarette in the darkness. She sent the solitary figure a sympathetic smile and hoped his insomnia wasn't caused by heartache, too. Then, rubbing her arms, she stepped back into the room and slipped into bed.

If Luke had been aware of her nocturnal wandering, he made no mention of it the next morning. Nor did he show any trace of resentment over their argument the night before. As usual, he was up before her, already shaved and dressed before she was fully awake.

He greeted her as if their disagreement had never happened, and as she showered and dressed, Nicole wasn't sure whether to be happy that he was ignoring their fight or frustrated that it apparently wasn't significant enough to bother him.

When he asked her what she wanted to do that morning, she suggested a shopping trip in downtown Waikiki. She was beginning to feel the effects of the sun on her back and decided to give the beach a rest for a while.

"I'd like to see the international market," she told him as they lingered over breakfast served at a table by the pool.

"You're not going to load up on all those shell necklaces, are you?" Luke asked mildly as he leaned back with a cup of coffee in his hand.

She gave him a scornful grin. "Now where would I wear shell necklaces in Portland? But I do like those wind chimes made of shells. I think they'd sound great hanging from my apartment balcony."

"Yeah, till we get one of our famous Oregon windstorms and you drive your neighbors crazy."

She laughed. "Well, I wanted something to remind me of the islands, and I think that would be perfect." She sobered, wondering if she'd want to be reminded of this place once this was over.

Luke must have thought much the same thing, since his expression changed. Putting down his cup, he said lightly, "Come on, then. If you insist on dragging me around all those junk stalls, we might as well get started."

As she rose to her feet, Nicole saw Tony detach himself from the railing alongside the pool. She should have been comforted by the assurance that he and Neil were within shouting distance.

But then, she thought as she followed Luke out of the hotel, she should have been a lot of things she wasn't. She should have been able to resist Luke's smile, instead of melting every time he looked at her. She should be worrying about her own safety, instead of wallowing in self-pity because he didn't return her feelings for him.

And she should be making the most of this free vacation and enjoying it while she could, because so far nothing had happened to suggest that Adams could be Adrian Merrill. Or if he were, that he would do anything to give himself away.

Maybe they were wrong, Nicole thought later as she wandered among the souvenirs piled high on the market stalls. Maybe Merrill didn't want Opal badly enough to blow his cover. Maybe he figured she wasn't worth the risk. In which case, she wondered, just how long was she supposed to go on parading around Waikiki in this ridiculous wig and getup before they realized that fact and recalled her back to the mainland?

She held a tinkling mobile of shells in her hand, swinging them gently to judge the delicate sound. "What do you think?" she asked Luke, who seemed more interested in the elderly wood-carver squatting on the ground between the stalls.

"Sounds okay to me," Luke murmured, still with his back to her.

"You're not listening," Nicole accused, "so how can you tell?"

He turned his head to look at her. "Okay, do it again."

She shook the wind chimes at him. "I don't know if they'll be loud enough."

He grinned. "They'll be loud enough in the middle of the night when everyone's trying to get some sleep."

She studied the creamy pink shells with a frown. "I guess you're right." After handing them over to the smiling woman behind the counter, she dug in her tote bag for her wallet. By the time she'd received the white package and her change, Luke had moved over to where two scantily clad young girls sat cross-legged on stools, weaving brilliantly colored blossoms into leis.

Nicole stood behind him and murmured, "Thank goodness. I was beginning to think you weren't normal."

He sent her a startled glance over his shoulder. "What's that supposed to mean?"

"It means that with all these half-naked women running around, this is the first time you've shown any interest in one."

She wished she could read the expression in his eyes when he said softly, "That's what you think. You just haven't noticed me looking."

Her stomach gave a little lurch when she wondered if he could possibly be talking about her. In the next instant, she irritably dismissed the notion. There she went again, reading things that weren't there.

Annoyed with herself, she walked quickly past the stalls to where she'd seen a display of stuffed animals. The toys were one of her weaknesses she rarely indulged. But, she decided, it was time to spoil herself a little. She had almost reached the end of the row when it happened.

She felt a vicious bump in the small of her back and gasped in pain. The next instant, she felt herself stumbling between the stalls. She grabbed a heavy curtain for support and found herself tangled in it, while rough, invisible hands tried to help her.

When she finally freed herself, she saw with a jolt of surprise that she was in a different aisle. Instinctively she whirled around, the wind chimes clattering in her bag as she swung it in front of her.

The hands hadn't been helping her at all. They belonged to a swarthy man with dark glittering eyes. His thin frame carried no weight, but the look in his eyes unnerved her. She hesitated a second too long.

As she plunged her hand into her bag, his fingers closed over her wrist and gave it as sharp twist. She hissed in agony and swung her foot up sharply against his shin.

In the two seconds he danced out of reach, her eyes searched desperately for Luke. The aisle seemed strangely empty of people, until she realized that the end had been walled off. She wasn't in an aisle at all but some kind of private alleyway between the stalls.

Again she stabbed a hand into her bag, and this time his foot snaked out and cracked against her elbow. Dazed with pain, she felt sick. She was up against an expert. Where in the hell was Luke?

She backed off, knowing her training in self-defense was useless against the kind of skill her adversary possessed. He lunged forward, and to her surprise, instead of grabbing her as she'd expected, took hold of her tote bag and tried to jerk it from her grasp.

She heard a commotion behind her but didn't dare turn her head. The blow to her elbow had numbed her right arm, and she twisted the handles of the bag around her left.

If he wanted her bag, she thought grimly, he would have to take her arm with it. She moved quickly, raising her knee, but again he sidestepped, still tugging desperately on the bag.

Pounding footsteps sounded behind her. For a moment, she froze, then her assailant lifted his head and with a muttered curse dived beneath a ragged curtain and disappeared.

Once more rough hands grabbed her, but this time they spun her around and she stared into Luke's familiar face. He wore an expression she'd never seen before. It shook her so badly she said quickly, "I'm all right. It's over. I'm all right."

Instead of answering, he dragged her into his arms. She could feel the thunder of his heartbeat against her breast, even while her own thumped madly in return.

"What happened?" he asked after a while in a voice she hardly recognized. "What the hell happened?"

Belatedly she remembered she was Opal Turner. It wasn't difficult to imitate Opal's breathy voice. She felt as if all her breath had been pumped from her body.

"Oh, honey," she said, pitching her voice as high as she could manage, "he tried to steal my purse."

Over his shoulder she saw a little knot of curious onlookers staring at her from the end of the alley, and beyond them Neil's head bobbing up and down.

Luke drew back and gave her a strained smile. The dreadful expression had faded from his eyes, but he still looked shaken. "Are you sure you're all right, sweetheart?"

She nodded. She caught a glimpse of Tony's friendly face in the crowd and began to feel a little better.

"Let's get out of here," Luke muttered and, keeping his arm around her, led her past the tourists who still sent covert glances her way as she edged past them.

Once outside in the sunlight, she gulped in air and managed a smile. "That was close."

"Too close." Luke's mouth looked grim as he put a possessive arm around her. "I'm getting you back to the hotel."

"No, I'm fine." He'd been genuinely worried about her. Whatever his personal feelings toward her, she couldn't mistake that haunted look in his eyes.

"Maybe, but we have to talk."

She knew better than to argue with that tone of voice. She waited in silence while he hailed a cab, and kept up a meaningless chatter about the shops on the way back to the hotel.

Once inside the suite, Luke went straight to the phone. He waited impatiently as the ringing at the other end of the line went unanswered, then cursed and replaced the receiver.

He glanced at Nicole, who sat on the bed, a wary expression on her face. The spasm of need that had bothered him for the past two days intensified. She'd kicked off her sandals and removed the wig, and she looked oddly defensive with her dark hair tumbled around Opal's garish makeup.

He wanted to take her away, far from the reach of all the dreary misery and horror that was part of her job. She was too warm, too compassionate, too sensitive to be mixed up in all this, yet he loved the strength and determination that made her good at it. And she was good at it.

She'd handled that thug like a pro, without a murmur, and after it was over she'd acted as calm as a sleeping tortoise. And God help him, he wanted her all the more for it.

He wanted her as he'd never wanted anyone or anything in his life before. He ached to hold her, to kiss her with an abandon that so far he'd managed to hold in check.

He wanted to end the agony of lying beside her at night. He wanted to make wild, wanton love with her, until all the passion and driving need was finally exhausted.

He made himself sit down on the couch. He would have to call in the guys. "I think we need a conference," he said as casually as his tension would allow.

She understood at once. "Isn't that risky?"

"Necessary."

She looked at him for a long moment. "It was only a purse snatcher."

"We don't know that."

"If he'd wanted to hurt me," she said steadily, "or even kidnap me, he could have easily done it. He was a kung fu expert. I'm convinced he just wanted my purse."

"Why you?"

She shrugged. "I imagine there are as many purse snatchers here as anywhere on the mainland. Maybe more. The tourists are thick as flies here. And you don't drive to Hawaii in a beat-up old car."

He knew what she meant. The majority of tourists in Hawaii had money. It made the risks worthwhile to someone desperate enough to snatch purses for a living.

Even so, he couldn't rid himself of the uneasy feeling that stirred the hairs on the back of his neck. It just didn't smell right. "So tell me exactly what happened," he said, hoping she could convince him that it was nothing more than a simple attempted robbery. A coincidence. Maybe that was it, he thought with a tug of anxiety. But there were just too damn many coincidences.

"There's not much to tell. It was all over in seconds, though it seemed longer than that."

He saw the hint of vulnerability in her face and again felt the tug of desire. "A hell of a lot longer," he agreed fervently.

"He hit me from behind." She pulled her knees up to her chin and wrapped her arms around them. He tried to keep his gaze away from the expanse of lightly tanned legs in the brief shorts.

"I stumbled with those stupid heels and kind of fell between the stalls. The next thing I knew, I was in this alley and he was standing in front of me. I went for my gun—" she frowned, hesitated, then continued "—and he kicked out, then grabbed my purse. That's all he wanted, I swear. Just my purse. I would have known if it had been anything else."

Luke let out his breath on a long sigh. "I don't know. It seems strange that just at that moment, someone stood in my way so I couldn't see what was going on. It was like a scene from a magic show. One second you were there, the next you'd vanished into thin air."

He swore, remembering the sheer, cold terror he'd felt at that moment. "I couldn't even see the guys. It was just luck that I chose to go left instead of right. I could have spent the next hour looking for you in that maze."

"I know. I have to admit I got nervous when I realized I was in some kind of alley. I did see Tony and Neil afterward, though. They were right behind you."

"Yeah." He combed his hair with his fingers. He still wasn't entirely convinced, but she could well be right. It could have been a simple case of purse snatching. And if it were, they still didn't have the proof they needed. If it weren't, then they would try again, and this time he'd be ready. He'd make damn sure he was ready.

He looked up when Nicole uttered a small cry of dismay. "My wind chimes! They're broken." She held up the crushed shells with such a look of devastation the knot inside him twisted in real pain.

"I'll buy you some more," he said, his throat tight.

She shook her head, dropping the pieces back into the wrappings on her lap. "It was a stupid idea, anyway. They would probably have broken on the way home."

He had to turn away before she could see the agony on his face. He had to get out of there before he did something really stupid. "Put your tumbleweed back on," he said gruffly. "I'm going to rent a car. We'll drive out somewhere and get out of the city for a couple of hours."

"I'd like that."

He heard her slip off the bed. He pretended to be busy sorting through his wallet until she'd closed the bathroom door behind her. Shoving the wallet back into his pocket, he strode across the room and picked up the phone, then waited a few moments before muttering a terse message into it.

He brushed past the bed and hauled open the window. He needed fresh air to clear his head. What he needed, he admitted as he leaned on the balcony, was a cold shower. But that could wait. They could both do with a break. Because he still wasn't convinced.

The back of his neck still prickled, and a gut feeling told him that somehow the purse snatcher and Merrill were connected. Merrill would want to be sure before he took the risk of having her picked up. And her purse would tell the whole story.

Luke heard the bathroom door open, and straightened. If her purse snatcher tried again, they'd know for sure. Twice would be too much of a coincidence. And if he tried again, this time he wouldn't find it so easy to get away.

The phone rang in the beach house on the windward shore. It took the crippled man a while to wedge the receiver under his scarred chin. He listened in silence for several moments before the necessity to speak tested his threshold of pain.

"Fool! You could have messed up the entire mission."

The voice garbled some more words in his ear. If it had been at all possible, he would have frowned. "When?"

He listened some more. "All right. And make it look good. We can't afford any more mistakes." He went through the process of replacing the receiver, but without the usual groan of pain this time.

Somehow the agony became more bearable, knowing he was this close. Say your prayers, Luke Jordan, he thought with a grunt of satisfaction. And say them out loud. Because soon you will be incapable of speech.

Not long now, he promised silently, and he'd have Jordan where he wanted him. He would make it last. He wanted to hear Luke Jordan scream the way he had screamed. He wanted to watch him writhe in agony, and he wanted to see the expression on that smooth, untouched face when Jordan realized what was about to happen. Once more the evil laugh cackled in his chest.

Nicole enjoyed the ride along the coast road. Luke, for once, seemed more relaxed. They even shared a joke or two as the little car sped along the narrow highway, winding its way through tiny villages and alongside secluded beaches.

They ate hamburgers in a restaurant overlooking the ocean, watching the breakers through glassless windows. They drank piña coladas sitting on the sand in the shade of leafy palm trees. And for a little while, Nicole could forget about Opal's voice and gestures and enjoy the luxury of being herself.

She leaned against the trunk of a coconut tree and closed her eyes. The sound of breakers washing onto the shore soothed her ragged nerves, and she was determined to make the most of this pleasant interlude.

"I think I could be happy living in a place like this," Luke remarked lazily.

Nicole curved her mouth in a smile but was too drowsy to answer him.

"Yeah," he went on. "A little grass shack on the beach would just do me. I'd have a boat, do a little fishing—"

"And you'd be bored to death within a month." She opened an eye to look at him. He was lying flat on his back, his arms pillowing his head. She felt an intense urge to lean over and kiss him, and had to restrain herself. Although she still looked like Opal, she no longer had the excuse of their pretense in this secluded spot.

"You think so?" Luke turned his head, a smile playing around his mouth.

She closed her eyes again, afraid of revealing too much to that astute gaze. "Yes, I think so. You're not the type to sit around doing nothing with your life."

"Oh? Then what type am I?"

She thought about it. "I think you're happiest when you're doing something for other people. You have a deep desire to be needed, to be useful. You have to know that you're making a contribution somewhere, and I think, deep down you're a lonely man, though you'd probably be the last to admit it."

He was silent for so long she thought he'd dozed off. She was drifting in a half doze herself when he said, "I miss being on the force."

She smiled. "I know."

"I've never told that to anyone before."

Her heart skipped, but she managed to keep a casual note in her voice when she answered. "Don't worry. I won't tell anyone."

"I know that."

Something in his voice opened her eyes. She met his gaze, and his smile stopped her heart.

"You're quite a woman, Officer Parker."

Don't, her heart begged. *Don't put all your hopes on a few lousy words.* It's the place, she reminded herself. The magic of the islands that everyone keeps talking about. It does crazy things to people's minds. It won't last. It can't last.

She forced her head back against the tree and closed her eyes. "You have your moments, too, Jordan."

He chuckled. "I'll accept that as a compliment."

She could hear the regret in his voice when he added, a few moments later, "I guess we'd better be getting back. I imagine Neil and Tony are wondering where we are."

Nicole sat up with a gasp. "Oh, Luke, I'd forgotten about them. They're probably frantic."

"I left a message on Neil's recorder to hold the macadamia nuts until we got back. He should figure from that that we're okay."

She relaxed. "You think of everything," she said, smiling.

"I try to."

He didn't return the smile, and she sighed, knowing that their brief respite had ended. They had a job to do, and she had a niggling feeling in the pit of her stomach that they were close to a confrontation.

Something about the attempt to steal her purse that morning still bothered her. She hadn't said anything to Luke because she couldn't quite put her finger on what it was, but her mind worried at it like a child's tongue with a loose tooth, and her uneasiness grew as they drove back to the city.

Luke called room service the minute they entered the suite, canceling their order of macadamia nuts. Nicole made a mental note to buy some when they went out again.

They spent an uneventful night dining at the hotel and strolled along the beach afterward, arm in arm and seemingly relaxed, while the tension between them was so thick Nicole's body ached with it.

She wished she could put it all down to the uncertainty of knowing just when and from which direction the next strike would come. The truth was, the source of her stress had more to do with Luke's kisses and casual caresses than the need to stay alert.

The quiet pleasure of the stolen hours that afternoon still lingered, and she was deeply reluctant to let it go. It hurt to know that Luke's responses were faked while hers were all too real.

She was glad when Luke suggested they return to the hotel. She knew by his voice that he, too, was edgy and uptight. She guessed that he'd expected some kind of move from Merrill and was disappointed that it hadn't materialized.

She wondered again why it appeared to be so desperately important to him. Sure, he had reason to hate the man. He had killed Luke's partner, after all. But she couldn't lose the feeling that there was more to it than that—something he wasn't telling her. And she had yet to find out why he had left the force.

She knew the two incidents had to be connected, but it seemed unlikely now that the rumors circulating about him were true. Knowing him as she did, she couldn't bring herself to believe that he'd lost his nerve.

Safely locked inside their suite, she tried to relax as she watched Luke call in the usual message confirming all was well. Even after erasing all trace of Opal from her face, and dressed in her shift ready for bed, she knew she was far too tense to sleep.

Instead of slipping into bed as she usually did, she walked out onto the *lanai* while Luke took his turn in the bathroom. The air seemed even more humid tonight, drenched in the fragrance of tropical blossoms.

She looked across at the rows of balconies opposite her, but she could see no moving shadows tonight. Either her late-night companion was sleeping better, or he wasn't yet back in his room.

A movement beside her gave her a start. Luke had stepped out onto the *lanai* without a sound. He still wore his pants but had removed his shirt. She dragged her gaze from his bare back as he leaned on the balcony beside her.

"It seems like a different place at night," he murmured. "It even smells different."

"I know what you mean." She had a word for it. A word she couldn't use. Intimate. Somehow the sultry darkness seemed to envelop them in a solitary refuge where nothing could invade their privacy.

She was being unrealistic, she knew. It was dangerous to think that way, yet somehow she felt more secure in the darkness, as long as Luke was by her side.

They seemed to share a certain closeness in the night, an intimacy that managed to surmount the stress of their job. She felt as if the night belonged to her. She could be herself, and as herself she couldn't ignore her feelings for the man standing next to her.

She glanced at him, wondering what his reaction would be if he could read her mind. Did he feel it, too, she wondered, or was it just a matter of wishful thinking on her part? Had they achieved any measure of progress in their relationship?

She decided to find out. Turning her back to the railing, she leaned against it and asked softly, "Luke, why did you leave the force?"

He looked down at his clasped hands resting on the railing. After a long pause, he said in a curiously flat voice, "I was responsible for a man's death."

Shock jolted her body. "What do you mean?"

He lifted his head and stared out at the restless ocean. "My partner, Mark Wilson, was killed in the raid on Merrill's warehouse," he said finally.

Nicole shook her head in bewilderment. "I know that. He was shot by Merrill, wasn't he?"

"Yes." He straightened, and she could see his knuckles gleaming in the moonlight as he gripped the railing. "You'll find out sooner or later, so I might as well tell you. Mark Wilson was Grant Sutton's nephew.''

Her shocked gasp sounded loud in the darkness. "But he never said—''

"I know." His voice filled with bitterness. "He hasn't mentioned it again since it happened. Mark's mother was Sutton's sister. Mark was her only child. After he was killed, she took to the bottle. Within a year, she was an alcoholic. She lost everything—her marriage, her home, her job. She's in some kind of home now. They say she'll never come out.''

"Oh, God." Nicole groped for the right words to say. "I'm sorry, Luke, that's a terrible thing to happen. But Merrill was the one who killed Mark Wilson, not you.''

Luke's laugh was pure contempt. "I was responsible for him. Mark was too young to be a detective—Sutton knew that. He promoted him because Mark accused him of holding back the promotion to protect him.''

He tilted his head back in a gesture of despair before going on. "Sutton was afraid that there was some truth to that. The boy was qualified technically, but Sutton wasn't sure he had what it took to deal with the pressures involved. He was afraid Mark would fold in an emergency.''

Nicole was beginning to understand. Her throat tightened. "And he did.''

"Yes." His pause this time was much longer. His voice echoed a harshness that frightened her when he spoke again. "Sutton assigned Mark to me. He said I was the only man he could trust to take care of the boy. Mark's first assignment was the raid on the warehouse.''

Nicole swallowed. "What happened?" She didn't really want to find out, but knew she couldn't stop him now.

"When Opal called me to let me know Merrill was moving out, we had no time to organize. We called in what manpower we had and made for the warehouse. We managed to get there before Merrill left, but he'd been expecting us. There was an exchange of gunfire, and the warehouse went up in flames.''

Luke's knuckles gleamed bone white on the railing. ''Merrill and his men were still inside. Mark was behind me as we made a dash along the side of the warehouse. We were trying to get to the doorway. We were almost there when Merrill stepped out. I yelled at Mark to stay put, but he panicked and started to run. Merrill got him right away. He fell almost at my feet.''

Nicole's lungs hurt from holding her breath. She let it out slowly on a sigh. Before she could say anything, Luke spoke again.

''I went down on my knees as Mark tried to get up. I couldn't believe that the boy had been hit. It happened so fast. I looked up. Merrill was still standing there with the gun pointed at him.''

His voice cracked. ''I froze. For one second, I had the gun in my hand and I couldn't lift it. One second, the space of a heartbeat, and that was all it took. Merrill shot again, and Mark collapsed in my arms. When I looked up again, Merrill had disappeared.''

Luke turned his head, and his eyes looked bleak and empty when he looked at her. ''I watched that boy die. Sutton trusted me with his nephew's life, and I let him down. I couldn't face working with him after that. So I resigned.''

Unable to stand that look in his eyes, she laid her hand on his arm. ''Luke, you must know it wasn't your fault. Even if you'd shot at Merrill, you probably wouldn't have saved Mark. What happened was part of the job. Sutton knew it when he promoted Mark, and Mark must have known it when he took the job. It comes with the territory. It could happen to any one of us.''

She was shocked when Luke whirled on her. ''I failed, dammit. I had Merrill right in front of me, and I froze. They all trusted me, and I let them down. I could have taken Merrill down and I didn't do it.''

He stepped toward the window and paused, looking at her over his shoulder. His voice was ragged with despair when he added, "I haven't had to use a gun since then. I don't know if I *can* use a gun again."

"Luke—"

He stopped her with a vicious shake of his head. "I killed Mark Wilson as surely as if I'd put the bullet in him myself. How does a man live with that? You tell me, because I've tried to find a way to live with it ever since."

Before she could answer him, he disappeared through the window, and she heard the slam of the door. She was alone, and in that moment felt a sense of failure almost as deep as Luke's.

He had finally told her. Now that she knew, she could understand what it had cost him to tell her. And why he had chosen to do so. He was suffering from massive guilt. In his desperate need, he had turned to her, and she had failed him. She hadn't been able to find the words that would release him from his terrible self-imposed prison of remorse.

Turning, she gripped the rail as he had done, while tears welled in her eyes. He hated himself so much that he had lost all trust in himself.

She stood for a long time, listening to the surf pounding in tune with her heart. The ache was almost unbearable, and the frustration of knowing she could do nothing to help him tore her apart.

Then she heard his key in the lock, and turned, her heartbeat racing with anticipation. She stepped through the window just as he opened the door.

For a moment, he stared at her, his eyes locked with hers in some wild, questioning appeal. She knew then what she could do—what she needed to do. For a little while at least, she could erase that terrible look from his eyes and ease the ache in her own heart. Wordlessly she held out her arms.

He took a step forward, then halted. "I can't make any promises," he said quietly.

"I know." She swallowed, trying to ease the ache in her throat. "It doesn't matter. Not tonight."

"Tonight might be all we'll have."

"I know that, too."

With a muffled groan deep in his throat, he strode toward her. Closing his arms around her, he lifted her off her feet. "Nicole?" he whispered, his gaze still questioning.

She traced his mouth with a gentle finger. "Yes."

The look in his eyes took her breath away as he lowered her onto the bed.

Chapter 8

Moonlight streamed through the open window, illuminating Luke's face as Nicole looked up at him. He must have grabbed his shirt on the way out, she thought with a far-off part of her mind. She reached for the buttons and began undoing them.

"Wait a minute," he whispered and straightened. Swiftly he pulled the drapes together, leaving a sliver of light to spread and diminish with the movement of the curtains in the breeze.

Coming back to her, he paused and looked down at her, his face just a blur in the shadows. "I want to look at you."

She waited, heart pounding, as he switched on a small pink lamp. The subdued light bathed his face, softening the harsh lines. He lowered himself onto the bed beside her, and she turned on her side, again reaching for the buttons of his shirt.

"Do you have any idea how much I want you?" he asked, brushing her cheek with his fingers.

"Tell me." She pulled his shirt free of his pants and pushed it off his shoulders.

"I'd rather show you. I've never been good with words."

She found the buckle of his belt and unfastened it. "Then show me."

"I have to get something straight first."

"I thought you didn't want to talk." She eased down his zipper and pushed his pants over his hips.

"This is important." He slid his hand down to the hem of her shift.

She caught her breath as his fingers touched her thigh. "Then you'd better hurry up and say it." She hooked her thumbs into the waistband of his briefs.

"I just wanted you to know—" His voice cut off as she worked his briefs down to his knees. The bed rocked while he kicked his legs free.

"Know what?" She had trouble forming the words.

He moved his hand up her thigh to her hip, bringing her shift with it. His voice sounded strained when he answered her. "This is definitely not in the line of duty."

She grinned and raised her arms, allowing him to pull off the shift. "I'm very glad to hear it." The words ended on a gasp when his hand found her breast.

"I just wanted to make that clear." He smothered any answer she might have had, his mouth covering hers in a hot, demanding kiss that wiped everything from her mind.

His fingers moved on her breast, sending shafts of intense pleasure rocketing through her body. She ran her hands down his strong, smooth back, her fingers tracing the bony indentation. She heard his sharp breath as she reached the base of his spine and followed the groove beyond.

He wrapped his arms around her, pulling her against him in a sudden fierce movement that took her by surprise. He pressed naked flesh against the length of her, burning her with his touch.

She arched beneath him, and it seemed as if she'd opened an oven door, releasing a smoldering heat that fueled his desperate need. He was no longer gentle with her.

When he asked too much, she made a frail attempt to prevent him from taking command of her body, but he persisted, proving to her that she wanted everything he could give.

He didn't ask what pleased her. Words didn't seem necessary. He knew where to touch, and the furnace he lit inside her engulfed her in a mindless vortex of emotions.

He created sensations she'd never felt before. She heard her voice making unfamiliar cries of pleasure, and the involuntary spasms of her body filled her with wonder at her response to his touch.

She raked his flesh with her fingers, loving the contrast of soft hair and smooth skin. While she still had the strength to assert herself, she explored his body with eager hands and mouth, finding a new excitement in his moans of arousal.

As he stroked her sensitive skin, his tongue tormented even more vulnerable areas, sending her deeper into a whirlpool of frenzy. She followed him through fiery channels of an excitement so intense she begged for release, but he seemed intent on making it last, and would not give in to her pleading.

Mindlessly she met his passion with a wild fervor of her own, caught up in the violent tide of emotion that seemed to drive them both. He showed her what he needed, and rewarded her with sharp sensual groans when she ventured beyond. Aware that he held nothing back, she gave with the same complete abandon.

Finally, just when she felt she could take no more, he rolled her onto her back. She was on fire, every nerve craving for release. She watched him stretch himself over her, and saw his slick body heaving with exertion. She heard his rasping breath, and the pressure in her own lungs threatened to explode.

Raising himself up with his arms, he stared down at her, and she knew she had never seen anything more beautiful than the flames of passion in his gray eyes.

As he slowly filled her, she raised her hips to meet him, taking all of him. Even as her own urgency built to fever pitch, she knew the moment his patience snapped. His wild, unmeasured abandon plunged her into a torment of fiery excitement. She fought for release with him, soaring like an eagle in an empty sky, leaving the world behind.

Joined with him, she crested the edge of the earth, until with a final shuddering cry she felt him spill over. And, as he buried himself deep inside her, she hurtled with him into endless, mindless space.

She lay for a long time in his arms, content just to listen to his breathing. Gradually the rise and fall of his chest beneath her cheek subsided to a more gentle rhythm, and she wondered if he was asleep.

Gently she moved her hand across his chest, tangling her fingers in the silky hair. He captured her fingers with his, pressing them to his skin so that she could feel his heart beating steadily beneath her palm.

She turned her face and pressed her lips into the hollow of his neck. His murmur of pleasure made her smile. "Were you asleep?" she asked softly.

"Resting. I haven't used that much energy in a long time."

The words formed on her lips and tumbled out before she could stop them. "Not since Opal?"

He went very still, and she waited, wishing miserably that she'd kept her mouth shut.

"I thought I told you it wasn't like that," he said at last.

She couldn't tell anything from his voice. "You did. I'm sorry. That was a stupid thing to say."

He turned his head, reaching her heart with the look in his eyes. "Not with anyone," he said quietly. "Not like that."

She smiled, the warmth of his words filling her soul. "Nor me." She leaned over and kissed him, then moved her lips to his throat. The subtle male scent of his skin stirred a response deep inside her, surprising her with its intensity.

She lay back on her pillow and began tracing a feathery trail from his throat down his chest. When she moved her hand over his stomach, she knew by his indrawn breath that already he needed her again.

He turned on his side, pressing his hips to hers to confirm her thoughts. "You don't satisfy easy, lady," he murmured.

She laughed softly. "Nor do you."

His kiss was long and lingering, and left her breathless. Again the heat consumed her as his hands moved over her, followed by the sweet torture of his mouth. This time her flight with him to the stars burned even brighter as she discovered new, acute pleasures his body could bring her.

When they finally lay spent in each other's arms, she drifted off into a contented sleep, only to wake again later to find the lamp still alight and Luke fast asleep beside her.

She propped herself up on her elbow to look at him. The sheet barely covered his hips, and unable to resist the impulse, she lightly traced a finger down the ridge of hair below his navel.

Waking at once, he pulled in a sharp breath and captured her hand. "You're going to make an old man of me."

She leaned over and gently bit his shoulder. "Can't keep up with me, hmm?"

He moved suddenly, making her gasp with surprise. His weight pinned her down as the mattress rocked beneath her. "There you go," he murmured against her mouth, "doubting my talents again."

"So how about proving me wrong?" She sucked in her breath as his hand moved over her belly.

"You're insatiable, Officer Parker." He teased her mouth with his tongue. "And thoroughly irresistible. Get ready for the demonstration of your life."

Afterward, as she drifted contentedly back to earth, he rolled onto his back, saying lazily, "We keep this up, and we won't be able to get out of bed in the morning."

"Yeah. What a way to go."

He grinned. "Too bad we can't spend the day in bed."

"Without food?"

He let out a mock groan. "You can think of food at a time like this?"

"I can think of food any time." She sat up, conscious of her empty stomach. "In fact, I'm hungry right now."

"You're kidding." He threw an arm across his forehead and squinted at her. "The kitchen's closed. It's got to be around four in the morning."

She reached for her watch lying on the table by the bed. "Four-thirty. Don't we have anything in the room?"

"How about coffee-glazed macadamia nuts?"

She grinned at him, slapping a hand lightly on his stomach. "Good thinking, Jordan. Where are they?"

"On the bar where Neil left them."

Swinging her legs out of bed, she reached for the cover, which had slid to the floor. She tucked it around her body under her arms and padded across to the bar.

The bag of nuts lay on the counter, and she picked them up. "Want some?"

He shook his head, his eyes glinting in the reflection from the lamp as he lay looking at her.

Her breath caught in her throat. Whatever happened between them after this, she thought, she would forever carry with her the memory of that look in his eyes and the magic of this night.

Popping a glazed nut in her mouth, she crossed the room to the window and stepped out onto the *lanai*. The soft breeze cooled her heated skin and slowed the rapid beat of her heart.

She crunched on the sweet, coffee-flavored nut, while the scented air bathed her in its exotic fragrance. Everything about this night seemed more intense, she thought. Even the stars seemed brighter. She dropped her gaze to the balconies across from her and saw a shadow move.

The same one she'd seen before. She could see the tip of a cigarette glowing in the dark. She jumped when Luke's arms reached around from behind her and pulled her back against him.

His mouth brushed the back of her neck. "Come back to bed," he whispered. "I'm lonely."

She turned in his arms and pulled in a shocked breath when she discovered he was still naked. "What are you trying to do?" she demanded. "Give everyone in the hotel over there a treat?"

He grinned. "There's something incredibly decadent about standing under the open sky without clothes. It brings out the animal instinct in me."

"Yeah? Well, you'd better get back inside before somebody calls out the vice squad and has you arrested for indecent exposure."

She was about to advise him that he could have an interested observer from the balcony, but his mouth covered hers as he pulled her back through the window. And when he dragged the cover from her body and pulled her close, he drove every rational thought from her mind.

By the time she remembered the insomniac again, she was too sleepy to mention it, and in the morning she had other things to worry about.

Luke awoke first, watching the faint flush of light behind the drapes turn from gray to yellow as the sun climbed in the sky. Nicole lay quietly beside him, her even breathing telling him she was still asleep. He turned his head and looked at her, a deep, ragged ache tearing through his heart.

She lay half on her side, turned away from him. The sheet was twisted around her waist, and beyond one smooth shoulder he could see the curve of her naked breast. The urge to touch her seared through him, and he turned his head away before he could give in to the intense longing. He had already done enough. He had taken advantage of her incredibly warm, generous nature. He had needed her, badly. So badly that when she had offered him what he craved, he hadn't had the strength to resist.

His body shuddered with the force of his sigh. He hadn't known it would be like that. Once he had tasted that kind of euphoria, it had been impossible to resist until he'd finally exhausted himself. And now they must both pay the price. He had to make sure it didn't happen again. He couldn't go on taking from her, knowing he wasn't capable of giving anything back.

Somehow he had to be strong. He wondered how he could make her believe that the night they'd just spent had meant nothing more to him than a casual diversion in the dangerous game they were playing.

Carefully he slid out of bed and snatched up his pants from the floor. Cursing himself for his weakness, he crept to the bathroom and closed the door behind him.

He hadn't meant it to happen. He'd been so determined it wouldn't happen. But then he hadn't expected to feel about her the way he did.

He leaned toward the mirror and scowled, running a hand over his scratchy jaw. He should never have given in to those feelings. He'd known it couldn't lead anywhere. Especially with a cop. He must have been out of his mind.

He moved over to the shower and turned on the water. He *had* been out of his mind. All those bad memories stirred up again; it was no wonder he reacted the way he did. He'd let his emotions overrule his common sense.

He was no good to her. He was no good to anyone. Once this was over, he promised himself, he'd get out. Start a new life. It was the only way he could learn to live with himself again. To get away from everyone and everything that could remind him of what happened. And that included Officer Nicole Parker. He stepped under the faucet, gasping as the cold water stung his skin.

Nicole lay listening to the rush of water, a smile playing around her mouth. She was tempted to get up and join him, but her body ached all over and, she admitted silently, though her spirit was willing, her flesh would need the best part of the day to recover.

And, she thought hopefully as she eased herself out of bed, there could be other opportunities. Although Luke's warning persisted in her mind, she chose not to listen to it. Everything was changed now. Surely he would see that? After the night they'd spent together, even a man as cautious as Luke Jordan had to admit they had something great going for them.

She hummed softly as she picked up covers and clothes from the floor. She didn't expect it to happen right away, she allowed, stuffing a macadamia nut in her mouth, but the barriers had been broken. It was only a matter of time.

The air conditioning chilled her body, and she pulled her shift over her head. Drawing back the drapes, she saw a sparkling blue sky and knew it would be another glorious day. If only she didn't have Merrill to worry about, she thought wistfully, she would be deliriously happy.

She heard a sound behind her and turned as Luke came out of the bathroom wearing only his pants. The emotion that surged through her at the sight of his incredible body robbed her of words.

In the next instant, she knew something was wrong. He didn't look at her as he crossed the room to the dresser and opened his drawer. "You'd better get dressed if you want breakfast," he said, his voice strangely polite. "They stop serving at eleven and it's almost that now."

Cold fingers seemed to be squeezing her heart. She took a step toward him and stopped, warned by the stiffness of his movements. "Luke?" she asked tentatively. "Is something wrong?"

He straightened and looked at her at last. She flinched at the indifference in his eyes. What could possibly have happened, she wondered, to wipe out all that emotion she'd seen burning in his gaze last night?

"Wrong?" He sounded defensive. "What makes you think something's wrong?"

She gestured miserably. "You seem . . . Last night . . ."

He shrugged, and she felt her heart being crushed like daisies under a careless boot. "That was last night," he said quietly. "This is today, and we still have a job to do."

She stared at him, and for a moment she saw her pain reflected in his eyes.

He spoke again, his voice ragged. "Nicole, I'm sorry. But I did warn you. No promises."

"Yes," she said, surprised at the cold calm that had settled over her. "You're right. My mistake." She picked up the wig from the dresser and thought she had never hated anything quite so much.

"I'll get dressed," she added, taking a pair of shorts and an orange top from the dresser. "But you go ahead and have breakfast without me. I'm not hungry."

"I'll wait for you here. We can have an early lunch."

"All right." She didn't have the willpower to argue. She still ached from his possession of her body. She couldn't simply wipe it all out of her mind as if it had never happened. Not as he appeared to, anyway.

She was almost glad when Opal's face once more stared at her from the mirror. It hid the devastation she knew must be visible beneath the makeup. He had warned her. *I can't make any promises.* He'd been honest with her. She'd told him it didn't matter. She had no right to blame him for the lie.

She was the one who had made the first move, the one who had expected too much. If only she'd known how much it would hurt.

Even then, she told Opal's reflection in the mirror. Even then, she wouldn't have changed anything. He had given her a night to remember, a night to measure against every future night. And he had promised her nothing more.

Sighing, she braced herself for the ordeal ahead. She would go on being Opal Turner for as long as he needed her, but Nicole Parker would from now on be locked away, far from his reach. She would not allow herself to be hurt like that again. She opened the bathroom door and prepared to meet the day.

Wandering around the Sea Life Park that morning, she went out of her way to draw attention to herself. She insisted on picking out the most prominent spots to take pictures of Luke. She made loud, raucous remarks, laughing in Opal's throaty voice while her heart ached.

She caught sight of the model pirate ship anchored in the lagoon and scrambled up the rigging, ignoring Luke's angry warning.

Perched precariously in the ropes, one arm hooked through to hold her steady, she waved gaily at him and sang out, "Okay, honey, let's take a picture for our future grandchildren."

When she finally came down, he took her arm and practically dragged her into the crowded restaurant where, he told her grimly, they were going to eat lunch.

She could tell his temper was close to boiling point. She was past caring. She wanted this job over and done with. She could no longer face the prospect of spending another night in the same bed with Luke.

In fact, she promised herself as she sipped on a tall, frosty, banana daiquiri, she would insist that he sleep on the floor for the remainder of their enforced association. From now on, the bed was off-limits.

The sandwich she'd ordered arrived, and she looked at it without much interest. Deciding she had to eat, she picked it up anyway and took a bite.

"So what would you like to do this afternoon, sweetheart?" Luke asked, his stormy eyes a startling contrast to his pleasant tone.

Nicole shrugged and stretched her mouth in Opal's wide grin. "Anything you want to do, honey. You know I'm just happy to be with you." She saw his eyebrow twitch and felt a small stab of satisfaction.

"We could go on that trip to Pearl Harbor," he suggested, giving her what passed for a smile. "That's if you can manage not to fall in the water."

She lifted her pencilled eyebrows. "What's that supposed to mean?"

This time he didn't even bother to smile. "Just that you seem a little—" he paused, while she waited with a blank expression carefully pinned to her face "—reckless today," he finished, scowling at her.

"Reckless?" Leaning forward, she muttered in her own voice, "I thought that was the idea."

The warning flashed in his eyes. "You know, sweetheart, we've been through all this once before."

She remembered his reaction after her display at the luau and smiled without humor. "I know, honey. But I'm getting bored. I need a little excitement, you know?"

She knew by the set of his mouth that he understood. She wanted Merrill to make his move, if he was ever going to. He had to know she was in Honolulu by now. In fact, she was beginning to think they were barking up the wrong tree. All they'd had to go on was a voice, and how well did someone remember a voice after two years?

"You might get more than you bargained for," Luke muttered.

Nicole didn't answer him. She was thinking about the attempt to steal her purse and feeling that something didn't fit.

If only she could remember what it was, she thought. Maybe they could have something to go on, instead of this interminable hanging around, waiting for something to happen.

"Ready to go?" Luke asked, breaking into her thoughts.

She flashed a look at his face and nodded. Reaching for her purse, she pushed her chair back and stood. Luke turned his back and had moved way ahead when a wiry body lurched into her, sending her hip crashing painfully into the table.

She uttered a low curse as empty glasses clattered and rolled. Snatching at the table to save herself from falling, she saw Luke turning back. With his muscles bunched into a half crouch, he scrabbled in his belt for his gun.

Screams shrilled in her ear, then with a vicious tug, lean fingers tore her purse from her hand. She made a grab at the figure flying past her, and her fingers caught the edge of his shirt.

He spun around, snarling at her like a wild animal while his hand chopped down on her wrist. She yelped and saw Luke leap forward, gun in hand. More screams filled the air as parents dragged children under tables, sending chairs crashing backward. One fell in Luke's path and tripped him.

The thief lunged past her, spinning her around, and she caught sight of Tony shoving past a terrified waitress. Then the lithe figure sprang onto a table and dived headfirst through the glassless window. She saw him roll to his feet, pause for a second and disappear into the crowd.

It was over so quickly she barely had time to breathe. She bit her lip as Luke's fingers closed around her arm.

"You all right?"

She nodded. Out the window, she saw Tony threading his way through the swarm of tourists outside, and knew he'd lost his quarry. "I'm sorry," she muttered.

"Let's go," Luke said sharply, and she realized people were staring at them as if they were Bonnie and Clyde. Seeing their horrified faces, she wanted to reassure them they were safe.

He gave her no chance to say anything, practically dragging her from the restaurant. They'd arrived at the park by cab, and Nicole saw with relief a couple of them waiting in the parking lot when Luke hurried her outside the gate.

"Well, it looks like you got your excitement now," he muttered as the cab carried them back to the hotel.

She sent him a sideways glance, her throat constricting when she saw the stark expression on his face. She leaned toward him and said softly, "I'm sorry he got away. But you can't blame that on yourself. You couldn't have shot at him, Luke. Not in that crowded restaurant. No one would have."

Obviously startled that she'd understood, he sent her a quick look. For a moment, she saw a flicker of warmth in his eyes. "Yeah. Thanks."

She nodded and straightened, trying not to take that spark and fan it into a fire. She was glad when they reached the hotel and she could concentrate on the next move.

"I don't think there's any doubt now," Luke said, closing the door of the suite behind him.

Nicole felt a quiver of excitement. "I guess not. Twice in two days is a bit too much coincidence."

"Merrill probably has your purse by now. After he's examined all the stuff we planted, he'll be convinced you're Opal."

His grim expression sobered her. "So now he'll make his move for sure," she said unsteadily.

Luke swore. "If only we could have grabbed the guy, we could have pinned him down. Now you've got to wait around like a sitting duck."

"That's what I'm here for," she reminded him gently. "We expected him to grab me. As it is, he's given us some warning."

"Yeah," Luke said, frowning, "that's what worries me. Merrill is much too clever to risk that without good reason."

She shrugged. "He just wanted to be sure, that's all. He probably figured it wasn't worth the risk until he was certain. After all, he knew Opal well. He may have picked up some differences we weren't aware of. As you pointed out, it takes more than looks."

She watched Luke pace around the floor, feeling his tension so acutely it reached out and enveloped her, too. "Twice," he muttered. "They got close to you twice and got away. They could do it again."

Realizing what worried him, she caught his arm, making him stop and look at her. "There's a lot of difference between taking a purse and taking a human being," she said firmly. "Especially one who'll put up the kind of fight I will. We have several counts on our side. For one, Merrill doesn't know about Tony and Neil. He doesn't even know that we know he's alive. He's figuring on us thinking this is simply coincidence."

She could see by his face he wasn't convinced. "I don't like it," he muttered. "Something is out of whack."

She thought about telling him she'd had the same feeling. Except she didn't know why. And she didn't want to worry him any more. She was afraid he'd do something stupid and try to pick up Merrill on his own.

"I'm going to ask for more protection," Luke announced, striding to the phone. "But I can't do it from here—it's too risky. I'll have to go to the station, and while I'm there, I'll put in a call to Sutton and give him a report."

He lifted the receiver. "I want you to stay put here. I'll have the guys in the hallway outside, just to make sure."

Without waiting for her answer, he stabbed the buttons. "Room service? We're out of macadamia nuts. I'd like some more right away. Yeah, the coffee-glazed ones."

"I'll meet them in the hallway and fill them in," he said, crossing the room to the door. He paused, his hand on the handle, and looked back at her. "You don't move from this room, and you don't open the door to anyone. That's an order, Parker."

She tightened her lips. "Got it."

He gave her a long look. "I'll be back as soon as I can."

She nodded. "I'll catch up on my reading."

He lifted his hand, opened the door and went through it.

Some distance away, a door opened in the house on the coast road. A wiry man with black hair walked into the darkened room and placed a purse on the polished table. At a signal from the thickset man seated in the leather chair, he turned the purse upside down and dumped the contents.

Merrill stared in silence at the miscellaneous items. After poking through the pile with a scarred finger, he pointed at a plastic card, and the man at his side reached for it. He held it under the full light from the lamp.

Merrill leaned forward and stared at the driver's license. Underneath the woman's picture, the name jumped out at him. Opal Turner. Leaning back, he nodded. The dark-haired man bowed briefly and slipped from the room.

Merrill grunted as he hooked the phone under his chin. He jabbed the numbers with a stunted thumb, then waited, his labored breath sounding harsh in the quiet room.

Finally a curt voice answered. Merrill drew a painful breath. "Where are they?"

The answer was what he'd expected. "All right. You know what to do."

He waited again for the answer. "No. We have to act immediately."

The voice asked a question.

"Whatever's necessary. Just do your part. I'll take care of the rest." He dropped the receiver onto the desk without bothering to settle it in place. It was time to move. At last the wait was over. Luke Jordan was about to face the worst moments of his life.

* * *

Nicole stared at the closed door for some time, then let out her breath with a soft curse. "Forget it, Parker," she muttered, kicking off her sandals. She couldn't waste time on what might have been; she had too much else to think about.

Things seemed to be heating up fast. She didn't know whether to be glad about that or sorry. She'd be happy to see this job finished and done with. The strain was beginning to tell on her.

It wasn't easy to strut around appearing unconcerned when she knew that someone could be out there just waiting to pounce on her like some wild animal watching its prey.

She dropped her sunglasses on the bed, then wandered over to the bedside table and picked up the magazine lying there. Flipping through the pages only confirmed what she already knew. She was much too jittery to read.

She threw the magazine down and paced slowly around the room. She wondered if Tony and Neil were stationed outside, and was tempted to check. Until she remembered Luke's orders.

Pulling a face, she mimicked his voice out loud. "You don't move from this room, and you don't open the door to anyone. That's an order, Parker."

She cursed again and angrily swept the magazine to the floor. She'd received the message loud and clear that morning. He didn't have to rub it in.

The bed rocked as she flopped down on it. The breeze caught the drapes and billowed them into the room. Nicole watched them settle back into place. Eyeing the sunlight reflected behind the thin fabric, she slid off the bed.

He hadn't said anything about the *lanai* being off-limits. After sliding the window all the way open, she stepped through. She could use some fresh air, she thought. Maybe it would help clear the memories from her mind.

She would need all her concentration now, she reminded herself. Somewhere out there, Adrian Merrill was waiting to grab her. Or his men were. She wondered uneasily how many he'd send. The same thought must have occurred to Luke, prompting him to arrange for more help.

Luke. She leaned on the railing and looked idly at the balconies across from her. How long would it take her to forget him? she wondered. How could she ever forget the way he made her feel, the incredible excitement his love-making aroused in her?

She would never look at a palm tree, or hear Hawaiian music, or smell orchids again without thinking about him. It would be hard to go on living in the same town, perhaps seeing him on the street, passing the Royal King knowing he was so near and so unreachable.

She heard the drone of a jet engine overhead and looked up, squinting in the sunlight. She'd left her sunglasses lying on the bed, she realized. She'd been wearing them so much lately, the dazzling light really hurt her eyes now.

She crossed through the window to get them. They were lying where she'd left them, and she picked them up and had turned back to the window when the phone rang. *You don't move from this room, and you don't open the door to anyone.* He hadn't said anything about not answering the phone.

She stared at it. It could be Luke with an urgent message. She agonized through two more rings before picking up the receiver. In Opal's voice she said cautiously, "Hello?"

"Is this the honeymoon suite?" a muffled voice asked in her ear.

Nicole frowned. It wasn't Luke. Was it Neil? Tony? "Yes," she answered at last.

"I have your coffee-glazed macadamia nuts," the voice said. "I'll bring them up straight away."

She relaxed her grip on the phone. Luke must have decided to send one of the men to her room. "Thank you," she said cheerfully, and replaced the receiver.

Crossing to the window again, she propped her sunglasses on her nose and stepped outside. At least she'd have someone to talk to while she was waiting for Luke to get back, she thought, her gaze longingly on the cool, blue ocean. She hoped it was Tony; he seemed the more friendly of the two.

She wondered if the friendly Hawaiian was married, and smiled, thinking about fat, chubby miniatures of Tony's smiling face. Feeling the sun burning the exposed edges of her shoulders, she turned to go back into the room.

She needed suntan lotion, she decided, then remembered it was in the stolen purse. She stopped short, her brows drawing together. Something else was in that purse. Her revolver. Would Merrill think it strange that Opal carried a gun?

Slowly Nicole turned back to the railing. She remembered again the first attempt to snatch her purse. She saw herself swinging around, her bag held in front of her. She'd known at once she was in trouble, and had made an instinctive move. A purely professional reflex. She'd gone for her gun.

How many women, Nicole asked herself thoughtfully, carried a gun in their purse? Yet her attacker had interpreted her move, almost as if he'd expected it. Twice.

She straightened, her pulse quickening as she went over it again in her mind. There was no doubt about it. The man had reacted immediately, as if he'd been waiting for the move and was prepared for it. That was what had bothered her at the time. She just hadn't thought of it until now.

She started pacing back and forth, trying to make sense of it. Okay. Merrill suspected she could be Opal, but wanted to make sure before he risked his move. Would he expect Opal to be carrying a gun? On her honeymoon?

Nicole shook her head. He might not be surprised to find one in her purse, but it was doubtful he would expect it to the point he would warn his man to watch for it. Maybe the thief was just being cautious.

She lifted her head as a sharp rap sounded on her door. She was just being jittery again, she told herself as she stepped back into the room. Removing her sunglasses, she crossed the floor and grasped the handle of the door. "Who is it?"

"Your macadamia nuts, ma'am."

Leaning forward, she peered through the peephole, then smiled when she recognized the man outside. She pulled open the door and looked into Neil's face. But when she opened her mouth to greet him, the words died in her throat.

His eyes looked at her blankly, without expression. Staring eyes...lifeless eyes. The seconds dragged by in slow motion as her gaze fell on the hairy arm clamped across Neil's chest, supporting his slack body.

Then, as if someone had flipped a switch, everything that followed spun into high speed. Even as her startled gaze flew to the dark face peering over Neil's shoulder, the police officer's body plunged forward, crashing into her and sending her stumbling backward into the room.

She stared in shock at Neil's still form at her feet, a dark stain spreading below his shoulder blades. Then the door slammed, and she jerked her head up to meet the cold gaze of a thin-faced man standing a few feet away. He held a revolver with a silencer fitted neatly on its barrel. His hand was perfectly steady as he aimed the gun straight at her heart.

Chapter 9

Luke paced up and down the white-walled office, wishing he could pin down the niggling worry that continued to plague him. A fan whirred noisily overhead, muffling the sound of traffic passing by outside.

Everything appeared to be going according to plan, he assured himself. It seemed certain now that Adams was Merrill. It also seemed certain that Merrill would now make his move, once he'd satisfied himself that Nicole was Opal Turner.

The fact that he'd gone to all the trouble of snatching her purse should indicate that he intended to kidnap her, which narrowed the risk of a bullet from a high-powered rifle, a fear that Luke had nursed right from the start.

So why did he have this feeling that Merrill was one step ahead of them? Merrill was clever but not that clever. They had covered everything, right down to the pack of antacid tablets Opal always carried for a nervous stomach.

Luke paused at the window and peered through the slats of the blinds. The parking lot outside shimmered in the heat, the blinding sunlight reflecting on the shiny roofs of the squad cars.

Maybe it was the gun in Nicole's purse that bothered him. But then it was feasible that Opal would carry a gun. Especially if she knew Merrill was still alive. Though she wasn't supposed to know he was in Hawaii. Opal Turner wouldn't have come within a thousand miles of the place if she'd known that.

Luke cursed and looked at his watch. Where was that damn officer? He'd promised to get in touch with the chief right away. The door opened behind him, and Luke swung around as a short, middle-aged man ambled into the office. His red face shone with perspiration, and his belly looked as if it had consumed more than its share of beer.

"Sorry to keep you waiting, Jordan," the policeman said with a smirk. "I guess everyone's on Hawaii time around here. I'm Captain Brad McLean."

Without returning the smile, Luke grasped the proffered hand. It felt sweaty and warm against his palm. "I did mention that it was an emergency," he said, trying to put a lid on his resentment.

"Yeah." Captain McLean strolled past Luke, leaving a faint smell of stale tobacco in his wake. He lowered himself into a swivel chair behind his desk and poked two stubby fingers into the top pocket of his shirt. "So what can I do for you?" He drew out a half-smoked cigar and stuck it in his mouth.

Hoping the captain wasn't going to light up, Luke explained rapidly what he needed. He could tell by McLean's expression that the man didn't fully comprehend the situation.

"You don't have any real proof that this guy, Adams, is the man you're after?" McLean asked, patting the paperwork strewn across his desk with the palm of his hand.

"We're as certain as we can be at this stage," Luke said, trying to control his rising irritation. "You must have the report from Oregon. I have two of your men working with me on the case."

"Ah, yes." With maddening slowness the captain shuffled some papers aside and unearthed a lighter. "Let's see, that would be Clements and Lopaka."

"Right. And two men are not going to be enough. I know Merrill and—"

"How you gonna prove this guy is the one you're after?"

Luke watched the flame of the lighter lick the stubbed-out end of the cigar. "I'll know," he said grimly.

The acrid smell of cigar smoke filled the small room. Little gray clouds belched from the corner of McLean's mouth, and he sucked on the cigar until the end glowed red. "I'm gonna need confirmation from Oregon," he drawled. "Can't release more of my men till I get it."

Luke's fingers curled in frustration. Leaning his knuckles on the desk, he said quietly, "There's a police officer out there risking her neck to bring this man in. She's in extreme danger. Your men are supposed to be guarding her. If anything happens to her, I'm going to hold you personally responsible."

McLean held up his fleshy hand. "Just hold on there, son. I'll put in a call to Sutton. Might take a minute or two. Why don't you wait outside? You look like you could use some air."

Luke felt his jaw tense. "I'll wait here," he said without unclenching his teeth.

"Suit yourself." The buttonholes on the captain's shirt strained to the limit as he leaned back in his chair and stretched his arms over his head before reaching for the phone.

"Get me the number of central in Portland," he murmured, adding, "Never mind," when Luke scribbled the number down on the back of a report sheet and shoved it at him.

Carefully McLean poked the numbers, and Luke jerked himself away from the desk and moved to the window. Shoving his hands into the pockets of his tan shorts, he made himself pull in a long, slow breath.

She'd be all right, he assured himself. She was locked in the suite, with Tony and Neil on guard in the hallway. She knew how to take care of herself, though he wished now he'd left his gun with her.

Behind him he heard McLean's slow drawl. "Yeah, Grant Sutton. When? Yeah, have him call Captain McLean, Honolulu PD."

Luke swung around as McLean dropped the receiver.

"He's not there," the captain explained unnecessarily.

"So talk to someone else," Luke demanded harshly.

The older man's round face lost its genial expression. "Now, wait a minute, son. I give the orders around here, and I'm not fully convinced—"

He broke off as Luke rounded the desk and leaned over him. "I'm going back to the hotel," Luke said softly. "I hope you have some more men out there within the hour, because if not, after this little lot breaks, I'm going to have your head."

He straightened and strode to the door. As he reached it, McLean muttered, "You wanna watch your attitude, Jordan. Making threats to a superior officer could get you in a lotta trouble."

Luke paused. "Not nearly as much as you'll be in if this thing backfires. That's a promise."

He strode out of the office, slamming the door behind him. His neck was prickling again. He couldn't wait around for Sutton to call. Something told him he needed to get back to the hotel, and fast.

He paused in front of the door marked Homicide and shoved it open. He pulled out his wallet from his back pocket and took out the badge Sutton had given him.

"I'm on assignment from the mainland," he barked at the surprised-looking woman seated at the front desk of the office. "I need a car right away." He flashed the badge, and she jerked her head at the wall behind her. Luke saw the rack of keys and strode around the desk.

"Have you got authority from Captain McLean?" the officer asked as he snatched a set of keys from the board.

Luke saw her reaching for the sign-out book. "Yeah. He's on the phone now. He'll clear me." He was out the door before she could reply. A few minutes later, he was speeding along Kalakaua Avenue, heading for the hotel.

On the twenty-third floor, Nicole stared in horror at the gun pointed at her. There had been many times during the course of her career when she'd been forced to pull her revolver. She'd never had to fire it in action, and she'd never looked down the barrel of a loaded gun before.

She knew without a shadow of a doubt that if she survived the experience, she would never be able to forget the cold, merciless fear that gripped her now.

Everything she had ever learned in training, every lecture, every practice, every mock attack she had ever dealt with hadn't fully prepared her for this moment. She'd been ready to put her life on the line for this job. She hadn't fully realized until now just how much she wanted to live.

She made herself look away from the gun and lifted her gaze to the face of the man who held it. He needed a shave, and his dark hair looked as if it hadn't been washed in a week. She'd seen that look in a man's eyes before. She wished she'd had time to say goodbye to Luke.

A low moan came from the man at her feet, and her stomach muscles contracted when she realized Neil was still alive. The knowledge pumped adrenaline into her veins, reviving her mind.

She was Opal Turner. Merrill could have killed her easily before this. He wanted her alive. As long as she kept that identity, she could stall for time. Tony had to be around somewhere; she hoped he'd miss Neil and come to investigate.

Fluttering her eyelashes, she lifted a hand that trembled all too realistically and laid it on her breast. "Please, don't shoot me. Who are you? What do you want? Money? I have money."

She wanted to distract him, but the dark eyes never wavered. He remained silent, but he watched her like a deadly snake, waiting for her to move.

She covered her mouth with her hand in mock dismay. "Oh, well, actually I don't. Have money, that is. You're not going to believe this, but my purse was stolen." She waved her hand in agitation. "They took everything."

She wished he'd say something. Anything. His silence was more frightening than anything he could tell her. "I don't know who this man is," she blurted out, pointing at Neil, "but my husband will be back soon. He has money. Lots of it."

"Shut up." He waved his gun at her, motioning her to sit on the gray velvet couch. She edged backward in her bare feet, keeping her eyes on the gun. Where was Tony?

The question had barely formed in her mind when a sharp rap came on the door, followed by two soft ones. Nicole's gaze flew to the door. Luke would have used his key. It had to be Tony. She had to warn him.

She started to get up, but a sharp jerk of the gun warned her to stay put. She thought about yelling, but the vision of a bullet plowing into her chest just about cut off her breath.

She watched the thug move backward, one hand behind him ready to open the door. He'd have to turn his back on her to deal with Tony, she thought, her mind racing ahead. For one fragile moment she would be out of his sight.

She'd have no more than a split second to act. But she had one advantage. He wouldn't be expecting a move like that from Opal. She eyed the distance across the thick carpet.

Neil lay on his stomach, and she couldn't tell if he was still breathing. She'd have to leap across him. A flying tackle behind the thug's knees should bring him down, but she had to do it before he got Tony.

She tensed her body, ready to spring. The crook reached the door and fumbled for the handle. Nicole met his cold gaze defiantly. Then, to her intense dismay, he pulled open the door and stepped forward, his gaze still pinning her down.

For one dreadful moment, she wondered if Tony was tied in with Merrill when she saw him come through the door. Then her spirits crashed when she saw the man behind him. He, too, held a gun, resting against the back of Tony's head.

Both gunmen wore surgical gloves, though neither had a mask. Nicole felt an icy chill when she realized the significance of that. They apparently didn't intend to leave any witnesses behind.

Tony's eyes flashed her a warning as he muttered, "Who are you guys? And who's she? What the hell do—"

The second man viciously smashed his gun into Tony's head, snapping it forward. "Cut the act," he snarled. "We know who you are."

"Shut up," his companion warned without removing his gaze from Nicole's face.

She hung on to her expression of shocked terror. "Well, I don't know who you are. Would somebody please tell me what's going on?"

At that moment, Neil moaned again and rolled onto his side. Nicole clenched her teeth in horror as the man watching her switched his gaze. Without changing expression, he lowered his gun and fired.

The slight pop sounded ridiculously quiet, considering its deadly purpose. Neil's body twitched once and was still.

Tony jerked around. "You bast—"

The second gun fired, and Nicole uttered a desperate cry of protest when Tony crumpled to the floor.

She was a police officer, she told herself. She was not going to fall apart. Her life depended on the next few minutes. As the man continued to watch her, the horror eased, to be replaced with a cold, deadly anger. If she was going to die, she decided with unnatural calm, she would make sure she took at least one of them with her.

She forced her memory to focus on Opal once more. "Look," she said, her voice trembling and breathless, "I don't know who you are but—"

"Lady, I'm not going to tell you again." The gun in the black-eyed man's hand jerked. "Shut up. One more word and you won't have any choice. Got it?"

She nodded, clamping her lips together. Thank heaven she hadn't taken the wig off yet, she thought, or she'd be dead, too. She would not allow herself to look at Tony or Neil. It was too late for them now. She had to concentrate on getting out of this alive.

The second man holstered his gun and crossed the room. He lifted the receiver and dialed, waiting for a moment before saying, "We're in. Yeah. Yeah. Got it."

Replacing the receiver, he showed his jagged teeth in a grin. "The boss says take her to the warehouse. I'll wait for Jordan."

Nicole's stomach plummeted. *Give it all you've got, Opal,* she told herself, and braced as the first man stepped forward. "I'm not going anywhere without my husband. I don't know who you are but—" The words ended on a gasp as the man's hand slapped her face so hard it rattled her teeth.

"Damn you, you son of a—" She cringed as the man lifted his hand again.

"The next one will be my fist, lady. Either you go out of here quiet and on your two feet, or we carry you out unconscious. Which way do you want it?"

She managed a fair imitation of Opal's pout. "Well, all right. But I'm warning you, when my husband hears about this—"

The second man's chuckle made an evil sound deep in his throat. "If your husband doesn't behave," he said unpleasantly, "the only thing he's gonna hear is the sound of my gun just before it blows his head off."

Nicole's stricken look was all too real. "You're not going to hurt him? What's he done to you? Why are you—" The bunched fist in front of her face cut off her words.

"Okay," her assailant muttered. "Now, we're going outta here real easy. You got that?"

She shot him a look of pure venom, but reluctantly stood, wincing as the man's fingers closed around her arm. She had to step over both bodies to reach the door. She hoped with all her heart that there weren't any miniatures of the friendly Hawaiians to mourn them.

It was up to Luke now. And all she had going for her was time. She had no idea how much Merrill knew. Perhaps the gangster figured Tony and Neil were private bodyguards and would have no idea the police were involved.

If Luke brought more men back with him, he had a chance, and so did she. If not... She wouldn't let herself think beyond that. Her job now was to play Opal Turner to the hilt. Either way, Merrill would have no mercy, but as Opal, she might be able to keep him talking long enough to give Luke time to find her.

She walked the length of the hallway, her arm in the grasp of her captor, and prepared to give the performance of her life.

Minutes later, Luke entered the elevator and punched the button for the twenty-third floor. His fingers drummed on the wall as he rose swiftly, silently cursing when the elevator paused at the seventh and ninth floors.

He barely noticed the other passengers. He was too preoccupied with worry, which was now escalating into fear. Why did Merrill bother to snatch Nicole's purse? It didn't make any sense.

His eyes flew to the indicator board above the door. Sixteen, seventeen... Something was wrong. If only he could figure it. Twenty, twenty-one... He'd have to call Sutton himself, he decided. He'd pick up Nicole and the guys and go to an outside phone....

The door slid open and he stepped out into the hallway. His blood ran cold. Where were the guys? They should be stationed at each end of the hallway.

His sneakers sank into the plush carpet as he trod past the first door. He tapped a signal on the second door as he passed it, the fear gnawing at his gut.

He was almost at the door of the suite when he stopped dead. Something had caught his eye, something small and dark on the carpeting, but only now had it registered. Praying it wasn't what he thought it was, he turned and retraced his steps. There it was, by the door of Neil's room.

He went down on his knees and touched the stain. His fingers came away sticky, and he didn't need to smell them to know what the stain was. He felt his heart turn over. Very slowly he got to his feet.

Moving silently, he crept to the door of the suite. He reached in his belt for his gun and drew it out, releasing the safety catch as he felt in his pocket for his key.

His stomach jerked when he saw another spot of blood at the base of the door. He put a screaming halt on his imagination. He needed his full concentration now. It could make the difference between life and death.

He knew he should be calling headquarters for backup. By the time he'd convinced that imbecile captain and got a unit out there, the trail would be cold. He hoped passionately that he wouldn't find what he expected to find. But if he did, he'd at least have a fighting chance of picking up the trail.

His hand held the gun rock steady as he eased the key into the lock with his left hand. Holding his breath, he turned the key and relaxed as the lock slid open.

He backed off three steps. He felt his body take on the peculiar calm that resulted from an adrenaline rush. His mind was crystal clear. Filling his lungs with air, he raised the revolver and placed his left hand under his right.

Raising his foot, he counted silently to three and then plunged forward, kicking the door back violently against the wall. He curled his body when he hit the floor, and rolled into the room, coming up on his knees, his arms straight out in front of him.

He fanned the gun left and then right. Nothing. The air in his lungs exploded when he realized the room was empty. Except for the two bodies lying on the floor.

The pain hit him hard, just below his ribs. He could see at a glance there was nothing he could do. He raised his head, listening. At least she wasn't lying on the floor with them. It was a faint hope, but a chance, nevertheless. It gave him an incentive to move.

He knew Merrill wouldn't leave any loose ends. He might have Opal, but he would certainly have made arrangements to take care of her "husband."

Carefully Luke edged toward the bathroom, kicking open the door as he went down in a crouch. Nothing. The closet. Still nothing. That left the *lanai*.

The window was open, exposing most of the *lanai*. Still, it left a narrow strip of wall wide enough to hide a man. Luke took a firmer grip on his gun. He no longer had any doubts about using it. One look at Tony had given him back his killer instinct. If it became necessary, he knew with a deadly certainty that he would pull the trigger.

He saw a pair of sandals lying by the bed, and for one second his mind touched the image of Nicole, then he jerked it back. He couldn't worry about her now. Not until he'd taken care of the immediate danger. He dropped to a crouch and crawled like a crab toward the window.

In the warehouse district near the waterfront, Nicole complained loudly in Opal's shrill voice as her guardian shoved her violently from the car. Her hands had been tied behind her back, and the rope bit into her wrists as she stumbled across the paved yard in the relentless grip of the gunman. The hot concrete seared the soles of her bare feet, and she limped in pain by the time she reached the entrance to a sizable warehouse.

Inside the empty building, the gloom contrasted sharply with the glare of sunlight outside. Even so, the heat was suffocating, the humidity intensifying the caustic smell of oil and gasoline fumes. Nicole fought down a sudden rise of nausea.

She could see several men in the far end of the warehouse loading cartons onto a truck. The rest of the building appeared to be empty, except for a pile of torn-up boxes and a few crushed beer cans lying by the entrance.

The man behind her gave her another shove, sending her stumbling toward the rear of the warehouse, where a narrow flight of wooden steps led up to a platform about twenty feet above the ground. She halted at the foot of the steps and looked up.

A light shone in the windows of the small office erected on the platform, and her stomach churned. This was the final test. All the hours of practice, the grueling repetitions, the constant walking, talking, gesturing—all were culminating in this one, final performance.

She felt a sharp prod in her back and spit out an oath at the man behind her. Then, holding her head up high, she mounted the steps, one by one. The thing they had most feared had happened. She was about to come face-to-face with Adrian Merrill.

Luke had done his best to prepare her in case the unexpected happened. She knew that now. She would give a performance worthy of him. She would be Opal Turner until the end. But she was determined on one thing.

If she lost, if Luke couldn't find her in time, she would not die as Opal. Even if she managed to fool Merrill, she would let him know who and what she was. If it was the last thing she did, she would rob Adrian Merrill of his final revenge.

She reached the top of the steps and waited, her heart pounding against her ribs, while the man at her side rapped on the door.

A voice muttered a harsh, "Bring her in."

The door opened, and a blow between her shoulder blades propelled her forward. She pulled up short in front of an empty desk. A man sat in a swivel chair, his back toward her. His bald head reflected the light from the single bulb hanging overhead.

Nicole's stomach quivered when she saw his angry red scalp. The folds at the back of his neck were covered with thick, scaly skin. She heard a silent echo of Neil's soft voice. *He told his lawyer he would see that face in his nightmares for the rest of his life.* As the chair began to turn, she braced herself.

Even so, she couldn't contain the gasp that escaped from her frozen lips as the man seated across the desk revealed himself. His features were unrecognizable under the shiny skin that stretched tightly across the left side of his face.

From beneath hairless brows, pale blue eyes glittered at her, almost hidden by eyelids that drooped halfway over them. A skilled plastic surgeon had obviously done his best, but the slits of eyes and ugly gash of a mouth intensified the evil that emanated from the shattered hulk of a once-powerful man.

Seconds ticked by while Nicole waited, scarcely breathing beneath that terrible scrutiny. The impatient growl of a low-flying helicopter vibrated through the roof of the warehouse, and the man behind her closed the door of the windowless office. It sounded to Nicole like the gates of doom. Certain now that Adrian Merrill could see right through her disguise, she waited for him to denounce her.

Air rattled in his chest as Adrian Merrill prepared to speak. His voice sounded almost normal when he said quietly, "It's nice to see you again, Opal."

In the honeymoon suite, Luke stood gazing in despair at the empty *lanai*. He couldn't believe Merrill had let him off the hook. Now he was facing a blank wall, with nothing to go on. And Merrill had Nicole.

Luke stepped back into the room and sank onto the bed, his head in his hands. No, he thought, not this time. Not Nicole. Somehow he had to find her. There was no way he could deal with this one. If he failed her, too, his life was over.

At that moment the phone rang, shattering the grin silence. He sprang for it, snatching up the receiver. Although he was praying to hear it, the sound of Merrill's voice sent chills down his spine.

"Hello, Luke. It's been a long time."

"Where is she?" Luke demanded. "If you've—"

"Relax, Luke. She's fine. In fact, you can talk to her."

Luke gripped the receiver, baring his knuckles as Nicole's voice came on the line. "Luke, honey? Isn't this a surprise? Fancy Adrian being alive after all. You can imagine the shock I got when I saw him. Of course, it was his voice I recognized, I—"

Her voice cut off abruptly and Luke's fingers clenched. She'd been trying to tell him she'd fooled Merrill. It was unbelievable at close quarters. She must have done a hell of a job.

His nerves tensed as Merrill spoke again. "Well, Luke, now that you know your wife is alive, perhaps you'll agree to be cooperative."

"As cooperative as your thugs were with these two men in my room?" Luke asked bitterly. "Let her go, Merrill. You can't blame her for betraying you. I forced her into it. She had no choice."

He heard a harsh sound and realized Merrill was struggling to pull air into his lungs. "I know that," Merrill said with an obvious effort. "I understand. That's why I'm willing to let her go. On one condition."

Luke's eyes narrowed. As much as he wanted to believe that, he knew Merrill too well to trust him now. "What condition?" he asked warily.

"That you come here to get her. I want you to look at me, Luke. I want you to see with your own eyes what you've done to me. I want you to spend the rest of your life living with the memory of my face, knowing that you were the cause of what I've become."

Luke shook his head. "And you'd be satisfied with that," he said dryly.

"I don't have that much longer to live, Luke. Things take on a different perspective when you're facing death. I want you to regret what you did. Yes, I'd be satisfied with that."

"And you'd let us both leave?" He didn't believe it for a moment, but he had to know where she was.

"You have my word." The horrible gasping sound of Merrill's breathing vibrated down the line.

"All right. Where are you?" Luke waited for several long anxious seconds before Merrill was able to speak. Then, as the man on the line recited the address, Luke scribbled it down. Thrusting it in his pocket, he snapped, "I'm on my way."

"Not so fast. I must warn you that if you attempt to bring anyone else with you or contact the police, she will die. Painfully."

Luke winced.

"And," Merrill added, "just in case you're tempted to test me, I should tell you that you'll be under constant surveillance."

Luke's eyes flew to the mirror. The front door still stood open, and as he watched, a shadow moved in the doorway. So that's where he was, Luke thought, furious with himself. He must have been at the end of the hallway, behind the exit door to the stairs.

"Don't do anything foolish, Luke," Merrill warned. "I'm sure you wouldn't want your wife to suffer as I have suffered."

Sitting tied to a chair in the warehouse, Nicole shivered. There'd been a wealth of hostility in that statement. She watched Merrill drop the receiver from his scarred chin to the table, and the thug who had brought her there replaced it for him.

"That should ensure he'll come quietly," Merrill told his man. "Go warn the others he's on his way. Everything's loaded. As soon as we take care of this little matter, we can be off."

Nicole was almost sorry to see the gorilla go. Much as she detested him, she hated even more being left alone with the grotesque presence of Adrian Merrill.

She didn't believe for one moment he was going to let them go. She could only hope that Luke would find a way to alert HPD. At least she was safe for the time being. Merrill obviously wanted the pleasure of killing them both together, or she'd be dead by now.

Again Nicole shivered, in spite of the oppressive heat. He probably intended to let one of them watch the other die. She tried not to make guesses at which one.

She jerked upright when Merrill said, "Now that everything's settled, you can dispense with the disguise."

Nicole blinked. "Disguise?"

Merrill conjured up a grating sound in his chest that resembled a laugh. "Oh, you were very good, my dear. You might even have fooled me, except for one small fact you and Jordan overlooked."

Nicole felt sick. "Adrian, I don't know—" She shrank back as the disfigured man pushed himself to his feet. Moving slowly and with considerable effort, he lumbered around the desk and stretched out a crippled hand.

With a sudden, sharp movement he took hold of the wig and ripped it from her head. "Officer Nicole Parker, I believe," he murmured.

She wasn't really surprised he'd seen through her disguise. But she was shocked to discover he knew her name. "How did...?"

The ugly laugh sounded again as Merrill shuffled back to his chair and lowered himself down. "Modern technology, my dear. I had a photo taken of you by one of my employees. All it took then was a fax machine and a very useful contact with the Portland Police Bureau in Oregon."

She slumped back in her chair. "How long have you known?"

"That you weren't Opal?" Merrill paused to gather breath. "Since the moment you arrived. No, before then. Since the moment you were booked into your hotel."

He leaned forward, the hideous gash that had once been a mouth stretched into the form of a grin. "You see, my dear, Opal Turner died some time ago. She made the mistake of believing she could hide in South America. I have many friends there. In fact, that's where I was...repaired."

He sat back in his chair, his light blue eyes squinting through his hooded lids making him look like some repulsive lizard. "The same people who put me together used their considerable imagination to take Opal apart." Carefully he shook his head. "It wasn't a pleasant death."

She would never have believed that in that hellish heat she could be so cold. She forced her lips to move. "Then why...?"

Merrill took several seconds to draw breath. "Why did I go along with your clever masquerade? I wanted to be sure of getting Jordan in my hands without fear of interruption."

He rubbed the back of one hand with his stubby fingers. "I wasn't sure at first. I thought he might have married someone who reminded him of Opal, in which case I would have simply had you killed and dumped in the ocean, then picked up your grieving husband. No one would have been the wiser.

"Once I saw Opal's name on the driver's license, I knew it was a setup and that the police had to be involved. Then I had to be a little more clever. I had to lure Jordan into my hands without him contacting the police."

Nicole swallowed. So that was why he had the purse stolen. She wondered how long it would take Luke to get there. Now that Merrill had achieved his purpose, he had no reason to keep her alive any longer.

As if reading her mind, Merrill opened a drawer in his desk. When he raised his hand, he held a small but deadly pistol. "I might have a little trouble pulling the trigger, but I can assure you my aim is as good as ever."

Nicole's stomach heaved as he aimed the barrel at her head. "You should be sending up a prayer of thanks that I don't have time to waste on you," Merrill added. "At least your death will be quick."

"Luke has already contacted the police," Nicole said, desperately playing for time. Surely Luke would be here soon, and she couldn't imagine he'd come alone.

"Yes, that could have been awkward. But he didn't know I had you then, and I was sure he wouldn't be able to make a move until he had the proof he needed. Once he realized you were gone, he still didn't know where you were. And he hasn't had a chance to talk to the police since I told him."

"How can you be sure he didn't call them after you talked to him?"

"Because, my dear, he won't risk your death." Merrill's eyes gleamed behind the scaly lids. "Oh, if you'd been just another undercover cop, he might have risked it. But you're not, are you?"

Nicole felt her face burn as she stared at him.

"No," Merrill answered for her. "You're much more than that. One of my men saw an interesting sight on the balcony of your suite, a little scene that convinced me Jordan would come hotfoot to your rescue."

Nicole closed her eyes. She saw again the glow of a cigarette in the dark and a naked Luke reaching for her from the French windows.

"No, my dear Officer Parker, Luke will be here in due time. Oh, it might take him a while, since I made sure he would be...delayed long enough to give me time to finish up here. Your dead body will be the first thing he sees when he arrives. It will make a fitting prelude for the ceremony to come." His thumb moved to the safety catch.

Nicole strained at the ropes holding her down and closed her eyes. She'd always known this was a risk that went with the job. She wished now she'd given it more thought. Her body jerked as the shot came, then her eyes flew open.

The shot hadn't come from the office but from outside. There were shouts, more shots, and she threw a glance at Merrill, who seemed frozen in his chair, his eyes concentrated on the door. It crashed open, and Merrill's shot flew harmlessly over the head of the figure in the doorway.

Nicole's heart leaped at the sight of Luke, his hair disheveled, his gray eyes wild with fury. Then she saw one of Merrill's men standing behind him, the barrel of his gun jammed against the back of Luke's head.

A sickening sense of déjà vu jolted her as the vivid memory of Tony's body slumping to the carpet sprang into her mind. Shutting the image out, she managed a wobbly smile as Luke looked at her.

Blood trickled down from a deep cut on his forehead, but otherwise he looked alert as he sent his steadying gaze across the room. "You all right?"

She nodded, but Merrill cut in before she could speak. "What happened?"

"He got Jake," the other man replied. "He's probably tipped off the cops."

Nicole watched, fascinated, as Merrill's face turned purple.

"Damn you, Jordan," the gangster snarled. "I might have known you'd cheat me out of my revenge."

"You want me to finish him?" the thug asked, releasing the catch on his automatic.

Nicole stopped breathing.

"No," Merrill howled. "Wait a minute."

Luke jerked his body in an attempt to get free and received a thud on the back of his head that rolled his eyes upward. Nicole cried out and Merrill swore.

The gangster hauled himself to his feet and shuffled around the desk. "I don't have time," he wheezed painfully. "They'll be here at any moment. Damn you, I don't have time." He looked up at the man holding a swaying Luke. "Tie him to my chair."

Nicole watched in helpless despair as the man took off his belt. Shoving Luke toward the swivel chair, he strapped his arms behind him and fastened them to the metal support at the back.

Merrill hobbled to the door and turned. "I'd planned a long, lingering death for you, Jordan. You cheated me of that, but you won't escape. You'll still have time to contemplate your death. The steps outside are wooden. They should burn fairly quickly. By the time you get free, if you get free, you'll have nowhere to go.''

He turned and pointed to Nicole. ''Take a good look at her face, Jordan. Pretty soon it's going to look worse than mine. Think about that as you wait to burn.''

He twisted his body and stumbled out the door. ''Lock it,'' he ordered, and disappeared from view.

Grinning, the other man lifted his hand in farewell, then closed the door, turning the key in the dead-bolt lock from the outside.

Chapter 10

"Luke!" Nicole struggled desperately against the rope that imprisoned her wrists. She saw him shake his head, then his eyes cleared.

"I'm okay," he muttered thickly.

"What happened?" Your head..."

"I got in the way of a ricocheting bullet. It's just a graze." He shook his head again. "I guess I'm out of practice."

"Did you call HPD?" Nicole asked urgently.

His breath hissed out. "Spoken like a true cop. Take care of the basics first. Yes, I called them. They should be here anytime."

"Why didn't you wait for them?"

"I couldn't. I didn't know what I'd find. I thought..."

She knew what he'd thought. She could see it in his face. She could see something else there, something she didn't dare let herself believe in. And now it could be too late. For the second time that day, she realized just how badly she wanted to live.

"I'm sorry," she said unsteadily. "I guess I blew it."

"You didn't blow it at all," Luke said, his voice harsh. "I did. I underestimated the enemy, and that's a bad mistake. But we don't have time to talk now—we have to get out of here."

Nicole felt a flicker of hope. "You got any ideas?"

"Yeah." He jerked his body back and forth, rocking the chair, then started to roll it on its wheels around the desk. "I'm going to turn my back to you," he said, grunting with the effort to keep the chair moving. "There should be a screw to adjust the back of the seat. These swivel chairs usually have them."

It took him a while to maneuver the chair's back toward her, but finally she could see the large screw just above his bound hands.

"It's there." With a flash of excitement she realized what he had in mind. "Wait a minute while I get twisted around," she said, tilting her chair on its back legs. "Then back up."

More precious seconds ticked by while Luke angled his chair toward her. She couldn't see that far over her shoulder and had to feel with her hands for the screw. Rope bit into her wrists as she strained to reach it.

Finally her fingers touched the serrated edge. "Got it," she announced in triumph. "Now hold steady."

The smell of raw fiber wafted over her shoulder as the rope chafed at her wrists. Ignoring the pain, she worked the screw loose, turning it a fraction at a time until it suddenly fell to the floor with a clatter.

"All right." Luke shoved the chair's back panel off the bar and lifted his hands free. He sprang to his feet, twisting at the loosened leather belt to free himself. Nicole could have sobbed with relief when he untied her.

With a muttered oath he dragged her into his arms and buried his face in her hair. "Oh, God," he whispered. "I thought—"

"Luke." Nicole's stomach lurched as she stared over his shoulder. From the base of the door, a deadly wreath of oily black smoke curled upward into the room.

Even as he turned, she could hear the crackle of flames, and the foul odor of burning rubber filled the room.

Luke swore. "He must have piled garbage on the steps," he muttered. "We don't have much time."

Nicole shook her head. "We're never going to break through that lock."

"We don't have to." Luke took hold of the metal frame of the chair back. "There's more than one way to open a door."

She watched in silent respect as he attacked the hinges of the door. The bolts inched up slowly, and her eyes began to stream as smoke coiled up to the low ceiling.

Luke grunted in satisfaction as the last bolt fell to the floor. With a hefty kick he sent the wooden panel swinging from the lock, giving them enough room to climb through.

Smoke poured into the room, stinging Nicole's lungs. Coughing violently, she felt Luke's hand grasp hers and pull her out onto the landing.

It was easier to breathe out there, but one look at the flames leaping up the staircase told her their escape had been cut off. She could feel the heat from the greedy fire, and the odor of smoldering wood made her eyes water again.

Luke peered over the landing at the ground below. "It's a long drop, but it's our only chance."

Nicole shuddered. "I can't do it. That's got to be at least twenty feet onto hard concrete."

Luke stared at her through the smoke, his eyes hard as steel. "I'm not going to let you burn to death."

"Luke, I can't do it. I'm sorry, I just can't." She could hear her voice rising in panic, but couldn't seem to control it. "Even if I lived through the jump, I could spend the rest of my life flat on my back. I couldn't deal with that." She looked up at him in desperation. "Could you?"

Her words were almost drowned out by the sudden roar that accompanied a burst of freshly fueled flames. The platform beneath her bare feet vibrated, hotter than the sunbaked concrete outside.

His expression grew desperate as he stared at her. Then he twisted around. Raising his voice above the roar of the flames, he said, "Across there. Another office. If we can beat the flames to it, we can make it down the steps to the entrance.

Nicole squinted through the smoke. "How do you propose to get there?" She was almost shouting now.

Luke pointed above his head. "The beam. It runs across the roof. We'll crawl across it."

Nicole looked up. Her stomach felt as if a hundred worms had taken up residence. The beam was no more than eight inches wide.

"Come on," Luke yelled, "we haven't got time to think about it."

He climbed up onto the rail of the landing and reached for the edge of the office roof. Hauling himself up onto it, he looked down at Nicole. "Get up here, Parker, and *fast*. That's an order."

Coughing in the smoke-filled air, Nicole climbed up on the railing.

"Don't look down," Luke yelled.

She jerked up her head and reached for his outstretched hands. With one mighty heave he pulled her onto the roof beside him. Putting his mouth close to her ear, he said firmly, "There's plenty of space above us. The smoke will fill in there first. Try to keep your head as low as possible, and don't breathe any more deeply than you have to."

He waited until she nodded, then added, "It'll take some time for the flames to reach the beam, so don't rush it. And don't look down."

Giving her a quick hug, he raised his hands and swung himself up onto the beam. Supporting himself with one hand on a cross beam, he reached down for her with the other.

She could do this, she told herself, fighting the crawling sensations that now invaded her entire body. She could feel cold sweat on her back and knew it wasn't from the heat of the flames.

"Come on, Nicole," Luke yelled. "Now!"

Closing her eyes briefly in silent prayer, she reached for his hands. Her stomach seemed to drop to her feet as Luke hauled her up onto the beam ahead of him.

Again he put his mouth close to her ear, and this time she clung to him, her fingers clenched in his shirt. "On your hands and knees," he commanded. "Move one hand and knee at a time. If you feel dizzy, wait a minute before going on. Whatever you do, don't look down."

Her teeth were chattering. She couldn't seem to stop them. Her eyes were clamped shut so tightly they hurt. She could see a screen in front of her. The simulator of an aircraft. The ground was rushing up toward her.... "I can't," she burst out, her voice breaking in sheer terror. "I can't do it."

"You must do it."

She could hear the desperation in Luke's voice above the roar of the flames. Something crashed below her, and she felt sparks stinging her bare arms.

"The steps are gone," Luke yelled. "Get out of there, Parker. Now!"

She shook her head. "I...can't. I'll just get dizzy and fall anyway. I'll never make it. You go."

"Damn you, Nicole, you're going."

She felt him tear her fingers from his shirt and shove past her. Now he was turning her, dragging her down to her knees. Her fragile support gone, she frantically reached for him and whimpered when she felt the grasp of his hand.

"Open your eyes," he yelled, "or you'll send me down with you."

She snapped open her eyes and fought the wave of blackness that swept over her. Luke faced her, balanced on his knees with one hand on the beam.

"I'm going to let you go," he said, his voice raised against the crackling fire.

Nicole shook her head violently, her fingers clamping around his hand.

"I'm going to crawl backward," Luke insisted, "and you're coming with me. We'll take it easy, okay?"

She was frozen in place, unable to move a muscle. Luke's face swam in front of her, and she closed her eyes. Her heart flipped rapidly as she swayed, then righted herself.

"Nicole!" His shout opened her eyes again. She saw his face clearly, his tense jaw, his eyes pleading with her.

"Trust me," he urged, his voice ragged and barely discernible. "For God's sake, Nicole. You have to trust me."

She stared into those desperate gray eyes. In some small terrified corner of her mind she remembered his voice from what seemed like eons ago. *They all trusted me, and I let them down.*

He would blame himself, she thought, tortured by the look on his face. She couldn't let him fail again. She had to do this.

"Please, Nicole. Let go of my hand."

She loosened her grip, then made a grab for the edge of the beam.

"All right." His grin barely made it, but it was enough. "Now, relax your muscles and shift one knee forward."

Slowly she moved her knee and felt her body sway.

"Keep going," Luke called out sharply. "Move with me. Keep your eyes on my face and feel your way along."

She heard him coaxing, encouraging, demanding, but had no idea of the words he spoke. She concentrated on his face and his voice, always inching toward him, intent on keeping up with him as he edged slowly back.

The roar of the flames seemed quieter now, the smoke less dense. Although aware of the rough splinters of the beam digging into her palms and her knees, she felt no pain. She felt nothing at all, only an intense, fierce determination to give Luke the only thing she had to give—her complete and total trust.

She was aware of a light somewhere below her drawing closer. A part of her mind heard sirens screaming, tires screeching, doors slamming. Shouts rang out below her, while the light drew ever closer.

All of it belonged in another world. There was only Luke, his voice and eyes drawing her, and the solid beam beneath her. Then he was reaching for her, lowering her until her bare feet touched the roof of the office below her.

She crumpled to her knees, shaking uncontrollably, and felt the thud of his feet beside her. Then she was in his arms, and the world once more became a reality of noise, smoke and confusion.

She looked up and touched his face, and her heart melted when she saw tears spilling from his eyes, creating shiny rivulets in his smoke-stained cheeks.

''Well done, Parker,'' he muttered, and hugged her in a fierce embrace that took the rest of the breath from her body.

Half-dazed with shock and exhaustion, she was only vaguely aware when he helped her off the roof and onto the landing. Men in helmets swarmed into the building dragging hoses with them.

A man climbed the steps to meet them. Strong hands took her and carried her into the clean, humid air. She felt the cool plastic frame of an oxygen mask as someone gently placed it over her eyes and nose. She caught a glimpse of a sultry blue sky. Then it was all fading…fading…and at last she could let go.

Luke sat in the ambulance, holding Nicole's limp hand in both of his. The medics had assured him she would be fine, but he would feel a lot better, he thought, when he saw her open her eyes.

They'd given her a sedative to ease the aftereffects of the trauma. They'd offered the same to him, but he'd refused. He wanted to stay awake until he knew she would be all right.

His lungs hurt, and his eyes wouldn't stop watering. He'd been treated for smoke inhalation at the scene, but he'd been better at holding his breath than Nicole.

She had, it appeared, taken in more smoke than he had. That and the effects of all she'd been through had taken their toll. His whole body ached with tenderness when he saw her face. She looked vulnerable and almost frail. Not at all like the tough, independent cop she worked so hard to portray.

He remembered something she'd said to him when they were still in his suite in Portland. *If two people love each other enough, they'll find a way to deal with anything. Including the pressures of a job, whatever they are.* He hadn't believed it then. Maybe he hadn't wanted to believe it then.

Carefully he rested her hand on her stomach and leaned back against the wall. He wanted to believe it now. He knew what it had cost her to put that much trust in him. He knew her feelings for him ran deep.

Was it possible, he wondered, that she could love him enough? Was he capable of that kind of love himself? Enough to deal with the kind of pressures they would face? He was still asking himself those questions when the ambulance pulled up in front of the hospital.

They made him wait in the lounge while they checked her over. He refused a similar examination. He was fine, he told them. Nothing a couple of bourbons wouldn't fix.

He tried to read a magazine, but after staring at a page for a whole minute without reading a line, he threw it down. He'd put it off long enough, he decided. He had to know if

Merrill was in custody. It should be over one way or another by now.

Pushing himself off the cool, plastic couch, he looked around for a phone. He saw a public booth at the end of the hallway and started toward it. He was halfway down the corridor when a familiar voice called out his name.

"Hey, Jordan. Where are you going?"

He spun around, shocked at the sight of the powerful physique and pale blue eyes of a grinning Grant Sutton. Disbelief shortened his tone. "Where in hell did you come from?"

The man with him wore a concerned expression on his red face. "Shoot, son, you look a mess." McLean rolled his unlit cigar from one side of his mouth to the other.

Luke barely acknowledged the police captain, merely flicking a glance over him.

"We did it Luke. We got him." Sutton stepped forward and grasped Luke's hand in his strong fingers.

"All right," Luke said unsteadily. "What happened?"

After insisting that Luke join them for coffee in the cafeteria, Sutton rapidly explained. Luke's call to the Honolulu precinct had generated immediate results. His guess that Merrill would try to leave by sea was right on target. While one squad raided the house on the seashore, another raced to the docks. The coast guard had been alerted and had rammed Merrill's boat as it tried to leave the lagoon.

"Adrian Merrill and his merry band of cutthroats are in custody," Sutton said, raising his foam cup in a toast. "And let's hope they're put away for a long time."

"But when did you get here?" Luke asked, still trying to take everything in.

"About an hour ago. I called your hotel but got no answer."

"Oh, God," Luke muttered, remembering the dead men. "Have you been out there?"

"I have," McLean said, his eyes reflecting his pain. "That's a lousy deal."

"Yeah." Luke leaned forward. "I'm sorry, Captain. They were good men."

McLean nodded.

"What about the one I got?" Luke asked urgently. "I left him tied up in the bathroom."

"We found him. He'd lost a lot of blood, but he'll recover in time to stand trial."

"Good." Luke felt a surge of satisfaction. "He's lucky I only winged him."

"Yeah." McLean coughed. "Good shot, son."

"Yeah. Thanks." Luke turned to Sutton in an attempt to change the subject. "So why didn't you let me know you were coming?"

"Well, I could've told you your boss was on the way," McLean said, taking the dead cigar from his mouth. "They told me when I called Portland. You were standing right there."

"Why didn't you tell me?" Luke demanded.

"Shoot, son, you didn't give me a chance. You went out of my office like a spitting tiger—" he jabbed the cigar in the air "—and you took one of my cars without authorization. That could cost you."

"I'll accept responsibility for Jordan's actions." Sutton sent Luke a look that warned him to cool it. "I didn't decide to come until yesterday," he added. "I got a report on the attempt to snatch Nicole's purse and figured things were heating up. I couldn't just sit there and wait. I wanted to be in on the kill."

Luke looked up as a tall, thin man in a white coat strode purposefully toward him.

"Mr. Jordan? Nicole Parker is awake. She'd like to see you."

Luke shoved back his chair. "She'll probably want to see you, too," he told Sutton. "Just give me a minute."

He waited for Sutton's nod, then followed the doctor's brisk stride down a sparkling clean hallway that bore the unmistakable chemical odor of a hospital.

His heart turned over when he saw her lying on the bed. Her head turned to greet him, and her eyes looked huge in her drawn face. Someone had cleaned all traces of makeup from her lightly tanned skin. She had never looked more beautiful.

After cautioning him not to stay long, the doctor left them alone, and Luke drew a chair up to the bedside and sat down.

She gave him her wide smile, and the ache inside him intensified. "Hi," he said softly. "How you doing?"

"Fine." Her voice sounded gruff, and she cleared her throat. "A little sore in a few places, but they tell me I can leave in the morning. They just want me to stay overnight."

He nodded, feeling a stab of disappointment. "That's probably for the best."

"I don't want to stay here tonight."

He knew what she was asking him. He wanted her so much. Too much. He reached for her hand, and it took all his willpower to say, "The doctor knows best. It's only one night."

He saw the regret flash in her eyes before she repressed it. "Did they get Merrill?" She watched him anxiously, relaxing with a sigh when he nodded. "Then it was all worth it, wasn't it?"

"Yeah," he said evenly. "It was all worth it." He made an effort to lighten his voice. "By the way, Sutton's here. He flew in this afternoon. He'll be in to see you in a little while."

"He is? I bet he's happy."

"Delirious."

"Luke?" Her eyes searched his face, as if looking for something that wasn't there. "I owe you my life."

He saw her lower lip trembling, and longed to take her in his arms. "Nah, you did it all by yourself. I just helped you along a little."

Her smile didn't quite make it. "It's not like you to be modest, Jordan. Not trying to squirm out of being a hero, are you?"

"If I'm a hero," he said unsteadily, "it's because you made me one. If you hadn't put your trust in me, I couldn't have done a damn thing to help you."

"I know." Her fingers tightened on his hand. "I knew you could get me across that beam. I wanted you to know it, too."

He was terribly afraid he was going to make a fool of himself and cry. He didn't know whether to be glad or sorry when a soft tap sounded on the door.

He heard footsteps behind him, then Sutton's deep voice asked, "So, how's my favorite detective?"

Luke watched Nicole's face as she looked up at her boss. He could tell nothing from her expression.

"Does that mean my promotion came through?"

Sutton nodded. "Good job, Detective Parker. I'm proud of you."

"Make that two of us," Luke said, stroking his thumb across the back of her hand.

"Thanks." Her eyes met his briefly, then switched back to Sutton. "What will happen to Merrill now?"

"I'll be taking him back to the mainland for indictment. We've got enough on him to keep him out of trouble for a while."

"He's a sick man," she said slowly. "He might not last long."

Sutton shrugged. "I'm not wasting any sympathy on him."

Nicole remembered something then, something she hadn't yet told Luke. Turning her head on the pillow, she said softly, "Merrill knew I wasn't Opal right from the start."

"I don't know how he figured it." He lightly squeezed her fingers. "Unless someone saw you on the balcony without your wig."

She shook her head. "He knew before that. Luke, Opal's dead. Merrill had her killed."

She saw his face whiten with shock, then he swore viciously.

Helplessly she sought for the right words to say. All along he'd denied any feelings for Opal, yet the look in his eyes mirrored stark despair. "I'm sorry," she said miserably.

"*You're* sorry!" He let go of her hand and stood, shoving his hands in his pockets. Turning to the other man, he said harshly, "Damn you, Sutton. Did you know this?"

"Luke—"

"The truth, Sutton. *Did you know Opal Turner was dead?*"

Nicole switched her gaze to Sutton and saw the answer in the hard glitter of his eyes. Frozen in shock, she held her breath as Luke muttered a vicious oath and pulled his bunched fists from his pockets.

"I ought to..." He made an obvious effort to control his temper. "So this whole thing was a setup. The whole damn deal. You put Nicole's life on the line, knowing Merrill could take her down anytime."

"It was a calculated risk." Sutton turned his back on them and moved to the window. "I was desperate. Merrill was sitting here, laughing up his sleeve at us, knowing we couldn't touch him. We had nothing on him. No proof that he was Adrian Merrill. If I'd let you come on your own, you couldn't have done anything legally. And if you'd been stupid enough to try anything else, he'd have picked you off like a speck of dust on his suit."

He turned back, his face grim. "I figured that if he saw Opal's double, he'd have to investigate. It would make him nervous enough that he'd at least have her checked out to find out what was going on. That's all we needed. Morris

Adams wouldn't have known who Opal Turner was. Adrian Merrill would."

"It didn't occur to you that he could have had us both killed?" Luke practically snarled the words.

Nicole shivered as Sutton shook his head. "I didn't think he'd take a risk and blow everything. After all, he knew Nicole wasn't Opal. He's a sick man. I figured once he'd realized the law was on to him, he'd make a run for it. And we'd be waiting."

Luke nodded, a dangerous light in his gray eyes. "You knew I wouldn't have gone along with all this if I'd known Opal was dead."

Again Sutton shrugged.

"And what about Nicole?" Luke demanded, his voice growing harsher. "Didn't she have a right to know?"

Nicole decided it was time she had a say in the argument, but Sutton beat her to it.

"I couldn't take the chance of her letting it slip. Hell, Luke, it's her job. It goes with the territory. This is the kind of business we're in. Sometimes you have to make some pretty desperate moves to get the job done."

"Yeah," Luke said bitterly. "I guess you do."

Nicole could keep silent no longer. "Look, you two, let's forget it, all right? We both survived, didn't we?" She felt a swift stab of pain as she remembered the scene she'd left in the hotel. "Which is more than can be said for Tony and Neil."

"Yeah," Sutton murmured. "That was unfortunate."

"Have they... notified the families?" Nicole asked after an anxious look at Luke.

Sutton nodded. "I guess so. Clements wasn't married, but his mother has been told. Lopaka had a wife and two kids—"

Nicole uttered a cry of dismay, while Luke swore again and turned away in disgust.

"If it's any consolation, Luke," Sutton said gently, "it was quite an empire. They were into all kinds of deals, from smuggling arms and drugs to illegal aliens. I wouldn't have risked people's lives simply for revenge. I hope you know that."

The two men stared at each across the bed, and as Nicole glanced from one to the other, she saw the look of understanding that passed between them.

"Yeah," Luke said quietly. "I know that."

Sutton stared at him for a moment longer, then nodded, apparently satisfied. "Well," he said, his voice several shades lighter, "it's going to take a while for them to clean up the suite, so I've booked a couple of rooms for you both on the sixteenth floor. You won't be flying back to the mainland until the day after tomorrow, so that gives you both a day's R and R in paradise."

Nicole smiled. "That sounds wonderful."

"I also brought your wallet with me from Portland. I figured you might need it. They're holding it at the front desk." Sutton leaned over and patted her shoulder. "Take care, Nicole. And good work. I'll arrange for a squad car to take you back to the hotel in the morning, and I'll see you when you get back to Portland."

He walked around the bed and held out his hand to Luke.

"Thanks, Luke. You did one hell of a job."

Nicole swallowed hard as the two men clasped hands.

"I'll wait for you outside," Sutton said as he opened the door.

Then he was gone, leaving her alone with the man who had come to mean the whole world to her. She watched him sit down in the chair again, and her heart ached for him. His wound had been cleaned and covered with tape, but his face still bore streaks of soot and his hair tumbled untidily onto his forehead. He looked tired, but when he looked at her, she saw an expression in his gray eyes that quickened her pulse.

"You look like you could use a rest," she said, her voice still sounding hoarse.

"Yeah. Neither of us got much sleep last night, remember?"

Remember? How could she ever forget? "It seems a long time ago now," she said cautiously.

He nodded. "I'm going to miss that big old water bed."

"So am I." She gave him a wobbly smile. "Maybe there'll be one in the new rooms."

"It won't be the same, though. I was getting used to being bounced in the air every time you tossed around in your sleep."

She tried not to read any meaning into his words. She'd been all through that before. She'd promised herself that she wouldn't let Nicole Parker near him again. And there was no more Opal Turner. For a brief moment she felt a pang of nostalgia.

"Well, I wasn't getting used to hearing you snore," she said lightly, determined not to dwell on the past. It was over. The sooner she accepted that, the easier it would be for both of them.

Luke pretended to be shocked. "Me? Snore? Not on your life."

"Loudly," Nicole assured him. "I thought it was a volcano erupting."

"I didn't think I'd slept long enough to snore." He gave her a long look that destroyed her breathing. Then he smiled, and she couldn't imagine how she was going to live without him.

He folded both his hands around hers. "I'd better let you rest now, or I'll have the doc after me."

She felt a ridiculous urge to cry. "It's going to be a long night," she said, her voice rough with the ache in her throat.

He stood, then leaned over and dropped a light kiss on her forehead. "Sleep well. You'll need your strength if you're going to make the most of your day tomorrow."

"Would you do me a favor?" She didn't know what plans he had for the next day, but he hadn't mentioned them spending it together. And her pride wouldn't allow her to suggest it.

"Sure." He straightened, looking down at her. "What is it?"

"Could you bring me some clean clothes in the morning? The ones they took off me are so awful."

"You bet."

He hesitated, and her heart started thudding in spite of her determination not to be affected by that expression in his eyes. "I've got a couple of things to take care of in the morning," he said slowly. "But how about I meet you for lunch by the pool?"

She could feel her smile spread across her face. "You paying?"

He grinned. "I've got a generous expense account."

"Well, in that case, I'd be delighted to join you for lunch."

He raised his hand and dropped it. "See you tomorrow, then. Around noon?"

"I'll be there." She watched the door close behind him and felt the threat of tears.

"Damn you, Parker," she muttered, groping for a tissue from the box on the bedside table. "You never cry. So don't start turning into a baby now." Reaction, she told herself as she dabbed at her wet cheeks. She'd been through a lot, after all.

She was glad of the sleeping pill they offered her. She knew that without it she wouldn't sleep. She also knew that it wasn't only the horror of the day she'd been through that would keep her awake, but the memory of a beautiful night and an ache deep inside that promised to last for a long, long time.

* * *

She awoke the next morning, refreshed and raring to go. A pleasant-voiced nurse with a wide smile brought her a gaily colored beach bag and a huge bouquet of flowers.

The card said simply, "Until noon. Luke." Staring at the small white card in her hand, Nicole made a decision. She had one day left. And one night. Whatever the future might hold for her, she would make this a day to remember.

She would spend the last hours of her time in Hawaii with him and live for each moment without thought for the future. For this short time at least, she would take all he was willing to give and give in return without reservations.

This would be her final farewell to paradise, and she would make it all it could be. And when it was time, she would store the stolen hours away in her memory, walk away and never look back.

She opened the beach bag and looked inside. Her heart melted when she saw the muumuu she'd bought for the luau. It was the only thing in her wardrobe that hadn't been bought specifically for her impersonation of Opal. And it was typical of Luke's thoughtful nature that he'd understood her need to be herself again.

He'd added underwear, and she smiled, imagining him going through her things, trying to decide what to include. He'd put in her toothbrush and toothpaste, a comb and a brush, and, for some reason, a tube of suntan lotion. The last item in the bag was brand-new, with the name tag still attached. She felt a lump form in her throat as she drew out a pair of white sandals with comfortable low heels.

The squad car arrived soon after, and once more Nicole found herself soaring up in the elevator of the hotel. She couldn't suppress the shiver as she stared at the button for the twenty-third floor, and felt immensely grateful for Sutton's quick action in relocating them.

The friendly policeman who had driven her to the hotel had given her the key to her room. As she wandered down the hallway, Nicole wondered which room Luke was staying in.

Her pulse skipped as she thought about her decision, and she couldn't help wondering if she'd be spending the night in his bed or if she'd just imagined the expression in his eyes when he'd looked at her the night before.

Inside her room she took one look at Opal's clothes folded neatly in her drawer and decided to pack them in the suitcase there and then. That done, she took her credit card and went down the row of gift shops that ran between the hotels.

In a fit of rebellion that she knew would cost her a week's salary, she bought a pair of pink shorts and a matching top, a pair of white jeans for traveling back the next day, a shirt to wear with them and a black swimsuit.

After only a moment's hesitation, she added a pale lemon sundress to her purchases. Feeling pleased with herself, she took everything back to the hotel room, washed her hair, put on the shorts and top over the swimsuit and went down to the pool to wait for Luke.

She didn't have long to wait. He arrived early. She saw him crossing the pool area, shading his eyes with his hand as he scanned the tables looking for her.

He returned her wave, then came toward her in his loose, easy stride, apparently oblivious to the interested glances from some of the women stretched out on lounge chairs by the pool.

She had to admit he was something to watch. He wore a pale gold shirt, unbuttoned to expose his chest to the waist. His white shorts bared his long legs, and he carried his sunglasses. His eyes looked even lighter against his tanned skin as he halted in front of her.

She saw the expression in them, and something cold touched her heart. For seconds she held her breath, afraid to say anything. Then he smiled, and she wondered if she'd imagined that bleak desolation she'd seen so clearly a moment ago.

"Hi," he said, sitting down in the chair opposite her. "I could use a drink. How about you?"

She nodded and wondered why those simple words seemed to hold such a ring of desperation.

Chapter 11

All through lunch, Nicole sensed a despondency beneath Luke's lighthearted chatter. Although she could tell he was doing his best to lighten up, her anticipation of the hours ahead dampened considerably as they shared an enormous seafood salad and fruit.

She thanked him for the sandals and received an abashed grin in response, but the bleak look still shadowed his eyes.

"What would you like to do on your last day here?" he asked when they'd both cleared their plates.

"Swim," she said promptly. "You have no idea how much I'm looking forward to spending the afternoon lazing on the beach with nothing more to worry about than premature wrinkles."

He smiled. "Sounds good to me. The beach it is. I've already booked dinner, if that's okay with you?"

She nodded, wishing she could feel more enthusiastic about the prospect. He was so good at maintaining that enigmatic expression. If only she knew what was going on behind it.

She'd held such high hopes for their last hours together, yet now she couldn't be sure what he wanted from her. Maybe she had imagined the warmth in his eyes yesterday. Maybe he was simply being extra nice to her after their ordeal.

She felt all the old insecurities return as she watched him sipping his coffee. She wasn't expecting anything beyond this night, yet now it seemed as if she might not have that, either. Something had happened since he'd left her the night before. It was subtle, yet she felt it as surely as if he'd spoken it out loud.

Unable to stand the uncertainty any longer, she took the plunge. "Did you see Sutton off this morning?" It was a polite way of asking him where he'd been, and she knew by his quick glance at her that he knew what her question really meant.

"No. I saw him last night before I came back here. I guess he left early this morning."

She nodded, feeling a knot of depression in the pit of her stomach. He didn't intend to talk about it. She was about to suggest they make a move when he said abruptly, "I went to see Tony's and Neil's families."

The knot moved to her throat. "Oh." Her fingers played with her mug while she sought for the right thing to say. She could imagine how painful those visits must have been. "I would have gone with you," she said at last.

"I know." He cleared his throat. "I thought it best if I went on my own. You've been through enough."

She looked up then and felt a chill when she saw the stricken look in his eyes. "You're not blaming yourself for everything that's happened, are you?" she demanded.

"No, not anymore. Sutton was right—it goes with the territory. It's something you have to accept when you're a cop."

She heard an odd note in his voice, and her uneasiness intensified. "I'm sorry," she said quietly. "It must have been an ordeal to talk to those poor people."

"Yeah." His long, brooding look chilled her, despite the hot sun on her shoulders. "It was the quiet way they accepted it that got to me. I could have understood it if they'd cried or yelled or...something."

He shifted in his chair and hooked his finger around his coffee mug. "But they didn't. Neither Tony's wife nor Neil's mother. They just had this terrible, frozen look about them, as if everything inside them had died, too."

Nicole's heart went out to them, to the grieving relatives and to the man who obviously cared so much. "It will get better for them," she said softly. "It's just the shock. It will pass."

He raised his eyes to her. "I wanted them to know that those men didn't give up their lives for nothing. I tried to tell them. How do you explain the reasons a man is ready to die for his job? How can you make them understand the kind of commitment that takes?"

She shook her head, feeling more helpless than she'd ever felt in her life before. She wished she could find the words to wipe that look from his face. "I'm sure they understand," she said carefully. "If they loved them, they understand."

"It doesn't stop the hurting."

"No." She was forced to agree. "I guess it doesn't."

He pushed his mug away from him with an impatient movement. "Well, I'm not going to spoil our last day here, so let's get to the beach."

She smiled, though her heart wasn't entirely in it. "Good idea. Last one in pays for dinner."

"You're on." He signed the tab the waitress had left on the table and shoved his chair back. "Do I get time to go and change?"

"Unless you're going in like that." She lifted the hem of her pink top to reveal her swimsuit below. "I came prepared."

He lifted an eyebrow. "You bought a new one?"

"Yeah. I got bored with Opal's bikini."

"Spoilsport. I kinda liked it."

"Then you wear it."

His grin came closer to normal. "Blue's not my color."

"Pity." She ran her gaze slowly up and down his body. "I think you'd look cute in it."

"I look cuter without it."

Her breath caught at this unexpected turnaround. "I'll second that," she said, giving him the closest thing she could manage to a suggestive look.

He leaned over and planted a light kiss on her mouth. "Hold that thought," he murmured. "I'll be right back."

She watched him leave, as did several other women as he passed them. The swift change of moods was typical of the man. She found it hard to keep up with them. What she found even more aggravating was the impossibility of gauging the meaning behind them.

So don't try, she advised herself as she settled more comfortably on her chair to wait for him. She didn't want to analyze him. She just wanted to enjoy him for the short time they had left together. As for the tomorrows, she would worry about that later.

He came back a few minutes later with a beach towel over his arm and a grin that told her he was determined to put his sobering thoughts aside for the time being.

Nicole went along with that wholeheartedly. She followed him as he stepped over legs and horizontal bodies to reach a few inches of space on the hot sand.

She helped him spread out one of the towels, then by mutual consent they decided to share it, since there wasn't a whole lot of room. Somehow, when she stripped out of her shorts and top, she felt more self-conscious than she had in Opal's skimpy bikini.

Maybe because she was now being herself instead of playing a part, she thought. Or maybe it was the appreciative glance that Luke ran over her body before she dropped to the towel and stretched out.

She closed her eyes, refusing to wear the sunglasses that had covered so much of her face the past couple of days. She was conscious of Luke lying down beside her, near enough for his legs to brush hers.

"I thought you wanted to go swimming," he murmured, his voice much too close to her ear.

She could feel the heat of him down the length of her body. "I do. But I thought we should establish our territory first, since the beach is so crowded."

"Good thinking, Parker."

She opened one eye and found him grinning at her. "Just don't go sneaking off while I have my eyes closed," she warned. "This is supposed to be a race, remember?"

He placed his open palm on his bare chest. "You have my word."

She relaxed, listening to the chatter of voices around her and the constant beat of the waves washing the sand. Some distance away a radio played the kind of lush music she liked best. The sun warmed her skin, and she let her mind drift lazily, until Luke grunted at her side.

"I don't know about you, but I'm beginning to burn."

He must have felt the shudder that shook her body. "I'm sorry," he said at once. "Poor choice of words."

She rolled over on her stomach, her peace shattered. "I guess it will fade in time. Though I don't know if I'll ever be able to hear that word again without remembering."

"It's not something you'll easily forget." He shifted onto his stomach, too, his shoulder pressed against hers. "But you're right—it fades with time."

She glanced at him, but he was staring straight ahead, and she knew he wasn't seeing the beach. She felt a twist of pain when she studied his strong profile and saw the deep grooves at the corners of his mouth.

She felt a different sensation entirely when she remembered that sensitive mouth moving over her bare skin. How well he knew her body now. And how well she knew his. "What about you?" she asked quietly. "Can you let it all go now?"

It was a while before he answered. "Sutton and I had a long talk last night," he said finally. "He seems to have found some kind of peace. I think he can finally lay Mark's ghost to rest."

"I'm glad." She waited, and when he didn't go on, she asked again. "What about you?"

She felt his sigh surface from deep inside him. "I don't know," he said, using his finger to trace a circle in the sand. "I have a lot of things to sort out in my mind. That's going to take time."

He looked at her then, and she saw the plea for understanding in his wonderful gray eyes. "I don't know how much time."

She hadn't realized what she was really asking until he'd answered it. She knew what he was trying to tell her. He'd said it before. No promises. He wouldn't ask her to wait, nor would she offer to do so.

She wouldn't waste time on false hopes; she knew the futility of that. Her heart ached for him, for both of them, but she managed to smile. "I hope your expense account can take care of dinner," she said, and shoved herself up on her feet.

He was right behind her when she hit the water, and his arms closed around her, sending them both sprawling into the waves.

She came up spluttering, and he surfaced beside her. Water plastered his hair to his head. "I consider that a dead heat," he said when he caught his breath.

She stood waist deep in the cool water, letting the surge of waves lift her off her feet before depositing her back on the sandy bottom of the ocean floor. "I think you cheated, Jordan," she said firmly. "I was definitely in before you."

He waded closer to her until his body touched hers. His expression sent her blood racing again as he rested his hands on her shoulders. "How about a new bet?" he suggested. "Last one in my bed tonight pays for breakfast in the morning."

She felt the shock waves ripple in sensual tingles down her body. "What is it about cops," she murmured, "that gives them such an incredible ego? What makes you think I want to go to bed with you tonight?"

He dragged her against him, his mouth muffling her protest. When he finally let her go, she had to cling to him to keep her balance. "Does that answer your question?"

The echo of his husky voice shivered down her spine. She touched the tape on his forehead with gentle fingers. "You figure you're up to it?" she teased. "I'd hate to cause a relapse. You know how insatiable I am."

"Yeah." He grinned. "That's what I'm counting on."

"It's going to cost you," Nicole said, gasping as a wave threw her up against him. "I'll need a top-notch dinner to build up all that extra energy."

"You got it." He set her away from him. "Now I'm going for a swim so I can walk out of here without losing my dignity. I don't need the whole beach to witness what you do to me."

He kept his promise. The dinner was everything Nicole could have asked for, and more. He'd chosen a restaurant overlooking the beach and had booked a table on the *lanai*, strategically placed in a corner beneath the gnarled branches of a broad-leaved tree. Their beaming waiter informed them it was called a *hau* tree.

Nicole was fascinated to learn that the ancient Hawaiians used the branches for cross-booms in their outrigger canoes. "I'd love to have seen the islands before they were civilized," she told Luke, her gaze on the rugged peaks of Diamond Head.

"I bet they were a lot different then." His smile teased her. "No fancy hotels, no mai tais, no exotic dinners on the beach."

"Except for the luaus," she reminded him.

"Yeah. Burned pig covered in sand, and raw fish."

She gave him a mock scowl. "Come on, Jordan, where's your sense of romance?"

"Okay, I admit it. There's something about palm trees and a warm sea at night that's definitely romantic."

Nicole couldn't agree more. Her skin tingled with the aftereffects of the sun and water. She felt healthy and incredibly alive.

She watched the setting sun reflect off the mountain's tawny slopes, turning it into molten gold against the purple-and-pink sky. Never, she thought, had she seen anything more heartbreakingly beautiful.

Until she looked back at Luke. She had never thought of a man in terms of beauty before, but now her entire body ached with the sight of him. He sat facing the sunset, his gaze on the white breakers curling in the distance. In the golden glow, his tan deepened to a dark bronze.

He wore his pale cream shirt open at the neck, and she felt a shiver of excitement as she remembered lying next to him, her lips pressed to the warm hollow at the base of his throat.

She could still feel his hard body, naked and hot against her hungry flesh. Her mind still breathed the exciting male scent of his warm skin and the taste of his mouth burning on hers.

She ran her tongue over her dry lips, and as she did so, he switched his gaze to her face. She must have revealed what she was thinking. She saw an answering warmth in his eyes as he reached for her hand.

"I like your hair pinned up like that," he said softly. "I like the dress, too. Yellow looks good on you. You look elegant tonight, Officer Parker."

"Thank you," she said lightly. "I do my best."

"Have I ever told you that you're a beautiful and desirable woman?"

Her shiver wasn't entirely due to the cool scented breeze wafting the back of her neck. Trying not to lose the light tone, she murmured, "Now you come to mention it, no. But don't stop now. I could listen to stuff like that all night."

"Yeah? Well, that's not what I had planned. I figure we're going to be much too busy to talk."

"Oh?" She looked at him with interest. "What do you have in my mind. Not another naked stroll on the hotel balcony, I hope?"

He studied her thoughtfully. "Hmm. Not a bad idea. But how about skinny-dipping on the beach?"

She shook her head. "Too public. I imagine dozens of other couples have the same idea."

"Yeah." He snapped his fingers in the air. "I got it. Slow dancing on the balcony, and we'll both get naked. That's what you call real dirty dancing."

Her laugh cut off as she remembered the silent watcher from the other night.

"What's the matter?" Luke said swiftly. "Did I say something wrong?"

"No." She reached for her wine and tasted the tangy chill of the excellent chardonnay. "I was just thinking about the cigarette I saw burning in the dark from another hotel balcony. I didn't realize at the time that it was one of Merrill's men."

"How come you didn't mention it before?"

"I was too occupied with other matters at the time."

Luke's eyes glinted in the candlelight flickering between them. "That must have been the one who took your photo. Sutton had him picked up. It was the same guy who carried up our bags when we arrived. Did you know Merrill had a picture of you faxed to Portland?"

Nicole nodded. "I'd forgotten about it until now. He said he had a contact in the police bureau. I should have told Sutton about that."

"Sutton already knows. Apparently someone disturbed the guy when he was taking the copy off the machine. The officer recognized the photo of you, but Sutton had already left for Hawaii. He got the message when he arrived here."

He made a sound of disgust in the back of his throat. "I still can't believe he pulled that scam on me, knowing Opal was dead. It was a hell of a risk to take."

"Well, as he said, that's what police work is all about. Taking risks." Nicole put her glass down. "Sutton isn't bothered by his conscience as much as you are."

Luke shrugged. "That probably makes him a better cop than I am."

"Not necessarily. I happen to think a conscience is just as important as courage. If not more." She gave him a look that she hoped would take his mind off the subject. "And you have more than your fair share of both. I like that, Jordan. I really like that."

His grin was her reward. "Yeah? Well, Parker, as you may have noticed, I like you, too. Now, getting back to the dirty dancing, what's your verdict on that?"

"I'll agree, on condition we do it in the room with the drapes drawn. I like my privacy."

"You got a deal."

His eyes promised her a lot more. The waiter interrupted her at that point, which was just as well, Nicole thought as she ordered the chilled cucumber soup and tiger prawns.

Much more of that conversation, and she'd be too carried away to eat.

He wanted to make the evening last, Luke decided after the waiter had cleared their table and it was time to go. He suggested a last stroll on the beach, and Nicole agreed with undisguised enthusiasm.

It was one of the things he liked about her, he thought as he took her small hand in his. She held nothing back. You would always know where you were with a woman like Nicole Parker. No games, no hidden resentment. Angry or excited, happy or sad, she said what was on her mind.

He looked down at her, amused by how much smaller she seemed without the high heels. Somehow he'd always thought of her as a tall woman. Though small wasn't exactly a word he would have used when describing her.

She had a heart big enough to hold the entire population of Oregon. Maybe the whole country. She'd talked about his courage, but hers was formidable. She had far too much guts for such a fragile-looking person.

Yet he knew that she was far from fragile inside. She was strong, determined to show the world that she was her own woman, even if she risked her life to do it.

He swallowed past the lump in his throat and squeezed her hand. He managed to smile when she looked up at him with her beautiful green eyes, and he wondered how long he could go on smiling after this night was over.

Then she paused and knelt to pick up something from the sand at her feet. He watched her tilt her head to one side while her slim fingers held the lovely, delicate shell to her ear. His breath caught in his throat, and something inside him snapped.

He reached for her chin, turning her face up to the moonlit sky, and settled his mouth on hers. It was supposed to be a gentle kiss, nothing more than a promise of pleasures yet to come, but when her arms crept around his neck and she pressed her soft body to his, the embers that had never quite died fanned into flames again.

He crushed her in his arms, his mouth desperately searching for the reassurance of her response. She parted her lips, and eagerly he took advantage of her willingness, his tongue hot and ruthless as he explored her mouth.

He felt her body responding to his onslaught. She moved her hips against him in a suggestive gesture that heated his blood. He couldn't get enough of her.... He had never wanted like this... hungered like this before.

He raised his head and drew in a rasping breath. "We'd better get back to the hotel before I ravish you in front of an interested crowd of tourists."

He could see the rapid rise of her breasts beneath the yellow dress. Her teeth flashed white when she smiled up at him. "That sounds interesting," she said, sounding breathless. "I've never been ravished before.'

"Well, lady," he said thickly, "prepare yourself. Because tonight you're going to be ravished."

"Do I get to do some ravishing, too?"

He almost groaned. "Whatever your little heart desires. Tonight I'm all yours, to do with as you will."

She grinned. "You been watching too many old movies, Jordan?"

He dropped his arms and took hold of her hand again. "What I've got planned for you hadn't been invented back then."

"God," Nicole said fervently, "I love it when you talk sexy." Her laughter mingled with his while they tramped up the beach, their footsteps quickening as they neared the hotel.

He had barely closed the door behind him when she grabbed the front of his shirt and began tearing open the buttons. "What are you doing?" he demanded, pretending to be shocked.

"Ravishing. I wanted to get a headstart before you..."

"Before I what?" Intrigued and delighted by her unexpected aggression, he let her drag his shirt from his back and stood passively while she unfastened his pants.

"Before I what?"

"Before you make me forget what I wanted to do."

Wearing only his briefs, he lifted his hands to her hair and pulled out the pins one by one until the silky mass settled over her shoulders. Then he waited, his heart thumping against his ribs, to see what she'd do next.

She stood facing him, her eyes holding his while she undid the buttons of her dress with slow, deliberate movements that just about drove him wild.

Letting the yellow fabric drop to the floor, she stepped out of it, then gave him a smile that almost destroyed the last of his control.

"Wait a minute," she said softly, and walked over to the clock radio beside the bed and turned it on.

He couldn't keep his eyes off her body as she leaned forward, tuning in some easy-listening music. He'd seen her in a bikini that revealed as much, if not more, than the lace-trimmed panties and bra that she wore now.

For some reason, she looked far more seductive at that moment than he'd ever seen her. He took a step toward her as she straightened, and felt his body tighten in anticipation.

"You wanted to dance?" she murmured, and held out her arms.

He paused, drinking in the sight of her lush curves before reaching for her. She came into his arms, her skin cool and smooth against his. She smelled as exotic as the gardenias and ginger blooms that spilled across the sidewalks of Honolulu.

He began to sway to the music, his cheek resting against her forehead, his flesh shivering with every contact of her body against his.

He felt her hands moving down his back, her fingernails drawing an exquisite trail of excitement over the swell of his buttocks as she eased his briefs over his hips.

His fingers found the clasp of her bra and freed her breasts, then stripped her of her panties. Her naked flesh felt cool against his burning skin as she moved with him to the intoxicating music.

Moving his hands over her enticing curves, he settled his mouth on hers while his body guided her slowly across the room. The music seemed to echo inside him, swelling and building until the passion raged to an unbearable pitch.

Her long, smooth legs collided with his, and her soft belly brushed him in an intimate caress. He felt the tips of her breasts harden against his bare chest, and his own body responded with a swift potency that destroyed his control.

He tried, he really tried to contain his impatience, but the torture of her smooth, naked body sliding sensuously against his chest and stomach built the smoldering pressure inside him, demanding release.

He pushed her down on the bed and covered her body with his. She made little sounds in her throat that blew his mind, and the pressure inside him threatened to explode. He fought his own need, taking the time to give her what she craved. He remembered what excited her, finding her sensitive spots with instinctive accuracy that arched her body in readiness for him.

Then the air erupted from his lungs when her fingers closed around him, and he could wait no longer. He took her hard and fast, a desperation driving him beyond all reason.

He felt her draw him deeper, tightening herself around him. Then he was lost, striving for that ultimate ride to a shattering pinnacle of pleasure, until at last he released himself inside her, his body shuddering in spasms of satisfaction.

It was over so fast, and yet it was only the beginning. As he lay with her locked in his arms, he promised himself that he would not let her sleep. As long as his strength held out, he would keep on making love to her, until he'd filled every corner of his memory with the special excitement that only she could give him. It was a memory that would have to last a long time.

Morning came all too soon for Nicole. She watched the sun creep up the drapes, spreading fingers of light to dispel the last of the shadows in the room.

Luke slept quietly beside her. She turned her head to look at him, a smile curving her lips. He lay on his back, with one arm flung across his forehead. A dark fuzz covered his jaw and upper lip, and sleep smoothed out the hard lines of his mouth. The sheet covered him to his waist, and she watched the rise and fall of his chest, listening to the sound of his breathing.

He had been relentless for most of the night. Every time she thought she couldn't possibly give any more, he'd lightly traced his fingers over her body until the excitement began to build again, and once more she'd been swept away by the passion. Her smile faded as she watched the room grow brighter. In just a few hours they would be on their way back to Oregon, and this lovely island would be nothing more than a memory.

In spite of everything that had happened here, Nicole told herself she would always remember the essence of Hawaii—the heady fragrance of the blossoms, the beautiful sunsets and the sound of whispering palm trees in the sultry wind from the sea.

But most of all, she would remember the teasing of a husky voice, strong arms holding her and a passion that she knew no other man could possibly equal.

She turned her head again, her heart skipping when she met Luke's steady gaze. "What were you thinking about?" he asked softly.

She wanted to tell him. She wanted to hold him until he promised never to leave her. She wanted to stay on this warm, tropical island and never think about Portland, Oregon, again.

"I was thinking about breakfast," she said, smiling. "I can't remember who was in bed first."

"Neither can I." He rolled onto his side to face her, his gray eyes studying her. "How do you do that?"

"Do what?"

"Manage to look so gorgeous first thing in the morning? I thought everyone looked like I do when I wake up."

Her laughter spluttered out, prompting a grin to spread across his face. "I should hope I don't wake up with a beard and mustache," she said, running her fingers across his jaw.

He grimaced and rubbed his hand over his chin. "Do you suppose," he murmured, "that if I nuzzled your belly, my chin would leave scratch marks there?"

"I don't intend to find out." She made a move to climb out of bed, but he caught her in his arms, dragging her back.

"Where are you going?" he muttered, and rubbed his chin across the small of her back.

"I'm going to order breakfast." She wriggled out of his hold, but he grabbed her, hauling her down on top of him.

"There's something you have to take care of first."

She felt him swelling against her belly and looked down at him in amazement. "And the man says I'm insatiable."

He grinned. "You know what they say. One more for the road."

He moved his hips beneath her, and she caught her breath. "Damn you, Jordan, I'm not going to be able to walk—" Her words ended in a gasp as his mouth found her breast, and then she forgot about talking at all.

*   *   *

"I've ordered the cab for one-thirty," Luke said as they sat by the pool later that morning. "That should give us plenty of time to check out."

Nicole concentrated on squeezing lemon juice over her papaya. "All right. I hope it's not raining in Portland. At least I'll have the weekend before I go back to work."

"Yeah. I'll be at the debriefing on Monday."

She looked up. "You will?"

Luke dug a fork into his hot cakes. "Yeah. Sutton wants a report from both of us."

She watched him hook up a chunk of pancake smothered in guava jelly. "You'll have a paunch by the time you're forty if you eat like that," she murmured.

"Well, I haven't got long to go."

His smile seemed a little tense, and she frowned. "You all right?"

"Yeah." He yawned at her across the table. "Just a little tired, though I can't imagine why."

She refused to let him unsettle her. "That's what you get for making a pig of yourself," she said calmly. "Everything in moderation, remember?"

"Everything?"

"Everything." She scooped out the last of her papaya. "That includes that disgusting sugar-loaded glop all over your pancakes."

"Are you always this concerned about other people's eating habits?"

"Only when it's someone I care about." She hadn't meant to say that. They had avoided putting their feelings into words.

She looked up at him and saw that his expression had changed. She knew him well enough now to recognize the guarded look in his eyes. "What is it, Luke?" she asked quietly.

He gave her a brief, wry smile that did nothing to settle her quiver of anxiety. "You don't miss much, do you."

"I try not to."

He dropped his gaze, and her throat tightened. She'd been expecting this, she told herself. Somehow she just hadn't realized how much hope she'd held on to, in spite of all he'd said. Impatient with herself, she prayed she wouldn't do or say something stupid.

"I was going to tell you on the plane," Luke said, "but this is as good a time as any."

She didn't answer but simply waited, aware of the dull ache spreading throughout her body.

"I'm going back on the force."

She stared at him, not sure how she felt. "That's wonderful, Luke. I know you've missed it, and I'm sure they've missed you."

He still didn't look at her, and the cold ache persisted. "Yeah, well, it was when I talked to Sutton. I'd been thinking about it off and on, but he brought it up that night, and we discussed it. He convinced me it was the right thing for me to do."

"And he was right." She leaned across the table to cover his hand with hers. "You're a good cop, Luke. And I know it's what you really want to do. I'm glad you made the decision to go for it."

He looked up then, and she saw something in his eyes she didn't understand. "It was because of you," he said, his voice not quite steady. "You gave me back my confidence. You made me believe in myself again."

Again the wry smile tugged at his mouth. "You told me you owed me your life, but it's the other way around. I owe you mine. I'll never forget that."

Gratitude. He was offering her gratitude when she wanted so much more. But then he'd never promised her more. She was the one who'd broken the rules. He'd laid it on the line for her, and still she'd let herself fall in love with him.

She met his gaze and now she understood the apology in his eyes. *Police work and marriages don't mix. You're better off if you have no one to worry about but yourself.*

The sun sparkled on his hair, finding the sun-bleached streaks at his temples. He looked so incredibly enticing and never more elusive.

She couldn't blame him for the pain. She could only blame herself. Somehow she found the strength to smile. "I guess that makes us even then, Jordan."

For a moment she thought she saw real regret in his eyes. "I guess it does."

She managed to get through the rest of the meal without losing her composure. Even when she finally escaped to her room and could spend a few minutes alone, she refused to let her mind dwell on her misery. There'd be plenty of time for that once she got back to her lonely apartment in Portland.

She packed the rest of her things and placed the oversized sunglasses on her nose. She might be able to keep the pain out of her face, but she wasn't so sure about her eyes. Then she rode the elevator down to the lobby, where she found Luke checking out.

The cab waited for them outside, and Nicole took her last, long look at the lush beaches and sparkling blue-green ocean before it all disappeared behind the towering buildings of the city.

She tried to make light conversation with Luke, but he seemed preoccupied and eventually relapsed into the brooding silence that was so typical of his temperament when they'd first met.

She bought a magazine at the airport and pretended to read while they waited for their departure call. It was easier than trying to talk to an unresponsive companion.

Things were a little better on the flight, though Luke's remarks were carefully restrained, as if he thought everything over before he spoke.

The only time Nicole saw a glimpse of the man who'd spent the night making love to her came as the plane began its descent. Without speaking a word, he took her clenched fist in his warm fingers and held it until the wheels touched the ground. She murmured her thanks but couldn't look at him.

To her relief, the sun shone in a clear blue sky over Portland's impressive skyline, and she didn't have to remove her sunglasses. She didn't look at Luke again until the cab deposited her outside of her apartment building.

"I'll take care of the cab," Luke said as she opened her purse.

"Thank you." At last she found the courage to meet his eyes.

He gave her his lopsided grin, and she nearly lost it then. "Don't worry," he said. "It'll go on the expense account."

She nodded. "I hope Sutton doesn't give you a bad time about that."

"If he does, you'll hear about it. I'll be at the briefing on Monday, remember?"

She had forgotten. One more nightmare to get through before she could finally write him off. "Oh, right. I guess I'll see you then."

"Yeah." His eyes crinkled at her. "I'll give you a hand with your luggage."

"No," she said quickly, "I can manage. It's only one bag."

"Okay. Have a good weekend."

"You, too." She scrambled out of the cab before her face gave her away. With a final wave she turned her back on him and trudged up the steps of her building.

She spent the weekend cleaning her apartment, expending as much energy as possible in the process. Even so, she couldn't make herself tired enough to sleep.

By Monday morning, she was exhausted, but the hours spent tossing in her bed hadn't been entirely wasted. At last she'd had time to think and to plan. It helped to put things back into perspective, and she'd actually regained an assurance she wouldn't have thought possible two days ago.

The last thing she had expected was that Luke would rejoin the force. But the decisions she had made earlier were now much easier to accept.

Once she had put on her uniform and fastened her hair back in the severe style she was used to, she felt like a different person.

She *was* a different person, she told herself as she looked into the mirror. The uniform and the hair were the same, but she looked different. Softer, somehow, and she'd lost that tense, driven look that someone had once told her made her seem distant and aloof.

Nicole gave her reflection a rueful smile. She'd spent a lot of years striving for recognition. The promotion she'd coveted for so long had always seemed just outside of her grasp. And now it was hers. But the price she'd had to pay for it was almost beyond comprehension.

If she'd known, Nicole asked herself as she drove to the precinct, would she have still gone through with it? She knew the answer to that when she walked into Sutton's office and saw Luke's lean body sprawled in a chair.

Yes, she assured herself, she would have gone through with it. For whatever the tomorrows might bring, the recent yesterdays had given her a new understanding of herself and a new appreciation for the complexities of a human being.

She had run the gamut of emotions, from horror and terror to sympathy and love, and had come through intact. She had experienced a passion that few women knew in a lifetime, and for a little while had enjoyed a glimpse of paradise.

She met Luke's gray gaze across the room and hoped it would be enough to sustain her through the bad days to come.

Chapter 12

Grant Sutton sat on the corner of his desk, his light blue eyes shrewdly appraising as Nicole seated herself in the vacant chair next to Luke.

"You should get a tan more often," he said, pushing himself to his feet. "It suits you."

"Thank you." She felt a momentary discomfort as she wondered what the two men had been talking about before she arrived but dismissed it almost at once. Luke, she was sure, would never mention their personal relationship. And neither would she.

Sutton sat down behind his desk and pulled a report pad toward him. "You'll both have to fill one of these out, of course," he said, "but I wanted to get a more comprehensive report from you both. I want to make sure Merrill doesn't wriggle out of an indictment."

"He was responsible for the deaths of two men," Nicole said anxiously. "Surely that should be enough?"

"He didn't actually pull the trigger."

"He sure as hell pulled the trigger of the gun that killed Mark," Luke put in. "And there's the little matter of Opal's death."

Sutton rubbed his eyes with his thumb and forefinger. "Well, we won't get him for Opal. That happened in South America. But as for Mark and the two HPD men, you were each an eyewitness to one of the crimes, so you'll both be expected to testify."

They seemed destined to be thrown together, Nicole thought as she listened to Luke answering one of Sutton's questions. She wondered if she'd ever be able to look at him without feeling the awful ache of regret for what might have been.

They had come so close. How could two people be so right for each other and yet so wrong? She jerked her mind back to Sutton when she realized he'd asked her a question and was waiting a little impatiently for the answer.

She kept her concentration riveted on the briefing after that, and by the time it was over, a dull ache had settled behind her eyes.

She had one bad moment, when Luke rose to leave and gave her a tight smile. "See you around, Parker," he said, his voice dropping to the husky tone she would never forget.

"Take care, Jordan." She stood and glanced at Sutton, who was watching her with an enigmatic expression on his rugged face. "I'd like to stay and discuss something with you, if you have time?" she asked him.

"Sure." He moved around the desk and offered his hand to Luke. "See you in court."

"Yeah."

She could feel Luke's gaze on her face but pretended to be engrossed in the report sheet Sutton had given to her. She held her breath until she heard the door close. When she looked up, she found Sutton staring down at her.

"What is it, Nicole?"

He saw more than he appeared to, she thought and had to struggle to keep her voice steady. The words came clearly in the quiet office. "I want to hand in my resignation."

Sutton rarely showed any emotion. His expression was impassive now as he returned to his seat. "May I ask why?"

She shrugged, not knowing how to explain. "I've changed my mind," she said lamely.

He seemed to be thinking that over. "You don't want to be a detective?" he asked at last. "You don't have to accept the promotion, you know."

"I know. It's not that." She sat on the chair and looked down at her hands, then made herself look back at him. "It was when I stared down the barrel of a gun that I realized it. I hadn't really given much thought to dying before. I've been in some pretty rough situations since I've been on the force. I've even been shot at a couple of times, but then it's always been over so fast I never had time to think about it."

His stoic expression unnerved her, and she looked away, concentrating on the toe of her shoe. "When I stood facing that gun, expecting to die any minute," she went on, "I asked myself one question. Why am I doing this?" Her breath shuddered out on a long sigh. "And I came up with the wrong answer."

Seconds ticked away while she searched her mind for the right way to explain it. "I've never been to Europe," she said finally. "I've never even seen the Grand Canyon. I don't know what it's like to sail a boat, or to ice-skate, or to fly down a mountain on skis."

She swallowed, took a breath and went on. "And I've never had a child. All of a sudden, when I thought I was going to die, I knew I wanted to be a mother. I want a child. No, I want lots of children. And grandchildren."

She flung out an arm in a gesture of despair. "I'm not prepared to risk losing all that. I'm thirty-one years old. And I'm chasing a ridiculous rainbow, and for what?"

She looked up and was momentarily taken aback by the look of compassion on Sutton's face. "I'll tell you what." She stood and leaned her hands on the desk. "To prove I'm as good as my brothers. Isn't that a ridiculous reason? I'm not risking my life because I want to be a cop. I'm doing it to prove a point."

"And now you've proven it."

"No, I haven't." She felt the tears threaten and tried in vain to keep them back. "All I've proven is that I can't take it. It's not what I want. I wasn't doing it for me. And now I want to live my life for me."

She felt a tear slide down her cheek and brushed at it with a furious hand. "Look at me. I can't even talk about it without bawling."

Sutton got slowly to his feet. "Don't sell yourself short, Nicole. You've got what it takes, all right. Don't consider yourself a failure just because you changed your mind about what you want from life."

He held out his hand. "I accept your resignation, Officer Parker, with regret. But I understand your reasons for doing so."

Giving him her hand, she managed a smile. "Thanks. I'll fill out the official forms."

"Do you know what you're going to do?"

"No." She turned to go, then looked back at him. "But I'm sure I'll think of something."

"Well, if you need a reference, I'll be happy to give you one."

"Thanks. I appreciate that."

Again she turned to go, but his voice stopped her. "Nicole?"

Something in his tone warned her, and she braced herself for his question.

"This doesn't have anything to do with Jordan, does it?"

She was proud of her composure. "Of course not. What gave you that idea?"

Sutton actually looked embarrassed. "I just wondered. Did you know he's rejoining the force?"

She nodded. "He told me."

"Did he tell you he's going to Nevada?"

She knew she'd been unsuccessful in hiding her shock. "As a cop?"

"As a deputy. I think he has a chance of making sheriff when the present one retires."

He hadn't told her. It shouldn't have hurt, but it did. "He'll make a good one," she said carefully.

"It was what he wanted. It's an isolated county, not much going on. He wanted out of the city."

"I know." She gave Sutton a wry grin. "That much he did tell me."

"I'm sorry, Nicole."

She looked into his sincere blue eyes and shrugged. "Yeah. So am I."

This time she escaped, and neither she nor Sutton mentioned Luke Jordan again.

Because of Merrill's ill health, he was given an early trial. Even so, the weeks in between dragged by as Nicole waited for the entire episode to end. She knew she wouldn't be able to overcome her feelings for Luke until she no longer had an excuse to see him again.

The day of the trial finally arrived, and she dressed with extra care in a conservative light gray suit. The moment she saw him, she knew nothing had changed. Maybe it never would, she thought miserably as she sat across from him in the courtroom.

The trial lasted three days. Although they exchanged greetings in passing, she didn't have an opportunity to talk to Luke until after the case was resolved. Either he left first, or she did, and it seemed as if neither one of them had anything to say to each other.

Merrill was convicted of the murder of Mark Wilson and of the attempted murder of Luke and Nicole. The men involved in the murders of Tony Lopaka and Neil Clements were held over for a separate trial, at which Nicole would again have to testify. As far as Luke was concerned, however, it was over.

Nicole walked out of the courthouse that afternoon and saw Luke waiting near the foot of the steps. She would have preferred not to put herself through the pain of talking to him again, but short of ignoring him, there wasn't much else she could do.

Even though she'd prepared herself for this meeting, the sight of his crooked smile almost destroyed her.

"Hi," he greeted her as she walked down the steps toward him. "How about a cup of coffee?"

It was the last thing she wanted. Yet she couldn't find the strength to turn him down. "You paying?"

His eyes searched her face. "You got an expense account?"

"Hell, Jordan, I don't even have a job."

He shoved his hands into the pockets of his pants. "Yeah, I heard you quit the force."

The light blue shirt he wore bared his throat, and she felt a swift stab of pain when she noticed he still had a tan. Hers had faded some time ago. She wondered how much time he spent in the sun in Nevada, then realized he was waiting for her to say something.

"I guess Sutton told you."

He nodded. "So, how about the coffee? My treat."

She shrugged. "That's an offer I can't refuse."

He took her to a coffee shop around the corner from the courthouse. The rich, mellow aroma of freshly ground coffee beans greeted her as he held the door open for her to enter.

She chose a table near the window. For some reason, she felt less vulnerable there. She let him order, refusing his offer of food. Any appetite she may have had vanished the moment she'd seen him on the steps.

"Tell me about your new job," she said when the waitress had brought two steaming mugs of espresso.

"Not much to tell. I drive around most of the day watching out for marauding possums."

She forced a smile. "Arrested any yet?"

"Nah. The little devils are always one step ahead of me."

"You never were very fast on your feet."

He pretended to be offended. "I can move when I want to."

Unbidden, a crystal-clear memory flashed into her mind. She could see herself dashing into a warm, green ocean, and two arms grabbing for her, pulling them both beneath the foaming water....

"It sounds boring," she said abruptly.

He was watching her with an odd, intent look in his eyes. "It isn't. It's small-town, down-home living, I grant you, but boring it isn't. People live in small towns like that—real people, not just bodies dressed in suits and faded jeans. They're people who have something to say and who are interested in what you say to them. People who care about other people more than they care about their cars, or houses, or their bank accounts."

She stared at him, not sure what to make of this unexpected declaration. "Well, Jordan," she said softly, "I'm impressed. That's the longest speech I've ever heard you make."

He held the look, as if waiting for her to say something else. Unnerved, she reached for her coffee. Avoiding his gaze, she lifted it to her lips and tasted the creamy froth.

"So, what about you?" he asked after a short pause. "Have you been looking for a job?"

She twisted her mouth in a wry smile. "Looking, yes. But not many people seem interested in hiring a thirty-one-year-old ex-cop. They're looking for secretaries, accountants, shop assistants. I either don't qualify or the job doesn't appeal to me. I guess there isn't much market for women who change a career midstream."

"Why did you quit your career? What happened to the woman who put her life on the line to make detective?"

She wondered when he was going to get around to asking that one. She'd been trying to decide how to answer it ever since they'd sat down.

She shrugged. "I left her behind somewhere in Hawaii. I just decided, after everything that happened, that I wasn't too excited about dying before my time. There was just too much to live for, and proving to my brothers I was as macho as they were wasn't worth the risks."

A group of teenagers exploded through the door as she finished speaking, and by the time they had settled themselves noisily in the corner behind her, she'd got it together again.

"I've decided to travel," she said when she could look at him again. "After the trials are over, I'm giving up my apartment and I'm going to work my way around the world. If I have to do menial labor to make a living, I might as well do it in interesting places."

His face hid from her anything he might be thinking. "The world can be a dangerous place for a woman on her own."

She uttered a short laugh. "If there's one thing the police force has taught me, it's how to take care of myself."

She saw a glimpse of regret flash across his face. "Yeah, I guess you can at that."

All at once she'd had enough. The ache that had slowly subsided over the past few weeks had returned, and she wasn't about to give it a chance to smother her again. She drained her coffee and put the mug down on the table. "Thanks for the coffee, Luke. It was nice to see you again. Give my regards to the possums when you get home."

She pushed back her chair and heard the scrape of his at the same time. She'd hoped he'd let her leave on her own, but he was close behind her when she stepped out into the bright sunlight.

People brushed past her in the late-afternoon rush for buses. People in suits and faded jeans. She gave herself a mental shake and turned with a bright smile to face him. "Goodbye, Luke. Have a good life."

His gray eyes probed hers, and she felt her heart turn over. "I'm not leaving until tomorrow," he said quietly. "I don't suppose you'd consider having dinner with me?"

Yes! her heart cried. I'll do whatever you want, just as long as I'm with you. "Sorry," she said briefly. "I've got a date." In desperation she glanced across the street. "There's my bus. Gotta run!" She flapped her hand at him, and blinded by tears, dashed into the traffic.

Luke watched her go, feeling as helpless as a caged lion. His entire life was disappearing in front of his eyes, and there was nothing he could do about it.

He spun on his heel, intent on finding somewhere quiet to think, and ran full tilt into Sutton's solid body. Cursing inwardly, Luke met the searching gaze of the other man and said lightly, "You following me?"

"I want to talk to you." Sutton grabbed his arm and shoved open the door of the coffee shop. "In here."

"I've just come out of there," Luke protested, but Sutton was obviously in no mood to listen to reason. Shrugging, Luke followed him to the table he'd just vacated with Nicole, and sat down.

Sutton glared at him across the table and muttered. "I saw Nicole leave."

Ignoring the swift stab of pain under his ribs, Luke nodded. "Yeah. We just had coffee together."

"I know. I saw you come out." Sutton gave a rapid order to the waitress hovering at his elbow, then looked back at Luke. "So that's it, huh? Just like that?"

Knowing it would be useless to pretend not to understand, Luke shrugged. "It's better this way."

"The hell it is."

Sutton's vehemence shook him. He could feel his eyebrow twitching as he met the ice blue gaze.

"I usually make it a habit to mind my own business," Sutton added curtly, "but when I see someone I like and respect make a fool of himself, I feel compelled to butt in."

"Even when it's not welcome?"

Sutton didn't flinch. "Dammit, man," he muttered, "can't you tell when a woman's in love with you?"

Luke fought down the quiver of hope. "Forget it, Sutton. That was just the effect of tropical heat. You know what that can do to people. Luckily it doesn't last. Most of the time they get their head on straight once they're back on home ground."

"And now you have your head on straight? Is that it, Luke?"

He felt his temper slipping and made a valiant effort to hold on. "Yeah," he said quietly. "That's it."

He winced as Sutton muttered a crude comment. "I never figured you for a fool, Luke," he added. "But if you're determined to see it that way..." He let his voice trail off as the waitress returned with his coffee.

For a moment, Luke hesitated, then decided to ask anyway. "Did she give you a reason for quitting her job?"

Sutton's face showed no expression. "Yes. But I'm not sure it was the real one."

Luke nodded, uncertain what to say to that.

"Why didn't you ask her?"

"I did." Luke shrugged. "I don't know if she gave me the real reason."

Sutton gulped down half his coffee, then set his mug on the table and swiped at his mouth with his napkin. "Look, tell me to butt out if you like, but I'm going to have my say. I might not know what's in Nicole's mind, but I know you,

Luke—and you can't fool me. I've always believed that if you want something bad enough to go after it, you'll get it. Why don't you try it? You might be pleasantly surprised by the result.''

He shoved his chair back and stood. "She's quite a woman, Luke. She's worth fighting for."

For a long moment, Luke stared up at his former boss. Then, as a surge of renewed hope lightened his heart, he smiled. "How come you're not married, Sutton? You're not a bad-looking bastard, and without that mean attitude you could be a great guy. You need a woman to soften you up a bit."

Sutton's face was expressionless when he looked down at him. "I had a woman once," he said quietly. "And it happens only once in a lifetime. Don't lose your chance at it. Okay?"

Luke shrugged. "I'll think about it."

Sutton shook his head. "What fools we mortals be," he murmured. "Good luck, my friend." He stuck out his hand, and Luke grasped it.

It was true, Luke thought. Somewhere along the line, they had become friends. "I'll keep in touch," he said, gripping the large hand firmly.

"Do that." Sutton gave him one last look, then turned and made for the door.

Luke sat there for another ten minutes, oblivious to the chatter and clatter around him. Lost in thought, he didn't notice the place gradually emptying out, and was startled when a sip of cold coffee reminded him how long he'd been sitting there.

He looked at his watch and then dug in his pocket for change, scattering it across the table before he shoved back his chair.

It took him another five minutes to reach his car, and ten more to drive to the apartment building where he'd dropped off Nicole all those weeks ago. It seemed like a lifetime now.

He hadn't planned what he was going to say to her. So much of it depended on what she had to say. But now he knew what he wanted. And one way or another, he intended to get it.

After parking the car outside the building, he retrieved a small package from the back seat, then spent another frustrating minute or two hunting down the number of her apartment. Finally he stood outside her door, his finger on the bell, and prayed she was there.

Inside the apartment, Nicole frowned as the bell pealed in her ear. She had changed into jeans and sweatshirt, her hair was a mess and she was in no mood for visitors. If it was a salesman, she thought irritably as she marched across her living room to the door, she'd give him her invasion-of-privacy speech.

She tugged open the door, rehearsing her opening salvo. Her jaw dropped at the sight of the man leaning casually against the doorjamb. The grave expression on his tanned face unsettled her even more.

"I thought you'd be halfway back to Nevada by now," she said unsteadily. Try as she might, she couldn't stop the sudden leap of excitement as she stared into his cool, gray eyes.

"I wanted to give you something before I left." He pushed himself away from the wall and handed her a small package.

Frowning, she looked down at it in her hands, not sure what to say. "What is it?" she asked finally.

"Why don't you open it?"

She didn't want to open it. She didn't want him standing there on her doorstep, looking so damn sexy and appealing. And the last thing she wanted to do was ask him in.

She stepped back and flipped her hand at the room behind her. "You'd better come in."

For a split second, she saw an expression in his eyes that made her pulse leap, then he stepped past her and walked into her living room.

She shut the door and immediately felt as self-conscious as if this were the first time they'd been alone together. Why was she doing this? she thought fiercely. Why was he doing this? What was he doing here, trampling all over her heart as if none of this had meant anything to him?

Regretting her rashness in asking him in and anxious to send him on his way, she ripped open the package. For a moment, she stared speechless at the tiny pink shells spilling into her hands, then as she lifted the string and the fragile song of the chimes filled her living room, she knew she was going to cry.

Damn him, she thought miserably. She'd held on all this time, and now she was going to let some stupid sea shells make her look idiotic and immature.

She swallowed down the lump in her throat and said carefully, "They're lovely. Thank you."

She knew he was looking at her, but she was afraid to look up, knowing the tears were hovering perilously close to the surface. He was much too sharp not to notice.

"I bought them in Honolulu before we left," Luke said, his voice sounding oddly strained. "I didn't get a chance to give them to you before."

She didn't answer. She couldn't. For a moment, she'd hoped...

"I was going to give them to you earlier, at the coffee shop. But you were in too much of a hurry to get away from me."

"I'm sorry," she said stiffly, her gaze still firmly fastened on the swaying shells. "I saw my bus and—"

"You didn't give me a chance to say what I wanted to say."

This time she heard something in his voice. Something that made her heart begin hammering against her ribs. Very slowly she lifted her gaze to his face.

He stood a few feet away, his hands thrust into his pockets, his expression as unreadable as ever. But his eyes held hers across the room, and suddenly she was struggling to breathe. "What...did you want to say?" she asked faintly.

He stretched out a hand toward her. "Come here."

Her legs felt shaky, and she took the three steps to reach him as if she were stepping over a fifty-foot chasm. Clutching the shells in one hand, she put the other in his and felt the warmth from his firm grasp spread throughout her body, catching fire as it reached her heart.

She was afraid to believe that look in his eyes, yet she couldn't tear her gaze away from his face.

He looked down at their linked hands, as if trying to decide what to say next. Then he looked up again, and her heart stopped. "I was going to ask you to marry me," he said evenly.

Shock held her speechless for a long moment. Then, as the unbelievable magic of his words soaked in, she could have sworn she was floating to the ceiling.

She managed to keep her voice steady when she asked, "So why didn't you?"

She saw apprehension written on his face and felt sorry for him. Didn't he know how much she loved him?

"When you said Nevada sounded boring and that you wanted to travel, I thought you'd changed your mind about...how you felt. I still intended to ask you anyway...."

He looked up then, and her heart melted at the uncertainty in his face. "But those kids came in, and there was too much noise and I knew it was the wrong place. I wanted to give you the shells, and I wanted somewhere special to ask you properly. Then, when I asked you to have dinner with me, you said you had a date—"

"Damn it, Jordan. You don't know anything about a woman, do you?" She'd finally lost it. She was crying.

He swore, then dragged her into his arms, and his mouth, warm, familiar and infinitely comforting, wiped out all the pain, the anger and the fear.

She leaned into him, seeking the comfort of his hard, lean body, and her skin quivered as his hands moved over her, soothing, caressing, searching her body as if trying to reassure himself that nothing had changed.

At last the need to breathe forced her to break away, and his eyes burned into hers as he looked down at her. "You haven't said you will," he murmured.

She couldn't resist teasing him. "Will what?"

His eyebrow twitched. "Marry me. You were supposed to fall into my arms crying, 'Yes! Yes!'"

"Oh, is that how it's done?" She grinned. "That only happens if you get down on your knees."

"If I get down on my knees, lady, you're coming with me. All the way to the floor."

"Sounds interesting." She pretended to consider it. "The bed's more comfortable."

The sparkle she loved to see appeared in his eyes. "Is that an offer?"

His voice had gone husky again, making her skin tingle. "You interested?" She pulled away from him and began undoing the buttons on his shirt.

"That depends."

"Depends on what?" She tugged the shirt from his jeans and pulled it open.

"On your answer. I can't make love to you unless you say you'll marry me."

She ran her hands over his chest, watching the flames dance in his eyes. "That's never bothered you before."

She gasped as he grabbed her and hauled her against him. "I'm determined to make an honest woman of you. But you'll have to hurry. As you can tell, I don't have a whole lot of time."

He shifted his hips against her, sending shafts of excitement up her body. Her defenses destroyed, she returned the pressure. "I'll marry you." She wrapped her arms around him beneath the shirt. "So what are you waiting for?"

Much later, as she sat with him on the couch listening to the provocative strains of *South Pacific*, she asked the question that had hovered in her mind ever since that first ecstatic moment of his proposal.

"Tell me," she asked casually as he wound his arm around her and pulled her into his side, "just when did you decide you wanted to marry me?"

"I'm not sure." He hesitated, then added, "I guess I knew we had something special going before we left for Hawaii. But it wasn't until you followed me across the beam and I realized just how much you were willing to trust me that I began to think that we could make a go of it together. Then I went to see Tony's wife and Neil's mother, and I saw what losing someone they loved did to them."

He shrugged. "I guess I got scared. I'd seen so many police marriages go sour, and I'd messed up so much of my life. I figured I was doing you a favor by getting out before I messed up yours, too."

She lifted her chin to look at him. "Why didn't you tell me all this in Honolulu?"

"I knew how easy it would be for you to change my mind. And I couldn't help being selfish enough to want that last day together. We'd never had time to spend on our own, simply because we wanted to be together. I wanted a special memory to take with me after I let you go."

"But didn't you think I had a say in the matter?" she asked gently.

"I didn't think so. Not at the time. I thought I had it all together. I was convinced I was doing the right thing. You know, the noble gesture."

He shook his head, uttering a short laugh of disgust. "All those weeks away from you, I couldn't stop wanting you. I realized then that without you, all that confidence and self-respect that you had given back to me wasn't worth a damn."

Choked with happiness and love, she couldn't answer. Then he stunned her by adding, "I'm willing to come back here, if that's what you want. I know Sutton will get me a job here in town. He'll give you yours back, too, if you want it. You said once that if two people love each other enough, they can deal with anything. I love you enough to know we can make it work."

If she'd ever needed proof of his love, she had it now. Shaken by the sacrifice he was willing to make, she waited until her composure had returned enough to let her speak.

Taking a deep breath, she said clearly, "I don't want my job back. I'll tell you what I want."

She sat up and rested her gaze steadily on his wonderful face. "I want children. Your children. I want a home, with dogs and chickens and a horse or two. And I don't care if it's in Nevada or Kalgoorlie, as long as it's with you."

He looked at her for a long, long time, his heart burning in his eyes. Finally he asked softly, "Do you have any idea how much I love you?"

She smiled. "Why don't you show me."

He did. Until she was breathless. Then he lifted his head. Looking down at her, he murmured, "Kal . . . what?"

She grinned. "Kalgoorlie. It's in Australia. My brother's a bush pilot out there."

"Ah." He nodded. "How's your family going to take to you marrying a cop?"